Heart of the Owl

Heart of the Owl

A Border Ballad

CATHERINE M. O'CONNOR

TCU PRESS
Fort Worth, Texas

Library of Congress Control Number: 2026021989

TCU PRESS

TCU Box 298300
Fort Worth, Texas 76129
www.tcupress.com

DEDICATION

For my brother Frank

CONTENTS

PART I TUCSON, ARIZONA 1930

ACKNOWLEDGMENTS

This novel is dedicated to my brother Frank whose loving support, humor, gentleness, and honesty have been a source of strength and joy for my entire life. You're the best brother ever and laughing with you is as good as it gets.

Thank you to my children, Claire and Patrick. It has been a beautiful journey to watch you grow, and your dad and I are so proud of the adults you've become. We love you and are so grateful for the love and support you give us in return.

And thank you to my husband, Jim, of thirty-one years. Life has thrown us a few doozies, but because of it, I feel closer to you than ever and my love and respect for you is boundless. We hit a home run when we found each other. Lucky me.

To my extended family and wonderful friends, thanks most of all for our shared laughter. You make life a joyful ride and I am grateful for each one of you. And I'll never forget the words of my friend, Thatcher. As a fellow writer, he knew that perseverance is a must. "Just keep going!" he said with his wonderful smile. I miss you, dear friend. To Betsy and Alison, your writing wisdom and caring friendship means everything to me.

A huge thank you to the TCU Press team for continuing to support my writing endeavors with enthusiasm, encouragement, and excellent guidance. A special heartfelt thanks to Dan Williams and Marco Roc for saying, "Let's give this another shot!"

Lastly, thank you to all the readers out there who have taken the time to read my novels. I feel a closeness to many of my characters, and when someone takes the time to get to know them, I'm filled with gratitude.

AUTHOR'S NOTE:

The song, "La Golondrina," the Swallow, that is quoted in the novel was written by Narciso Serradell in 1862. The song was has been recorded in many versions since, but the source for English and Spanish translations used in this novel was from sheet music found on the IMSLP website (International Music Score Library Project) https://imslp.org/wiki/La_golondrina_(Serradell%2C_Narciso). This particular arrangement was for piano and voice and titled "La Golondrina, The Swallow Fantasia." The arranger was A.F. Heckle and the sheet music publisher was Houston: Thos. Goggan & Bro., 1900.

Border Ballad
(verse 1)

Listen and hear
what I am about to sing,
these events of the boy and the great owl.
And do not say it's not true.

PART I:

Tucson, Arizona
December 1930

CHAPTER 1

ANTONIA

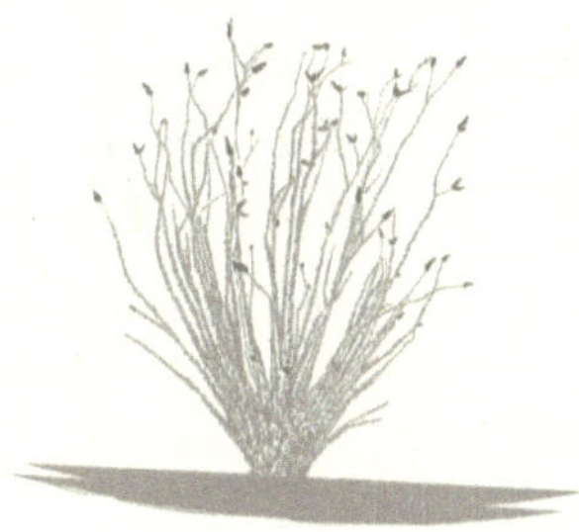

A squeaky door was the stick of dynamite that led to the implosion. She had complained before, grumbling mostly, but this time her tone was as hot and fiery as the cast iron skillet and spitting bacon that she stared down upon.

"For God's sake, just oil the hinges. You're gonna kill Pancho or me the way you wield that gun around like a madman when it's nothing but the wind causing that heinous squeak."

Elton's face turned flame red as though his head was about to explode.

"Hell no! I'm not oiling that damn door! It's my burglar alarm," he said. "There are nutjobs all around this neighborhood, and I'm gonna—" but before he could finish, she cut him off.

"Good God, Elton. The craziness in your head," she said.

"You're calling *me* crazy?" Elton said.

Pancho was eating breakfast, and his eyes shifted back and forth like he was assessing the intensity of an approaching storm. When Elton threw down his napkin, kicked his chair, stomped out the side door, then roared the LaSalle's engine under the porte cochere, Antonia clenched her temples between her fingers and gritted her teeth. An all-too-familiar scene: spinning car tires, a spray of dust and gravel at the end of the driveway, screeching rubber on Tupelo Street, then silence.

She wiped her hands on her apron then turned to Pancho and tried to change the subject with an upbeat lift. "Ready for school?"

As Pancho nodded, she studied his eyes. Their sudden sparkling brightness or their cloudy misting had always been the tell-all to his mind and heart. But at this moment, his eyes were cold and hard like marbles as if all emotion had been tamped down into the pit of his being.

She put her hands on his shoulders. "Everything's okay," she said in her well-practiced voice.

But *nothing* was okay.

Pancho grabbed his book bag and ran out the door without saying a word. She didn't blame him. Lately, things had turned bad.

Now alone, Antonia angrily doused breakfast dishes in hot soapy water and launched into her increasingly frequent diatribe about what a mistake this so-called marriage had been.

"You're a paranoid, bigoted, cheating drunk!" she shouted to an empty kitchen.

"You said you loved me, your 'blond beauty,' you called me. What a performance! Turns out you only married me for the money and that damn—" She stopped mid-sentence, shook her head, scooped up a handful of soap bubbles, threw it at the window, and watched it slide down the pane leaving a silvery film in its wake. She dropped her chin and gripped the sink edge with a vice-like hold and added, "And Pancho—his Mexican blood eats at you like a canker."

As she scrubbed dried egg yolk off *his* plate, she became even more enraged.

"And if you ever call Pancho my 'little bastard' again, I'll . . ." She raised the plate high in the air and smashed it on the linoleum floor. With a gloomy expression, she stared at the shattered aftermath for a minute before taking a deep breath and retrieving a broom and dustpan from the closet.

By the time she had swept up the ceramic shards that slid to the far corners of the room, she had resolved that Elton was not all to blame. She had fallen partially for his handsome face and his salesman's charm but mostly for his three-bedroom brick bungalow, the sapphire-blue GM LaSalle in the garage, the smooth lawn, neatly clipped shrubs, and his savings account—the result of his rising success at the car dealership. These were the things she had convinced herself would create a better life for her and Pancho. It had all hinged on a choice and an agreement.

But it wasn't until she dumped the shards into the trashcan under the sink that she spilled her last words in a venomous concoction of fear and ferocity.

"It's over, Elton! O-V-E-R! I don't need you or your dirty money. I will care for Pancho on my own." Then she collapsed into a chair, put her head between her hands, and clenched her hair as though she were hanging onto clumps of grass on a slippery slope.

This wasn't the first time she had felt this way. That same full body ache and cramping had reared up just after she had told her father and stepmother about the bulge in her belly that several months later would become Pancho. That moment, from twelve years ago, now felt distant—but still chilling. As she remembered, it was more like a bad scene in a play versus real life.

STEPMOTHER (shouting): Sixteen and pregnant? And to a Mexican farm hand?

ANTONIA (quietly): We want to get married.

STEPMOTHER (arms flailing): Married? I'll bet he does. So, *we* can foot the bill, and he can become a US citizen then ditch you.

ANTONIA: He's not like that! You don't even know him.

STEPMOTHER (head shaking): You can really make a mess. Just like your mother.

FATHER (begging): Settle down, Lyla.

STEPMOTHER (wagging her finger): Don't tell me to settle down, John. She's *your* daughter. Fix it!

FATHER (drops his head): I will. Enough.

STEPMOTHER (points toward the door): Get out of my sight!

ANTONIA (turns and leaves in tears)

Remembering that scene, Antonia had one festering regret. If only she had mustered the courage to say what she was thinking—"You're a cruel witch!"

CHAPTER 2

PANCHO

Pancho no longer went straight to school after one of these thundering episodes between his mother and Elton. Instead, he headed down the driveway with books and lunch in hand, and after a few steps, he glanced back to be certain that his mother had left the kitchen window where she usually waved goodbye. Her "*adiós* post" she called it.

If the coast was clear, he'd sprint back toward the house and station himself behind an oleander hedge in the side yard, under the eave, where he made little parachutes out of white flowers and waited.

There, he would check his watch—a gift from his mother on his recent twelfth birthday—and wait a full twenty minutes to be certain that Elton didn't return like he had once before. On that horrible day, the day Pancho had noticed the bluish rings around his mother's throat that she had tried to hide with a scarf, he drafted a handwritten statement with pen and paper.

I, Pancho O'Rourke, do solemnly swear that I will never allow that to happen again! Then with eyes wide open facing his new truth, he poked his finger with a straight pen, squeezed it to reveal a red droplet, then sealed his signature in blood.

Only after twenty minutes—the time it took for Elton to drive to work—did Pancho feel safe to dash for school. The consequences of missing the final bell were hefty, but he was used to absorbing the blow—a tardy slip, a trip to the headmaster's office, needling-under-breath comments from his tablemates, an hour of study hall, and at home, snide remarks from Elton, sharp words from his mother about lollygagging, and lastly no dessert.

No dessert was the worst part—especially when it was chocolate pie. He didn't mind the headmaster's office because he hardly ever saw Mr. Sterling. He usually saw Mrs. O'Brien, a plump, gray-haired receptionist with a gentle smile, who tore up the tardy slip, winked at him, and gave him a piece of butterscotch candy, because as she said, "We're brethren—I'm an O'Brien, you're an O'Rourke—we Irish stick together."

Study hall wasn't so bad either. He'd sit in the corner and finish his homework while others, mostly boys, goofed off. An occasional spitball to the forehead was humiliating, but he forced himself to laugh to keep the predators at bay. Whining or complaining was out of the question—he'd end up with face full of mushy wads.

School definitely had its pros and cons. He didn't go there for the other kids—not for Tim Johnson, Philip Larkin, or Ben Chase who called him little fart for being small or Geronimo because of his brown skin. He didn't have the courage to tell them he was part Mexican, not Apache, because more name calling would have followed. And he didn't go to school for Priscilla, Margaret, or Lucy who basically ignored him like he was two grades below—too short and skinny to be a seventh grader. As he recalled, there'd been only one interaction with that group of girls—that was when Priscilla snapped her gum, stared at him, and without smiling said, "Your eyes are *huge*!" He didn't know whether to say sorry or thank you, so he said nothing. And that was that.

The main pro at his private school was library period where he had a quiet corner and stool for reading books like the *Call of the Wild* and *The Adventure Boys*. In that corner, he inhabited other worlds and imagined himself running wild and free with the pack or exploring distant lands for treasures. There he was strong, courageous, brave.

At least school was predictable. Home was the problem.

And just yesterday, home had taken a painful twist.

Pancho's job was to take out the trash, and when he raised the lid, he saw something small and yellow poking out from under Friday's discarded newspaper. He blinked, not believing his eyes, then his heart stopped.

It lay limp among a collection of loose feathers—the canary Pancho had bought with his allowance money a few years back. Piper was his name, and his home was Pancho's room where the cage door was left open for him to fly about. Piper would flit from the curtain rod to lamp then back to Pancho's outstretched finger, but sometimes he would flap his wings against the windowpane in a way that tore at Pancho's heart—as though Piper wanted something more.

Several times Pancho had thought of setting Piper free, but now it was too late. And now he was furious, sad, and numb with guilt. He should have seen it coming when Piper swooped down the hallway and into the living room. It had been almost funny—the way Elton cowered and waved his arms like a windmill as Piper hovered above. *Go Piper!* Pancho had thought.

But yesterday, after he gently picked Piper from the trash, cupped him in his hands and buried him under a mesquite tree, nothing was funny, and everything was sad.

Had he cried under that mesquite? Bawled. Did he tell his mother? No. Fights were dangerous.

But he mostly wondered why Elton hated him so much.

CHAPTER 3

THE ESCAPE

It was the next night, a Saturday, after Antonia's kitchen soliloquy and official severance statement, that she made her move. As Elton lay face down and snoring among twisted sheets, she packed her belongings. Though she could barely see, she felt her way from their bed, past her lace-covered dressing table, toward the closet, but didn't risk turning on the light. Instead, she groped in the dark for things that felt familiar—a wool skirt, two blouses, two pairs of stockings, underwear, an extra slip, and shoved them into her satchel. She only packed the necessities and was careful to take nothing that might give Elton any clues.

Earlier, she had sprinkled a half dose of sedative compound into his third whiskey then greased the hinges of the screen door—that *squeak*, the proverbial last straw—the sound that made Elton sit bolt upright in bed, fumble for his pistol under the mattress, hold the .45 at arm's length and creep down the hall and shout, "Who's there? If you don't get outta my house, I'm going to blow your head off."

She felt no remorse about the sedative—it was a safeguard for extra time. She was sure he would remain passed out at least until noon, and when he awoke, he would assume they were at church. She was confident with that part of her plan. The rest she'd have to make up as they went along and do her best to hide any worry from Pancho.

As Pancho waited for her, his room was mostly dark except for the glow from the streetlamp that spilled over his white bed linens and cast a halo of light around his small frame. Perched on the edge of his mattress like a winged creature scanning a moonlit landscape, he sat straight-backed, wide-eyed, and perfectly still as he listened for any signs of movement. His eyes, black pupils within a ring of yellow-flecked hazel, were unusually large making his other facial features—a delicate nose, small ears, and thin-lipped mouth—look miniaturized and doll-like.

He had done exactly as she had said. He was dressed in a white shirt, gray trousers, navy peacoat, green clip-on tie, black socks, and held his brown lace-up church shoes in his lap. Though she had said nothing about bringing books, he had cinched three in his book strap and looped the belt three times to secure it in his right hand.

The door to his room was slightly ajar when a curled finger appeared and beckoned him. He stood up, gripped his book strap, tucked his shoes under his arm, and tiptoed toward the door. In the hall, he searched the darkness for his mother's soft-featured face, but all he could see was a pale finger pressed against rosy lips. Following her lead, he slid in his stocking feet over wooden floorboards as smoothly and quietly as if he were on ice. As he passed his bathroom and the yellow glow from the lightbulb within, he could see that his mother was wearing her long wool gray coat, a purple scarf, and carrying an overstuffed canvas satchel.

When they got to the kitchen, he whispered. "What time is it?"

She didn't say a word but waved for him to follow. At the kitchen door, she gingerly slid the latch until it unlocked, turned the brass doorknob, and opened the screen door just wide enough for them to pass through then gently closed it behind them.

Outside, the air was brisk, and he rubbed his small hands together until they turned pink and breathed nervously creating a rapid string of vapor puffs. She sat down, patted the concrete stoop, and motioned for him to sit and put on his shoes. As she bent over and slipped her feet into her pumps, her blond hair rolled off her back and covered her face so that he couldn't see her expression.

He poked her gently in the soft tissue of her arm. "What time is it?"

Without answering, she grabbed his hand and moved forward with urgent strides. He leap-stepped to keep up with her pace, and it wasn't until they reached the driveway's end that she finally responded.

"It's a little after midnight and just like we talked about, we're going on a trip. I'll tell you more later."

"Is Elton coming later?" His usual voice was high-pitched and tinged with strain.

"No," she said. "Just you and me," and when he relaxed his shoulders, she gently raked her fingers through his straight dark hair then forced a tight smile. He furrowed his brow. This wasn't her real smile. The real one was much wider and curled up at the edges, and he wasn't sure what this one meant.

When they took a left on Sonora Street, Pancho didn't look back at the house he had lived in for twelve years. Not at the barrel filled with an assortment of balls that Elton had bought—baseballs, basketballs, footballs—team sports stuff that Pancho could care less about. Not at the bicycle propped against the garage wall that, to his embarrassment, was sized for a fourth grader but still fit him.

All that stuff belonged to the kid he was leaving behind. He felt no remorse to be rid of that boy—the one who had banged pots and pans, weaved around furniture, and streaked between Elton's fists and his mother's body to distract; the boy who learned to keep a pail full of water in the bathtub, so he could douse Elton and allow his mother to slip from Elton's grip; the boy who sprinted toward the door while his mother desperately shrieked for him to *RUUUUUN* as Elton stood sputtering and shock-faced with water dripping from his chin and ear lobes.

That boy was behind him—the boy who was always fearful of what might happen. He stopped in his tracks and closed his eyes tight for a few moments trying to erase all of it from his mind. Suddenly, his eyes snapped open like he had heard a voice from the future.

He leapt forward and tugged on his mother's coat and announced forcefully, "I don't want to be Pancho anymore. I want to go by my real name—Francisco!"

Antonia tilted her head, "But you've always been my Pancho. Why?" she said.

"I don't like him," then he tightened his fists. "I hate him!"

He stood straight-armed, rigid, and enraged as his mother hugged him tightly.

Her voice quavered, "I'm sorry, Francisco. Please forgive me. I love you—you're everything to me."

Antonia didn't want to spend money on a cab, but she had no choice. That time of night, a boy and a mother alone? Easy target.

Within ten minutes, they arrived at Tucson's train station with its brick façade and red tile roof, then walked briskly under the loggia toward the entry door. Their surroundings were mostly quiet except for other taxi engines purring in cue, and the soprano trill of insects that swarmed the corners of the station's vestibule. It wasn't until something grazed Antonia's ankle and leapt up her skirt that the quiet was pierced.

"Dammit to hell!" Antonia shouted then slapped at her skirt until something small, wiggly, and black dropped at her feet.

Bending down, Francisco scooped up the bug and cupped it in his hands, leaving a peephole for her to see inside. "Look. It's just a cricket."

Antonia ran her fingers through her hair and glanced from side to side to see if anyone had witnessed her embarrassing outburst then spoke in an exasperated tone. "I know, Pancho, I mean Francisco, let it go now, please. Crawling things, you know how I hate them."

She knew crawling things had never bothered Francisco—caterpillars, snakes, lizards were of great interest and even more so were the birds that ate them. He was familiar with all the desert species—woodpeckers, cactus wren, flycatchers, hawks. She had witnessed him poring over a field guide that he had repeatedly checked out from the library. Why birds? She had no idea.

She turned hurriedly. "Come on," she said, then grabbed the station door handle and jerked it open.

The cavernous, high-ceilinged space was empty except for a few sleeping bodies on wooden benches. Outside, a train puffed like a breathing dragon.

When they approached the ticket counter, a red-eyed salesman raised his head as if he had been awakened from a deep sleep.

"Where to?" he mumbled.

"El Paso," she said. "The Argonaut."

He scratched his wiry fringe of gray hair and yawned. "You missed the Argonaut. Left over an hour ago."

"An hour ago? I thought it left at 12:40 a.m.?"

"The Golden State's next. Sitting outside."

"How much is the Golden State?"

The man studied a schedule chart intently like the question had never been asked. "$1.50. Fifty cents more. Leaves in a few minutes. You arrive at 5:15 a.m.—if there are no delays."

Antonia shook her head in desperation. "We can't afford that."

The ticket salesman took off his cap and rubbed his hand over his bald head. "Look, lady, I ain't your personal accountant, and I don't set no fares. You can go back home and catch the Argonaut tomorrow or take the Golden State tonight. Whataya want?"

A booming voice rattled the station's paned windows.

El Paaaaaaaaaaso . . . track threeeeeee!

"Okay, the Golden State," she said. She opened her change purse and dumped a pile of coins onto the counter and pushed them toward him.

Track threeeeeee! Allllllllll Abooooooard!

"Hurry, Ma," Francisco shouted. "It's about to go."

With a pained expression, the man sorted through the coins. "We got two, four, six, nine quarters . . . four dimes . . . looks like five nickels . . . then five, six, seven . . ."

Antonia shuffled her feet as though she was standing on hot coals. "Please, Mister. Give us the tickets!"

The man shook his head and shouted back. "You're short! By three pennies. You ain't got no bills?"

Antonia's face flushed. "I do but they're tucked away . . . I didn't think I'd need them."

Francisco patted his pocket. "I've got a penny!"

The man groaned. "Just take 'em for Pete's sake. Go!"

"Thank you!" Antonia spun on her heels. "Hurry, Francisco!"

They ran through the waiting room, down a long corridor, and burst through the doors and onto the covered platform.

Last callllllllllllll track number threeeeeee!

"How do we get there?" Antonia said.

Francisco looked to his right. "Way down there. That bridge, I guess," and he made a beeline in that direction with Antonia following close behind.

As they mounted the steps, Antonia saw the conductor check his watch, swivel his head from engine to caboose then step inside the train. When they reached the top of the bridge, the train released its breaks—*pshooooo.*

Antonia frantically waved her arms, "Wait!" then stopped, dropped the bag, and shucked her shoes.

"I got the bag!" Francisco yelled and scooped it up. "Come on!" Both scrambled down the stairs.

Barefooted, Antonia sprinted next to the train waving and flailing her arms. When she looked back, Francisco was close behind, so she grabbed the rail handle, pulled herself onto the first step, then turned and shouted, "Toss me the bag!"

Francisco hurled it and when it hit her arms, she bobbled the bag, and something fell to the ground with a clunk—gone.

"Grab my hand!" she shouted.

She had a loose grip when the train started chugging faster—*fshooo, fshooo, fshooo*—and when his fingers slipped from hers, her mouth dropped open and she screamed, "Run!"

That word propelled him like it had so many times before. He ran faster, faster, faster, then with a burst of energy, he lowered his head, shoved off his left foot, and thrust his body forward. Suddenly, he was airborne with his book strap trailing behind.

When he hit the train landing on his toes, the book strap followed with a thud. For a moment, they were speechless. Then Antonia gasped, "Oh my God, Francisco. That scared me to death!"

"I did it!" Francisco shouted. "Did you see me?"

She looked at his shining face, gripped his shoulders at arm's length then hugged him tightly until he wriggled free.

He was giddy with excitement. "I flew!"

Antonia laughed, "You hopped so far—just like a grasshopper!"

He turned his head sideways. "A grasshopper?"

She smiled even more broadly. "Yes," she said. "Just like a little grasshopper."

He wrinkled his eyebrows. "But it was more like flying—like a falcon or an eagle taking off."

"Well sure, I guess . . ." she said, "I just meant, you know, a grasshopper can jump a long way for its size."

Francisco's shoulders slumped.

She knew it—his sensitive spot—his size. "I didn't mean to hurt your feelings. I'm sorry." She turned toward the train door and pulled the handle. "Let's find a seat."

Her legs were wobbly as she walked down the aisle. They had barely made it, and it was just the beginning of their escape. What else lay ahead?

CHAPTER 4

TRAIN RIDE

Francisco found an open bench, plopped down, scooched toward the window then stared outside as they whirred past flickering city lights then into darkness. Despite his mother's apology, he was still smarting from the grasshopper comment. Why was he so small? His mother was tall, and his grandfather, John O'Rourke, was tall too. Francisco knew because of a picture he had found while searching for a piece of gum in the kitchen drawer. It was stuffed in the back under a stack of papers. In the photo, his grandfather was with Elton. They were both standing in front of a shiny, new-looking car. Elton was smiling; his grandfather's expression was sour like he had eaten a persimmon.

"He's tall like you," Francisco had said.

"Yep," Antonia said without any further elaboration.

Francisco was jerked back to the moment when his mother cursed, "Dammit!" She frantically shuffled through her bag.

"What are you looking for?" he said.

"That thing that fell out, my—" She stopped herself then suddenly blew through her lips. "It's okay—*phew.*"

Still preoccupied with the "little business," Francisco nudged her. "Was my dad short?"

Antonia sighed. "A bit. But listen, you don't need to worry about that. Kids grow at different rates. Just give it time. You'll probably spring up in a year or so, and before you know it, you'll be taller than me."

"Really?"

She smiled. "Yes, really," she said, then she closed her eyes.

He mumbled with the intention of her hearing. "I wish I could meet my real dad."

Her eyes popped open like she had heard a clap of thunder. She put her hand on top of his and squeezed it gently. "I know, Francisco, I know. Maybe someday . . ."

"Where is he?"

"I don't know. All I know is that he had to go away—back home to Mexico before you were born—he had no choice."

Someday, he thought. She had never hinted that it might be possible. He looked out the window and his heart raced. Could it really happen? Then suddenly he was struck with fear. What if he doesn't like me—like Elton?

He remembered the cricket that he had tucked in his coat pocket, back at the train station, when his mother wasn't looking. When he grazed his hand over the cloth, he felt it move inside. Worrying that it didn't have enough air, he removed the handkerchief that he had stuffed inside to keep it from hopping out then cupped his hand over the pocket opening. He could feel the cricket's tiny legs tickling his palm.

"Don't worry, friend," he whispered. "I will let you go once we arrive. You'll be in a new place just like me."

His eyes grew heavy, and he drifted off to sleep.

Antonia tried to sleep but couldn't as the train whirled through the desert landscape slowing only momentarily for the small-town depots that flashed by their window like vague and streaky images from a worn-out, black-and-white picture show: Esmond, Cruz, Vail, Pantano, Empire, and Mescal in the first hour, then Benson, Dragoon, Cochise, Wilcox, in the second.

She shifted from side to side trying to get comfortable, but the heat in the railcar was blasting, and sweat pearled on her upper lip. She shed her coat but still felt as if she were covered with a heavy blanket due to the unknowns that lay ahead.

And Francisco's plea—to know his father—had hit Antonia in the gut. She knew it would come up sooner or later because lately he had been asking more questions. So here it was—boom! Now what?

She had told him many times that his father—Mateo—was kind, gentle, tender, but had little else to add because she knew nothing of Mateo's whereabouts. The "fix it" plan had been swift—immediate deportation.

Her father had spoken to her on the day it happened. Standing before her, in a funeral-esque gray suit, he wore a stern expression. "He's gone. Not coming back. Time to move on."

She had screamed so loud that he took a step back like he had seen a ghost.

"How could you?" Antonia had said between sobs. "You wouldn't even let me say goodbye? You're as cruel as her!"

He stuttered. "It's for the best."

"Who's best? Lyla's best?"

He said nothing for a moment then cleared his throat. "You'll stay with my sister in Albuquerque until you have the baby, then you'll put *it* up for adoption."

The word stung. *It.* Like it was a pest, not a child. She couldn't believe her ears. "So, I have no choice?"

He rubbed his hands together. "No."

She had started crying uncontrollably. He reached out to touch her arm, but she pushed his hand away. "Leave me alone."

After he left, she lay there imagining what had happened. Knowing her stepmother's vehement disgust with the situation, she felt certain Mateo's departure had been layered with threats. She didn't believe her father was capable of harmful deeds, but it was possible that others might do the dirty work for him. She had been scared to death for Mateo—he was gone from her life like he'd never existed.

And to this day, she knew only one thing that could be a clue to his whereabouts—she would pursue it with caution to protect Francisco. The last thing he needed was more pain. And her own feelings were in play. What if Mateo was married and had a family? Twelve years had passed, so it was probable. Would he even want to see them?

Her mind swirled. Focus on the immediate, she thought. Her plan? Find a place to rest until daylight, then pursue the clue—the hotel near the rodeo grounds. If it still existed, it was probably off the beaten path, not downtown. Maybe they could afford to stay there for a few nights while she looked for a job. The money she had would go fast.

Her other concern? Elton. He might come after them and had reasons for sure. When it came to money, Elton had a nose like a hound dog.

Antonia had nodded off but was abruptly awakened when the conductor shouted, "Union Depot—El Paso!" She looked at her watch—5:16 a.m., and it was still dark outside. The station was quiet except for a man who yelled profanities and stumbled around waving a beer bottle in the air. Not the place to rest, she thought.

She noticed a young man unlocking the door of a restaurant with a sign above that read "Harvey House."

"Excuse me," she said. "Is there a church nearby?"

The man turned her way with an eagerness as if he were grateful to encounter a pleasant face bearing a look of sanity. "Yes, Ma'am. St. Patrick's. About a ten-minute walk from here on Mesa Street. Can't miss it. Has a bell tower like this station—and is the same red brick."

"Thank you," she said, "And also, do you know of a hotel near the rodeo grounds?"

He tapped his finger against his chin and moved his eyes between her and Francisco. "Hmmm . . . Hotel Luna is the only one I can think of . . . but if you're thinking of staying there, I don't know if it's the best spot for a lady like you and your boy. That side of town can get a little rough, being near the rodeo and all. And it does have a . . ." He waved his hand in front of his nose. "You know horses, cows. Maybe you should try downtown instead?"

"Appreciate your help," Antonia said, not wanting to reveal that a cheap hotel was all they could afford. So, it still existed. The place where Mateo used to stay as a seasonal worker at the rodeo.

Now she was nervous about what she might find there.

CHAPTER 5

BELL TOWER

To Antonia, each step felt like a mountain leading to the doors of the cathedral. The spent adrenaline, sleeplessness, and worry about the future made her feel like the walking dead. The twenty steps upward, tall wooden doors—more like barricades than thresholds—and the looming brick towers felt more daunting than welcoming in the darkness of predawn. And inside felt even colder and darker than outside.

"Let's find a spot to rest for an hour or two," she said as she reached for Francisco's hand and led him down a dimly lit aisle toward the northern transept.

Francisco's eyelids fluttered as they passed a wrought iron stand with tiers of flickering candles in red votives lined up like a Christmas choir, and he stopped to warm his hands. His face glowed golden, but for the first time, Antonia could see that he had grown thinner, more frail, and hollow-cheeked, and suddenly she saw the full weight of what her and Elton's anger had done to Francisco.

As he stared at the light, Francisco whispered. "Why El Paso, why this church?"

She sighed, "Because it's far away, and—" She stopped herself.

"And what?"

"Nothing," she said. She couldn't tell him everything. Not yet.

Francisco stood quietly for a moment and didn't take his eyes off the orangish-white light. "But what if he comes looking for us?"

She raised her chin trying to shore up her fractured confidence. "I'll figure it out, don't worry," she said, but her voice sounded timid. Her sketchy backup plan—a retreat into Mexico—had no direction, no clear lines, nothing.

The only thing that felt firm was her commitment to protect Francisco. She knew Elton. He was tenacious, and he wouldn't give up easily if he wanted something. Elton had entered the picture just a few weeks after Antonia gave birth. Though Antonia had planned to give the baby up for adoption, when she saw Francisco's sweet face for the first time, she knew she could never do it. It was Mateo's face with his beautiful, bright eyes. Eyes that made you feel as though you were looking into unknown worlds. And there was that soul-melting feeling—love—the one thing that she had yearned for in her own childhood.

So, when Antonia put her foot down about keeping the baby, her father made arrangements that were nonnegotiable. Marry Elton immediately.

And for Elton the benefits were enticing: a new car every year, monthly payments to care for Antonia and Francisco, and the promise of partial ownership in the car dealership if Elton followed through—until Francisco was eighteen. If he didn't, the deal was off.

But Antonia knew it wasn't just the money that would propel him to search. For Elton, it was also pride and getting the last word. *Pride*—the one thing she and Elton fully shared. She had purposefully not reached into the mason jar in the pantry behind the jellies and canned goods and slipped out a few twenties, not because he would notice, but because she wanted to owe him nothing.

And here they were in this church with a fresh but frightening start. She watched Francisco as he held his index finger above the flame just high enough to feel the heat but not close enough to burn.

"It's because of me, isn't it?" he said.

She touched his shoulder gently then tenderly tucked a strand of his hair behind his ear so she could see his expression.

"No," she said. "It has nothing to do with you—it's me and Elton, that's all." But she could tell by his blank stare that he wasn't convinced.

"Let's go rest until it lightens up, then look for a hotel," she said.

She intentionally selected a pew close to the chapel altar away from the homeless snoring bodies in the nave, but as she rested her head on her satchel that held her only possessions and pulled her knees to her chest and felt Francisco's socked feet touching her hair, she shivered with the recognition that she and Francisco were anything but separate from the others—they were the same.

Francisco awoke from a light sleep when a hunkered down old woman clamored into a pew two rows in front of them and talked in a language that he couldn't understand as if she had arrived from a faraway land or maybe a distant planet where mumbo jumbo was understood. When he sat up to look at her, she stared right back at him and waved her hand like she was banishing him from her world.

Mmgrabla . . . grshiba . . . phsss

Her rattling on kept him awake, so he slid down the slick seat and gazed at the jewel-colored glass, soaring white columns, statues of angels and Jesus with his arms open and raised. Everything around him seemed to lift his eyes upward, and he wanted to explore these higher places. He tiptoed along the marble floors toward the crossing, climbed five narrow stairs leading to the pulpit, but upon reaching the top, discovered that he was too short to see. The wood paneling that surrounded him was like an unscalable cliff preventing an ascent to the top. He crept back down the stairs and with his arms folded against his chest scanned the choir and caught sight of a stool with soft velvet padding. Lifting the stool, he quietly mounted the stairs again, positioned the stool near the pulpit edge, then stood on his toes, and though only the top of his head and eyes breached the precipice, he could see layer upon layer of white arches and a vast display of shining organ pipes in the distant upper gallery.

Higher, to the bell tower, he thought. He had seen it from outside with its soaring spire that appeared to mingle amongst the stars.

With light feet, he quick-stepped down the center aisle then searched the narthex for doors or hidden stairways that led upwards. In a dark corner near the back, he found a small narrow portal only two feet taller than himself. His imagination reared up. Did a hunchback live here?

He remembered the day—back when he was five in front of the movie theatre—when his mother had quickly pulled him away from a poster advertising an upcoming feature. "Come on, Pancho" she had said. "You're too young for that."

But he couldn't forget the image—the *Hunchback of Notre Dame*—Quasimodo—kneeling, chained to a pedestal like a wild animal, with flame red hair, one eye bulging, the other swollen shut. It was both horrifying and fascinating.

He gently turned the brass handle and tugged, but it didn't budge. Glancing around he whispered, "If I were a key where would I be?"

He ran his hand along the underside of a bench beside the door—nothing. Then he raised the corner of woven mat at the foot of the door but found only dark speckles of mouse droppings—drats!

Shoving his hands into his pockets, he paused for a few seconds. Suddenly, he whipped his hand outward like a pirate unsheathing a sword and pointed to the ledge above the door. "Aha!"

He scampered on top of the bench, steadied himself, then ran his fingers across the molding but came up with nothing but dirt and dust. He looked over his shoulder. Behind him was a small square window—maybe there? Again, he stroked the surface of the sill, but again found nothing.

Resting his elbows on the sill, he cupped his chin in his palms and stared outside into the dark shadows of a juniper tree. Its branches swayed in the breeze like it was waving to someone across the garden. Beyond the garden wall, in the glow of streetlights, he could make out a few low brick buildings—storefronts—but he couldn't see the wording on any signs except for one that had a rickety overhead lamp that swung in the wind—YATES C—FE. Loose and dangling, a letter clanked against metal, and though the window was closed, he could hear the squeaky, eerie sound.

Then he heard something eerier. It seemed to emerge from the top of the juniper—a distant rustling at first—but as it got closer, the rustle transformed into something more rhythmic, more powerful—*whoosh whoosh whoosh.*

In an instant, it was before him spanning the entire window—splayed feathers, outstretched wings, sharp open beak, fierce golden eyes. When he raised his arms to cover his face, his body lurched backwards and teetered on the bench edge, and just when he thought he was going to tumble to the floor, he waved his arms in wide circles regaining his balance then thrust his head forward towards the window and found himself locked eyeball to eyeball with a beast. Neither he nor the giant owl blinked.

Suddenly, the owl swiveled his head to the right, and Francisco turned his head in the same direction. Their motions seemed synchronized by some primal connection. He paused, recognizing the moment for what it could possibly be—a message, a sign, given directly to him from an owl. He took a deep breath and gently pushed the blue curtain that framed the window aside. On a hook, attached to a long green ribbon, was a shiny brass key.

His knees were shaking as he opened the door then closed it behind him and stared upward into a dark cylindrical structure with a winding staircase. Like he was being swept up through a chimney by a windy force, he ascended the stairs in a whirl, taking two steps at a time, round and round, circling upward, upward, until his last leap. With feet firmly planted, and adrenaline coursing, he gasped at what he saw.

Everything: twinkling stars loosely sprinkled across the early dawn sky. Mountains to the north, a dark blue against a slightly lighter blue sky . . . a sliver of a moon cradling a bright shining light . . . a hint of pink to the south just above the horizon . . . flickering yellowish lights across the surface of a dark ribbon-like form. Gridded streets stretching out in an endless checkerboard.

And above him was a giant bronze bell with a long-knotted rope dangling down. He touched the rope's rough surface, gripped it, and tugged, but the bell didn't budge. He tugged again, with more force, and heard a slight squeak from the bell's hinges.

"Who's there?" a low gravelly voice shouted.

Francisco jumped—was it the hunchback or maybe someone worse? He pressed his body against the tower wall and slid towards a corner. Shuffling feet came closer, closer, closer. His heart thumped against his chest like a pounding bass drum. Then a light, bright and blinding. He covered his face with his arms, frozen, trapped, perhaps to be launched over the tower edge, flailing, screaming, then *splat*.

"You are not supposed to be up here," the voice growled.

Francisco said nothing but prepared to make a dash toward the stairs.

"You found my key, I see."

Francisco tilted his head slightly, dropped one arm, and squinted into the blinding light.

"Either you're clever at finding things, or I'm a predictable man." The voice had changed its tone. "Don't be afraid."

The light dropped away from Francisco's face and onto the brick floor, and even though it was dim, Francisco could see that the man was old and stooped—but he wasn't bare chested with a tattered cloak, and his face wasn't lopsided with one eye bulging. Instead, he wore a cap, baggy pants, a wool jacket, and his features looked soft and gentle.

"Did you come to see the bell?" he said hoarsely.

Francisco nodded.

"Then I credit you with an admirable curiosity." The old man gazed up at the bell and pointed. "1805, see the date? Cast in France, brought to Mexico on a Spanish ship, then ended up here. *Mi abuela* I call her."

Francisco relaxed and looked up at the giant bell. "Your grandmother? Why do you call it that?"

"Because she's over fifty years older than me," the man said, then he turned to Francisco. "And how old are you, son?"

"Twelve," Francisco said.

"Well, that makes her over a hundred years older than you." He smiled.

Francisco was amazed. He imagined a Spanish sailing ship in a raging storm, the captain at the helm holding tight to the wheel, his face grimacing against battering rain and gale force winds, his curses and shouts to his crew, "*Aaar* . . . man the ropes, secure the bell, you scallywags," as waves breached the bow, and the bell clanged amid pitching seas.

The old man's voice brought Francisco back to the present. "The dawn is beautiful, isn't it? That's why I'm here. To see the sunrise before ringing the bell."

"That's your job?" Francisco said.

"Yes, I'm Javier," the man said gently. "The bell ringer, the trash collector, the gardener, the floor mopper, the cobweb broomer, the window cleaner, and the duster of everything."

"You must be important," Francisco said.

The man smiled and nodded. "*Sí, mi amigo*, very important."

Francisco looked at him with a serious expression. "I found some spots you missed when looking for the key. I can show you where it is so you can wipe it up."

Javier laughed. "Yes, later. Not now. There are more important things to consider at this moment, but first I must know your name."

"F-F-F-Francisco," he stuttered, as if he were not completely familiar with his new self—whoever he was.

"Ah, Francisco. A courageous name," Javier said. Then he took a deep breath, held his chin upward and blew out a long string of mist that glowed like a comet in the emerging dawn light. He turned his head and directed his attention to the southeast as if he were searching for a companion. "Out there," he said and pointed, "just next to the fading moon is Venus. Do you see her twinkling? My dawn friend. My goddess of beauty. She will remain with me for a few more weeks, but then I must say goodbye." He put his hand over his heart. "I will miss her, but true as a soulmate, she won't leave me forever. She'll return in a few months, and I'll greet her on spring evenings when the acacias are blooming in the church garden."

Javier put his hand on Francisco's shoulder—even though it was cold out, the old man's hand felt warm like a distant sun.

Javier pointed. "And those out there are the Franklin Mountains," then he raked his finger further south, "and that is the Sierra de Juarez range beyond the river in Mexico. The river, do you know its name?"

Francisco shook his head.

"*Rio Bravo*," Javier said. "The Rio Grande as they say here—in your country. So, you see just over there is my country—so close."

"How close?"

Javier chuckled. "You are a thinker." He paused and gazed toward the river. "My house—my wife, my children—are over there, less than a mile from this church."

The light had begun to change, and the eastern horizon was a bright pink, then orange above with streaks of dark gray like giant brush strokes across a magnificent canvas.

Javier clapped his hands together. "It's almost time!"

"Time for what?" Francisco said.

"To ring the bell." As Javier moved toward the rope, something caught his eye, and he stooped to pick it up.

"What is it?" Francisco said.

"An owl's breast feather," Javier said, and he handed it to Francisco. "A gift for you. My family believes that the owl is the protector of our children. My great-grandmother, as a small child, was saved by an owl. When she was just two, she wandered away from home, at night, deep into the desert. An owl led her parents to her. They found her sleeping in the sand, near a cluster of Spanish daggers—unharmed. The owl was her protector and the Spanish dagger her guards. Ever since then, our family has believed that our human souls and the owls are connected."

Francisco held the delicate feather and ran his index finger over its soft tips. "I saw an owl outside the window near the key. It flew right up to where I was standing. At first, I was scared, but it just sat there and didn't fly away. By turning its head, it showed me where to look for the key."

Javier studied Francisco as though he were examining a newly identified relic then cleared his throat but didn't say anything.

"Have you seen the owl up close too?" Francisco said.

Javier smiled. "Not like you, but she is my friend. She keeps the pests away in the garden, and the feather I gave you is hers. She's a great horned owl, and you see, she is already at work—looking after you," and he smiled. "You must keep the feather someplace safe."

Francisco thought for a moment then tucked the feather into the inside pocket of his jacket and patted his chest.

Javier nodded in approval then pointed toward the bell. "Now, we must get on with our business."

He looked Francisco up and down. "It's a very heavy bell, but I can see that you're strong . . . I'll hoist you up, and we'll ring it together."

Javier struggled on the first attempt, but tried again, holding Francisco's hips and raising him up. Francisco reached for the rope and gripped it tightly, one hand above the other, then secured his legs around the rope's dangling end.

"Hold tight, *mi amigo*," Javier said.

Javier held on to the rope and pulled downward with a great thrust. Francisco swung upward, the bell rocked once, but didn't ring.

"Again," Javier shouted. "Throw your weight!"

This time with all his strength, Javier pulled, and on the downward haul, the clapper hit bronze, and the bell's reverberating ring ricocheted off the tower walls then pealed out with a *dooooooooong*!

Javier let go, and Francisco flew upward with a *whoosh* then downward again, his feet grazed the ground, then up. Javier spread his arms wide and belted out a joyful laugh.

"Fly, Francisco, fly!" Javier shouted.

Unleashed and swinging with the bell's weight, Francisco let his mind take flight. He imagined the rope stretching in length as he swung wider and wider beyond the boundaries of the steeple walls, further, further, outward!

"Hang on," Javier yelled.

Francisco held on tight with one hand and reached out with the other then threw his head back absorbing the cool light of the stars as he swept south then upwards past the shadowy depths of lunar craters then even farther toward Venus—the apex of his flight—where the brightness made him blink, and where he touched a sparkle of the planet's light before swooping down again toward the rippling currents of the river then ascending upwards past the bell tower where Javier stood waving his arm as if he were pulling Francisco across the sky toward the mountains.

Javier laughed and shouted, "You are free!" and the sound of Javier's voice echoed off rocky cliffs as Francisco's feet grazed the fragrant tips of the giant fir trees and created a flourish of crystalized mist as he sped upwards and swooped above the tallest peak where he could see the entire mountain chain zigzagging across the desert and feel the warmth of the pink eastern sky. Here, at the top of the peak, the great horned owl awaited him then spread her giant wings, took off, and glided beside him as the great bell clanged below.

Underneath the bell, Javier watched as Francisco swung back and forth, up and down, kicking his feet, laughing, with wide eyes glittering in the morning light.

Francisco shouted. "I'm soaring, Javier! With the great horned owl!"

Javier was stunned, and it took him a minute to recognize what he was hearing. His breath caught in his throat, and he put his hand over his heart. He looked up—heavenward—then out across the river, then whispered. "*¿Es posible?*"

Hearing the bell, Antonia awoke, rubbed her eyes, then looked around for Francisco—he was gone. Panic gripped her.

She jiggled the old woman in front of her. "Have you seen my son?"

"*Bumballab garum shrum,*" the old woman muttered and brushed Antonia away with her arm.

Antonia ran to another pew where a man was sitting. "My son, have you seen him, twelve years old, dark straight hair?"

The man shook his head absently.

She walked quickly to the back of the church. The narthex was a swirl of movement with shuffling feet, whispering voices, veiled faces, fingers dipping into water, genuflects, but Francisco was nowhere in sight.

She threaded her way through the moving bodies like she was swimming upstream through schooling fish.

Outside it was almost light, and she stood at the top of the steps looking to her right and left in a state of frozen fear not knowing which way to turn. Maybe he was in the cloistered garden to her right, or maybe he took a walk down the street or was he in the parish hall looking for something to eat? Then a shiver ran down her spine—Elton.

She grabbed shoulders and arms as a crowd mounted the stairs. "My son. Francisco, he's wearing a peacoat, white shirt, green tie. Please someone help me find him!"

A woman in a yellow coat with two toddlers, one squirming in each hand, glanced around with an empathetic eye, then a young man in a suit offered to go scout the parish hall, and a grandmotherly older woman who seemed to think that the cloister was a possible hiding place marched off with an upright posture and long strides like a soldier securing the perimeter.

All the while, Antonia shouted into the streets.

"Francisco, Francisco, where are you?"

Then a voice came from above.

"*Maaaaaaama.* Look at me!"

She spun around trying to see where the voice was coming from but was bewildered to find him nowhere.

"Francisco, where are you?" she shouted again.

"Up here, *Maaaaama!*"

Antonia looked up and saw something popping above the tower walls, rhythmically, and she recognized his small face and black mop of hair.

He shouted with a joy that beamed like a bright star. "Up here! I'm ringing the bell. I touched Venus!"

She held her hands up to her mouth, took a deep breath, then stood with her eyes closed and her face tilted upward into the yellow sky.

She whispered, "Thank you."

CHAPTER 6

HOTEL LUNA

Walking down Mesa Street in the early morning hours, Francisco didn't elaborate on his mind's wild ride—about touching Venus or on his trip past the moon, or his favorite part about gliding with the owl, because his mother definitely wasn't in the mood.

Instead, he purposefully stayed a few steps behind her as she scolded him for wandering off.

"You scared me to death, Francisco. Never ever do that again!"

"I was just exploring and—" he said, but he didn't get the chance to mention meeting Javier because Antonia interrupted him.

"Never ever!" she said, then she stopped, held both of Francisco's hands, and looked him in the eye with an intensity he had never seen before. "Promise me!"

He dipped his head, "I'm sorry, I promise," and continued to walk quietly behind her as they trudged southward through the center of downtown where multistoried brick and stone structures—hotels, banks, department stores, theatres—lined both sides of the street and then further south, where the density of downtown gave way to a quieter neighborhood with rows of two-story brick apartment buildings and narrow laundry-filled courtyards.

It wasn't until they had crossed over the tracks where Antonia snagged her high heel between two railroad ties that they came to a stop. She held onto Francisco's shoulder as she bent over, slipped her foot out of the shoe, and jerked the heel from its lodged position while mumbling a few damns and bloody hells. He didn't remember his mother cursing so much in the past, in front of him at least, but lately these expletives rolled off her tongue like they were part of her being, passed down through her Irish ancestry.

Beyond the tracks, the road narrowed and turned to dirt. Dense clusters of low-slung shacks lay ahead appearing to have risen from the surrounding piles of junk and scrappy vegetation. Walls made from tin panels, wood pickets, and mud-smeared cobbles supported loosely thatched roofs.

A thin Black man, in worn-looking clothes, emerged from one dragging two barefooted toddlers as they hung onto the straps of his suspenders. When he started to run, the suspenders stretched and snapped back, and the children fell to the ground in a pile of giggles.

Francisco waved and laughed at their squirming giggly mass as Antonia shook her head and scanned street signs at intersections. "So many tree names—Poplar, Birch, Cedar—but not a tree in sight."

At the corner of Rosewood and Wyoming, two men in wide-brimmed hats argued. One held a red hen under his arm and shouted, "*Pollo* mine!" and the other gritted his teeth and vehemently grabbed at the hen. "Your *pollo* skinny, mine fat like this one!"

When they pushed each other, Antonia tugged on Francisco's coat, and they crossed the street to steer clear of the ruckus, but a Chinese woman almost ran them over as she wheeled around the corner pushing a cart piled high with bruised apples. She called out in a high-pitched voice—*píngguǒ, manzanas!*

Francisco smiled at a swaddled baby that was strapped to her back as a girl in a tattered gown and oversized boots sprinted from a brick doorway then gently pinched the baby's cheek and squealed *goo goo ga ga*.

The woman laughed. "Rosa, you pinch my baby . . . I pinch you!"

The girl tee-heed then twirled in a circle. "If you can catch me!"

The early morning excitement—playing children, barking dogs, scurrying chickens—was invigorating to Francisco, and he had a sudden instinct to escape his mother's serious mood and join a game of tag that swirled up like a wind witch before him. And for some strange reason, he wasn't afraid to try. Ever since meeting the owl and Javier, he felt different—as if he were lighter on his feet and could breathe, smell, and hear more clearly.

He caught himself as he took an enthusiastic leap forward. Don't, he thought, you're already in a heap of trouble. So he considered quieter options. He reached into his coat pocket and cupped the cricket in his hand then squatted and opened his fingers. "You'll like it here," he whispered. "*Adiós*, friend."

By then, Antonia was several strides ahead, so he ran to catch up. For a while, they walked parallel to a railyard with long lines of engineless, rusted-out freight cars. He had already counted seventy and craned his neck to see ten more as they veered off Missouri Street onto Madera then walked another five blocks and turned right on Luna. It wasn't until they stopped in front of a two-story brick building another two blocks down that Francisco spoke up.

"Is this it?" he said.

His mother sighed. "I'm afraid so."

Francisco stared at the crescent-shaped neon light that blinked intermittently, flashing a milk-colored haze over a mural painted on the building's façade. The mural depicted a night sky—dark blue background with sprays of tiny white stars and a few planets—some fiery looking, others light blue, icy.

He was overcome with something he couldn’t explain. It felt like the events of the early morning were somehow connected to the here and now, and he wondered in awe if the moon or Venus—or maybe the owl—had guided them to this very hotel.

As his eyes drifted over the galactic display, he didn’t notice his mother studying their environs with shifting eyes.

Antonia’s assessment? Filth mixed with debauchery. All around were crushed beer cans, assorted discarded bottles, and the overwhelming smell of things gone rotten, and worst of all, urine.

So, this is the place, she thought—her only clue.

She remembered the moment vividly when mention of this place came up. It was the first day they’d met. A summer evening. She had come to see the foal—just four weeks old, a rusty brown with a white blaze on its nose. When she entered the barn on her family’s ranch, the setting sun cast an orange glow onto the hay-covered floor.

Mateo had his back to her and was feeding the mare a bucket of oats while her foal nursed.

“Hello,” Antonia said.

He jumped. “Ay, you scared me.” Then he laughed.

“I’m sorry, I just came to see the foal.”

He ran his hand over the mare’s flanks. “The baby’s beautiful, but she is too. And she’s a good mama—very patient.”

Antonia nodded and watched for a moment without speaking, caught up in the tenderness of the scene.

“You seem to have a way,” she said. “I’ve never known that mare to be so calm. With me, she’s usually biting or ready to give me a swift kick.”

He laughed. “Yes, she does have a temper at times.”

"Do you have your own horse?"

"No, I'm a city boy—Juarez. But I used to work as a hand at the rodeo grounds in El Paso during the season. That's where I learned to love them."

She listened as he told her about his favorite horses—quarter horses named Elroy, Snafu, and Solo. "'So-Slow,' the cowboys called him. He was a good horse though. My favorites weren't the ones that bucked the cowboys easily. Everybody liked those—good draws for top points. I liked the ones that nobody wanted to ride. There's no use for a bucking horse that's no good at bucking. Most are sent to slaughter. I felt bad for them, so I gave them special attention."

"Did you like the job?" she said.

"Sort of," he said. "Long hours. Four in the morning till after midnight every day for a month. Pretty exhausting. Mostly, I slept in the stalls or sometimes at a hotel down the street where a family member of mine worked. She would sneak me a key to an empty room when they weren't full. The hotel was hardly fancy, but it was better than the stall. One thing I liked about it was the mural out front—a brilliant night sky with a flashing neon moon. Strangely, it seemed to offer hope."

He laughed, "But the inside was another story."

And now Antonia stood face to face with the mural just like Mateo had. This is it, she thought. The only crumbs I have.

The front door of the hotel was barred and locked, so Antonia rang the dirt-smeared buzzer. Below the buzzer was a laminated handwritten notecard that said, "Don't ring twice. We ain't deaf."

When no one came for five minutes, Antonia pushed the button again with a look of exasperation.

While they waited, Francisco stretched his neck backwards and pointed to the biggest star on the mural. "Do you think that big one's Venus or the one closer to the moon?" he asked.

Antonia didn't answer but instead tapped her foot impatiently and looked up toward a second-floor window where she heard voices.

A dog barked and someone from behind the door said, "Another blind customer, Paco. Can't anybody read?"

"I can read," Francisco said and stepped forward.

The door cracked open, revealing a slice of a face. It had one eye that was smeared in violet above the lid, and there was a partial mouth with lips the color of blueberries.

The crack grew wider, and now the wrinkled face of a gray-haired woman appeared revealing a sideways smile. She spoke to the dog that poked his nose through the crack. "Look, Paco, we got us a tiny little customer."

Antonia suddenly appeared behind Francisco, and the woman's smile dimmed.

"A man at the train station said you'd be open by now," Antonia said.

"My name's Loretta, and we are open, but I'm old and slow and would appreciate a little patience. Nobody has patience these days. They think they can whistle, and you'll come running like a jackrabbit. And mind you, I'll come when I feel like it." Then she paused and raised her eyebrows. "*If* I feel like it, that is."

The old woman waited for her message to sink in then looked down at Francisco and added, "But seeing this little prince has cheered me up." She opened the door wide for Antonia and Francisco to enter.

The entry foyer, a hallway about five feet wide and twelve feet long, was covered with dark wood paneling that was shredded and split where the wall met the ceiling. Yellowed rodeo posters were tacked on both sides along with a few "Wanted" leaflets that featured blurred images of scraggly-looking faces. When Francisco stopped to examine a leaflet that was taped at his eye level, his mother beckoned for him to follow into a slightly larger lobby with a long, narrow desk, two straight-backed wooden chairs, and a table tilted to one side.

Loretta waved her arms. "Welcome to Hotel Luna where luxury and cleanliness is our motto." She laughed and revealed two gold-capped teeth.

Ugh, Antonia thought, looking around at the cobwebs in corners, the shredded gray carpet, and then back at the old lady. Maybe staying here was a bad idea. And was this a member of Mateo's family?

She must be rich, Francisco thought. Not only did she have rings on every finger—with sparkling stones—but her teeth were made of gold. Never before had he seen gold teeth, and she had two. As he considered their value—in the thousands or maybe more—Francisco felt Paco's warm breath at his ankles, and he bent over to scratch behind the dog's ears. The dog groaned with pleasure and looked up with soft eyes of attachment.

Antonia spoke flatly, "We'll need a room for a few days."

Loretta smiled. "Well of course. Anything for this precious little one." She cleared her throat and lowered her voice. "And his mother I presume?"

"Yes," Antonia said.

Loretta raised her eyebrows again. "And his mother's name?"

Antonia lifted her chin and said, "Mrs. Flynn."

Francisco looked up with surprise—Flynn? He was about to say, "Who's that?" when Antonia pressed down hard on his foot with her shoe and gave him a look.

"Ouch," he mumbled.

The old lady noticed the exchange then squinted and looked at Antonia skeptically. "Are you *suuuuure* its Flynn?"

Antonia nodded.

Francisco wiggled his toes to see if there was still life in his right foot and wondered. Why the fake name?

Loretta took a deep breath, and the smell of stale cigarette breath wafted their way. "Well, Mrs. Flynn, it's your lucky day. We do have a room for you and your little angel. On the second floor, just up the stairs and to your right. It's one of our best as is suitable for a visitor from heaven." She gave Francisco an exaggerated wink.

Why do old ladies always wink? he thought. And the endless pet names that this lady was using was weird—*little angel, little prince, precious little one*—like he was a character in a toddler's fairy tale. He avoided any more eye contact and instead glanced around the room. Everything seemed slightly tilted and splintered as though an earthquake had shaken the building, but no one had bothered to make repairs. The stairs to the second floor were sloped and rickety. The plaster ceilings were filled with aimless roving cracks.

Rusty horseshoes were nailed into the molding above every door, a large brass clock shaped like a sun hung on a wall. Its face was yellowed, and the second hand was stuck on six. Gravity had won the battle over wheeled mechanics.

But there were other things that added a bit of cheer—colorful rectangles of perforated paper depicting doves and angels strung overhead from one wall to another, a banner of a white butterfly, a terrarium with a half dollar-sized ceramic turtle and fake moss and tiny palm trees. And there was a smell—smokey, earthy, plant-like. What is it? he thought.

Even with its slanty awkwardness, there was something about this place that intrigued Francisco. Perhaps there was a hidden story and everything that surrounded him was a clue.

"Please give us the keys, and how much for tonight?" Antonia said.

Francisco could tell his mother was losing patience, but the old lady wasn't fazed and cheerfully pulled a key off a hook and clutched it tightly in her hand.

"That will be three dollars, ma'am."

Antonia reached for the key.

"Sorry, money first. Hotel policy," Loretta said.

Antonia sighed, and as she counted out bills, Loretta dangled the key in front of Francisco. "Here you go, Master Flynn," she said.

Francisco blinked. No one had ever called him Master. Even though he liked the sound of it, he tried not to show it. And now, not only was he a master, but he had a whole new person—Francisco Flynn. A newly planted seed ready to sprout. He held the key in his palm and examined the brass tag with the number 203 then tucked it safely in his pants pocket and was intensely aware that this was the second key in a matter of hours that had come his way.

Once they ascended the stairs, Francisco ran down the hall searching for 203. "Down here," he yelled. It was the last room on the right in a hallway that smelled of mold and musky old furniture. When he unlocked the door, room 203 was pitch black. He fumbled around for a light switch just inside the door then clicked it on—it barely lit the room.

Antonia groaned. "No window?"

What had been a window was now boarded-up with plywood, and there was a scurrying scratching sound behind it.

"Tell me no," Antonia said. "Rats?"

Francisco cocked his ear and heard more than just scratching. There was also a muffled high-pitched chatter. He tapped on the wood and the creature stopped making noise. "It's probably a bird scouting out a place to nest."

"How do you know it's a bird?" Antonia said.

"I just do—I know about birds 'cause of Piper," Francisco said. His face dropped, and his mother looked at him.

"I'm sorry, Francisco. I meant to say something earlier, but I got caught up in our trip. Elton said he got loose and flew off."

Francisco looked down. "Yeah." He didn't want to get into it. It hurt too much.

"I'm sure he'll be happy out with the other birds—at least he's free," she said.

Francisco said nothing. He wanted to forget *all* of it. Everything that was behind him. So he diverted his attention to the one thing that gave him comfort—the owl feather in his pocket. He needed a safer place for it and remembered the leather strand and metal trinket that served as his bookmark.

While his mother huffed and fumbled to find a light in the closet, he turned his back to her, plucked a thick wool thread from the hem of his coat and tied a double slip knot around the feather's quill, then lay the leather strip on the bed and cinched the woolen thread around the leather strand. He tugged on it to make sure it was secure then looped the leather strand around his neck and tucked it beneath his undershirt.

He didn't plan to tell her about the feather or its purpose—it was too risky. Though she might let him keep it, there was also a chance that she'd make him toss it. "Wild birds carry disease," she had once said when he found a blue jay feather in the yard, pushing him toward the hose to wash his hands.

This feather was too important. It was their protection against Elton and any other bad stuff. He would keep it close.

CHAPTER 7

PEARL-HANDLED DERRINGER

It was hard to tell what time it was when Antonia awoke to a poke and Francisco's voice. In this windowless room, it could have been midnight or midday.

"Wake up, Ma. It's time for breakfast," he said. "The birds are chirping outside, and I'm hungry."

Antonia mumbled, emerging from a dream, then suddenly sat up. She scanned the room then flopped back down with a groan. "Ugh—what a dump." She took a deep breath and wondered if this had been the room where Mateo had slept. How could this place possibly be better than a horse's stall? She closed her eyes momentarily and admonished herself over her privileged criticism. This is your life for the moment, she thought. Get used to it.

"I'm going down the hall to the bathroom," Francisco said. He stood looking at her in his white t-shirt and oversized jockey underwear that made his skinny legs look like sticks protruding from a flour sack.

"Lock the door behind you," she said. "And come straight back."

"Okay," Francisco said with a drawn-out yawny voice.

She knew he would be a few minutes because he always lingered during toilet time. Why she didn't fully understand because most other times his attention moved from one thing to another as though his eyes and mind were in a race to see all. Perhaps it was the safety of a locked door or the book he took with him—or both.

While he was away, she methodically organized her things. She lay her blouse and skirt on the bed, pulled her girdle up to her waist, slipped her feet into her silk stockings, clipped her stockings to her girdle, then tucked her pearl-handled derringer behind the girdle lacings, and cinched it tight. It was the derringer she thought she had lost in their frantic scurry to board the train. From here on out, she'd make sure it was available but safely stowed.

The coldness of the barrel against her skin gave her a shiver. She had never owned a gun and had purchased it, reluctantly, the day before while Francisco was at school. Her justification? Unknown and potentially dangerous times ahead. Even though carrying it made her edgy, she had convinced herself that it was the one thing she could count on for protection. And she didn't want Francisco to know about it either—such bold steps might cause him to worry. He had been through enough.

She had been the only woman in the gun shop. Several men glanced at her with intrigue, but one gawked while he caressed the stock of a shotgun laying on the glass counter.

"Your old man cheating on ya?" he chuckled.

His tone and arrogance reminded her of Elton, and though she wanted to clock him, she said nothing.

The salesman looked at the man. "Shut up, Ed," then turned back to her. "This little derringer's a beauty—good ladies' gun," the salesman had said and winked. "Small, elegant, and fits nicely in your purse," as if she were in a department store shopping for a decorative cosmetic bag or a little bejeweled mirror.

Ready to get out of there, Antonia quickly replied, "I'll take it." Even though the cost would put a dent in what little money she had.

Back in the hotel room, she tucked her rolled up wad of bills into her bra, and by the time Francisco came back, she was fully dressed and brushing her hair.

He scratched his bottom under his jockeys and said, "What are we going to do next?"

Antonia responded quickly and like a well-rehearsed actress, she spoke with a clear, clipped confidence. "I'm going to find a job. Something that will work for both of us—where you can be with me."

"But will I go to school?"

"No, not now. Maybe later."

When Francisco grew quiet, she tried to sound cheerful and added, "We'll get books. I'll help you learn. And when you get smarter than me, we'll figure out what's next."

He stood on his toes with an excited expression. "Can I pick out the books myself?"

"A few of them," Antonia said and smiled feeling relieved that she had steadied him for the moment. "So, which book were you reading in the bathroom?" she asked.

"It wasn't a book," he said. "It was a magazine—*Boys' Life*."

"I didn't know you liked *Boys' Life*. Did you bring it with you?"

"No, it was just in there. I was reading about bears, and cougars and . . ."

Antonia's mind drifted. Strange, she thought, for a *Boys' Life* magazine to be in this hotel with no kid in sight.

Before leaving the hotel to find breakfast, Antonia approached Loretta who sat hunched over a newspaper, working the crossword with a pen in one hand and a cigarette in the other. The old woman didn't look up until she heard Francisco cough.

She peered over a pair of half glasses with purple rhinestones arrayed around the frame and immediately smiled at Francisco while ignoring Antonia. "Ah, my prince," she said. "How did you sleep, little one?"

Francisco looked at her from under his dark bangs. "I'm twelve," he said. "Not a kindergartener."

Antonia glared at him. "Francisco, your manners."

Loretta's lips turned into a thin line of red lipstick as her smile flattened. "Hmm, well, my apologies."

"It's okay," he said, and his attention averted to a millipede that inched across a ripped linoleum floor tile.

He squatted and watched its tiny legs at work then whispered, "I wonder what all those feet sound like to you. Are they loud like a marching army or quiet like you're wearing tiny pairs of socks?" As he reached out with his index finger to touch it, he heard a shrill voice.

"Don't touch! It's poisonous!" Loretta squealed.

Francisco looked up and blinked with a surprised expression.

"It's not a centipede," he said. "It's a millipede and they don't sting. Look, see?" He touched the creeping insect, and it curled up in a ball.

Loretta coughed. "Oh, I see . . ." she said, ". . . quite the little expert . . . oops . . . I mean expert . . ." then she mumbled under her breath with a sour expression, "*Un niño precoz*," and abruptly turned her attention to Antonia.

"How can I help you, Mrs. Flynn?"

"I'd like to inquire about a job. Maybe here at the hotel?"

Loretta stared at her. "You don't look like the type to clean toilets," she said behind a plume of exhaled smoke. Loretta's gray hair was pulled back in a messy ponytail, and purple-dyed strands framed her worn and wrinkled face. As she took another drag from her cigarette, smoke curled under her nose, and her black eyes turned into dark slits.

Antonia straightened her back and raised her chin. "I'll do whatever it takes—for my son and me."

Loretta looked her up and down as though she were considering the purchase of a feisty mare of questionable breeding, then let out a fake chuckle.

"You're running from something aren't you, sweetheart?"

Antonia straightened her back and pushed her hair behind her ears. "I need work."

There was an awkward silence as Loretta picked up a small clay bowl with painted images of blue agave and tamped out the glowing tip of her cigarette until a final braid of smoke dissipated. "Well, let's see, there's the . . ." She paused and continued, " . . . or maybe the . . ."

Light from the front door with its barred glass cast striped shadows across her faded pink blouse.

"The what?" Antonia said impatiently.

Loretta waved her palm like she was swishing a fly. "Ah no. I forgot that Consuela already has a maid. Perhaps Reina at the theatre ticket booth? Mind you, she always smells like popcorn, not necessarily a bad thing, but it ain't fine perfume."

Antonia took a deep breath then blew out. "It's okay, I'll figure it out."

Loretta held up both hands and with a sudden terseness said, "Just a minute. Sometimes a person needs time to think." Then she cradled the ashtray in her palm and rubbed her thick fingers over the colorful fired imagery. She laid it gingerly on the counter, got up, disappeared into an office, and closed the door.

Through the thin door panel, Antonia heard her voice. "Operator? Oh, Ruby, *hola.* Listen, sweet cakes, hook me up with Ray."

Outside, there was barking, the hotel door opened, a chill blew through the corridor, and a bundled-up Chinese man shuffled through the lobby.

When Loretta returned, she had a freshly lit cigarette hanging from her mouth, and her newly applied lipstick was bright and shiny. "Couldn't get hold of him, but he'll be here at the hotel at 11:00," she said. "I'll introduce you. His name's Ray. He eats lunch here every day, and he might have a job idea. Trust me, you'll need more dough than you think. Things ain't cheap in this touristy town, and I get the sense that you're used to comfort."

"I may not be who you think I am," Antonia said.

"We'll see," Loretta said. She dropped her head and mumbled smugly to herself, "Desperation and compromise can be cozy cousins." Suddenly, she looked up with a forced cheerful expression.

"And your first name?"

"Antonia."

Then she turned to Francisco. "And remind this old lady, you're Francisco, right?"

"Yes."

She reached under the counter and pulled out two packages of candy and laid them on the counter: a box of Sugar Babies and a Three Musketeers bar. "You choose," she said. "A present—to ask forgiveness for my mistake."

Francisco didn't hesitate and pointed to the Three Musketeers.

Loretta smiled. "My favorite as well," she said. "The Sugar Babies are tasty, but they get stuck in my teeth."

Francisco smiled. "I like your gold teeth. They're pretty."

Loretta laughed joyfully, reveling in his high compliment.

"Is there a bakery or a grocery nearby?" Antonia asked.

Loretta twisted her lips. "Take a left on Luna, and about five blocks down and two over, you'll find a few shops south of the stockyard. Just follow your nose and watch your step. Cow patties everywhere."

"Cows?" Francisco said. "Can we go see them?"

Loretta threw back her head and belted out a laugh. "You can't miss them!"

"We will be back at 11:00," Antonia said. "Thank you."

She had tried her best to sound polite, but she wasn't sure she could trust this lady or this man she was about to meet. Though Loretta had offered Francisco candy, how could Antonia know she wasn't after something?

CHAPTER 8

LORETTA

Loretta immediately tried to call Ray again and when he picked up, she didn't bother to say hello. "There's a woman staying at the hotel with a boy. I don't know much about her, but she needs work. She's blond, a real beauty. She's got a rich girl look about her—nothing sleezy. You need to talk with her and check her out. For you-know-what."

"Right," Ray said. "A beauty, eh?"

"Yeah, blond hair that curls over her shoulders like a movie star. No one would suspect. Of course, she'll need some work, but I'll cover that. And the boy, oh my. He's a doll. Together they're perfect." Loretta's voice turned to a whisper. "I've told her you might have some means of employment but gave no details."

"What makes you think she'll do it?" Ray said.

"She's got that desperate look. And I don't think she'll find any decent work around here 'cause there ain't none to be found. This town is crashing like everywhere else—New York, Chicago," then she snickered. "Except for a few businesses—thanks to our good friend prohibition." She paused a moment. "And I think something messy has happened in her life. I'm pretty sure she gave me a fake name."

"Hmm . . ." Ray said.

"She's coming back to meet with you at 11:00. So be here and don't wear that old brown shirt with the holes in it. You need to look tidy but not too fancy. Wear something with a little color but not too much. You don't want to look like a fiesta."

Ray sighed. "Oh, Loretta. You and your designer ideas. I'll wear what I want to wear," he said. "Just like I always do."

Her voice got shrill. "That's what I'm afraid of—that you'll screw this up! She *has* to trust you. I'm telling you, this may be our big chance!"

Ray took a deep breath. "I'll see for myself. Goodbye, Loretta." After they hung up, Loretta looked around the lobby to make sure no one was there, then scooped up Paco, positioned his front paws over her shoulders, spun him around, and giggled gleefully. "Paco, my sweet *perro*, she could be the one!"

Her giddiness was cut short when she thought of Francisco. He seemed to be a sweet boy, but also especially observant and curious. That could complicate things.

She needed a dual strategy for success—be kind to the child. Then maybe the mom would notice and start to trust.

CHAPTER 9

MOO

Outside, in the chill of the morning, Francisco raised his nose, sniffed, then pointed. "Smells like that way." He reached for Antonia's hand and pulled her along. "I'm starved."

They skirted along the railroad tracks, past a collection of boarded-up brick warehouses and came upon the gates of the stockyard.

"So many cows!" Francisco said and pinched his nose with his fingertips.

Within a cacophony of moos, one cow stood atop a manure pile that to Francisco looked two stories high. The cow stretched its neck and bawled as though it had reached the mountaintop and was admiring the view.

Past the stockyard the smell cleared. "Thank God, I can finally breathe again," Antonia said. "I'm not sure I can handle manure with eggs."

Francisco added, "It wasn't that bad, it's just grass and a little gas."

Antonia smiled.

Heading south, they came upon a small park with a few trees and scraggly patches of lawn within a field of packed dirt. No children played on the rusty swing set or the pull-up bars, but the benches were filled with lumpy figures under gray blankets with mussed-up hair and protruding chapped feet.

Francisco ran to the metal pipe bars, shimmied up an eight-foot pole then grabbed the cross bar with both hands and yelled, "Watch!"

He did six chin-ups and pushed himself to do one more, gritting his teeth and grunting. After the bottom of his chin touched the bar, he dropped to the ground, took a deep breath, and looked at Antonia.

"Well done," she said. But he felt like he deserved a little more enthusiasm, like "Wow, you're strong!" or "Look at those muscles!"

At the south edge of the park, a street vendor called out to them.

"Fresh empanadas!"

They walked toward the smell of fried dough, and as they got closer, they saw a short squatty old man thrusting his weight and pushing a cart with a yellow-and-white striped canopy and wobbly wheels. Francisco noticed a rusted horseshoe dangling from the post of the vendor's wagon, and like a cowbell, it clanged against the post with his every step. The gray-whiskered vendor wore a navy wool driver's cap that cast a shadow over his eyes, but his cheeks had a chapped rosiness.

"*Hola, Señora,*" he said as he lowered the cart. He took a deep breath and wiped the perspiration from the back of his neck with a dingy white towel that was draped over his shoulder.

He pointed to a menu that dangled from a chain. "I have pork and chickpea or beef, raisin, and pecan. My wife makes them." He rubbed his stomach. "*Muy bueno.*"

"How much?" Antonia said.

The old man pointed to a sign. "A dime for two, *por favor.*"

Antonia handed him a coin. "Pork please."

"*Gracias, Señora.*" He gave her a sparsely toothed smile and wiped his greasy hands on his apron before wrapping two in a piece of newspaper.

After paying, Antonia scanned the park for a place to sit then headed toward an empty bench in the sunshine next to what appeared to be a remnant of a rose garden. Only a few scraggly stems remained, and a clump of paper napkins stuck to their thorns.

Before Francisco turned to join her, the old man raised his cap and gave Francisco a wink with eyes the color of sea mist. "You're good on the bars, *muy fuerte.*"

"*¿Fuerte?*" Francisco said.

The old man held up his arm, pushed up the checkered sleeve of his shirt, flexed his muscle, and a bulge the size of an orange emerged from ripples of wrinkles. "*Fuerte.* Strong."

Francisco smiled as confidence swelled inside, and suddenly he felt less hungry for food and hungrier for conversation. He pointed at the horseshoe. "Why do you have that?"

"For *buena* luck."

"Good luck?" Francisco said.

"Yes, very good, *mi amigo*. You must forgive me. Around here, we mix our English and Spanish like it is one."

"I know some from school," Francisco said. "*Yo tengo que ir al baño.* Our teacher made us say it in Spanish every time we had to go to the bathroom."

The old man chuckled. "That's good, very good." He nodded at the horseshoe.

"That shoe belonged to a horse named *Papalote*—twenty dollars I won on that *caballo*—most money ever for me. She ran like the wind before a thunderstorm—swift, *rápido*. She was beautiful too—black and shiny."

Antonia called for Francisco. "Your food's getting cold, come on."

"Better go," Francisco said. As he turned to run, the old man called after him.

"*Adiós,* Francisco."

Francisco stopped in his tracks and whipped around. "How did you know my name?"

The old man smiled broadly. "I had a hunch. My brother Javier—the bell ringer—told me about you, and you fit his description. Your *ojos*. I could tell right away."

"My eyes?" Francisco's eyes were wide and sparkled in the sunshine.

"*Sí,* they are big, bright—handsome." The old man leaned over the cart and held out a hand. "*Me llamo* Gabriel."

Francisco heard a *urrrrrrip urrrrrip chew chew chew* above and looked up as a bright red cardinal landed at the top of the striped canopy's peak.

"That's my friend," Gabriel said. "He follows me picking up empanada crumbs."

Francisco smiled, "I like birds. When I met Javier, I also met the owl that lived in the church garden. I've decided that if I could be a bird, I'd be an owl. How about you?"

"Tough question," Gabriel said. "Songbird or bird of prey? I must think on it. If you come back for empanadas again sometime, I'll have an answer for you."

Clouds were moving swiftly across the sky. A giant puffy one blocked the sun at the far end of the park, and its shadow drifted toward them, turning everything in its path momentarily gray. When it passed over, Francisco felt a chill, but the sun returned with a flash of light.

Francisco reached out to shake Gabriel's hand. It felt soft and cushiony like pillows, and for some reason, Francisco didn't want to let go. He felt something magical passing between them. In the distance a church bell rang.

Francisco laughed. "It's Javier!"

Gabriel smiled and looked at his watch. "*Sí, mi amigo*. Eleven o'clock. He's right on time."

When Antonia and Francisco returned to the hotel, two scruffy looking Hispanic men wearing jeans, cowboy hats, and boots stood talking with Loretta while rolling dice. Loretta had an orange marigold tucked behind her ear and looked at Antonia and tilted her head to the left.

"He's out back," she said. "Francisco can play dice with us." She pointed. "Grab that stool, Francisco. You can roll 'em for me."

Francisco beamed. Antonia frowned with a clear message.

Loretta spoke to the men. "Boys, we'll finish this game *mañana,* and I'll take the rest of your money." She elbowed the youngest one. "Don't break your neck on Tamale. He's a feisty old bull."

The men snickered and tipped their hats. "*Hasta luego,*" one said, and walked out.

Loretta turned to Antonia. "Okay if Francisco escorts me to the store? It's just around the corner."

Antonia's mind raced—so much was happening at the same time. There was the possibility that Elton might be searching for them, and who was this new person she was about to meet? "I don't think that's a good idea."

"It's okay, Ma," Francisco said. "I'll take good care of Mrs. Loretta."

Antonia shook her head and mumbled. "Well, that's not exactly what I meant—"

Loretta stopped her mid-sentence with a glance. "Yes, with him along, I should be fine. And it's no more than twenty steps down the street."

Antonia took a deep breath and sighed, feeling her better judgement slip away. "Okay."

Francisco ran to the door to open it for Loretta then said, "If you need some help, you can hold onto my shoulder."

As they moved away, Loretta looked back at Antonia and patted her heart. "We won't be long. He can keep me company at the front desk when we return. When you're finished talking, he'll be right here with me."

"Thank you," Antonia said. She followed them outside and watched warily as they disappeared around the corner. Panic set in like a thunderbolt, and her heart pounded against her chest. *Am I crazy—letting Francisco out of my sight?* Elton could show up at any moment and snatch him.

CHAPTER 10

FIREBALL

Francisco walked with exuberance in his step. He wanted to show this grandma type his best side, and he wanted her to like him. So far, it was working—she had given him a Three Musketeer's bar. Perhaps there would be more to come at the store. And he had to admit that there was something about her that he was starting to like too. She was treating him as though he was older than twelve—like suggesting he join in with the cowboys in the game of dice—with real money at stake.

He pointed northward in the distance. "When I saw those mountains earlier, they were purple and blue—the same color as your eye lids and those purples stones on your glasses. Pretty."

"Really?" she said, and she raised her eyebrows and smiled. He thought he saw a faint pink rise in her cheeks.

"*Muchas gracias,*" Loretta said.

Right behind them, Paco trotted and sniffed at the empanada remnants on Francisco's fingers, and when the dog boldly took a lick, Francisco didn't shy away. Instead, he stopped and scratched behind the dog's ears.

"I've never had a dog," he said.

"Why?" Loretta said. "Every boy needs a dog."

"My stepfather didn't want one. He didn't like the . . . you know . . . in the yard."

Loretta laughed. "Yes, the 'you know' is not much fun to pick up, but the dog is worth it. This one here, he's old like me and blind as a mole, but his hearing's good. His bark sounds fierce, but he's a lover not a fighter."

Francisco gave him another pat, and Paco licked his hand again. "I like animals," he said.

"Mmmm . . ." she said. "I see you do, and they like you too."

Loretta looked at the dog and pointed back towards the hotel. "Go home, Paco! Guard the castle, you loveable mutt." She let out a chuckle that turned into a brief deep-throated cough.

Francisco waited until she finished, then asked, "Have you ever read the *Call of the Wild*? There's a dog named Buck that once was gentle, but he learned to be fierce to protect himself. I have the book."

Loretta cleared her throat. "You should read it to me sometime. You enjoy reading?" she asked.

"Yes," he said. "And I found a magazine in the bathroom this morning, and I read about people who fly—planes I mean. And how people study birds to design airplanes—their wings, feathers, their body shape. I read the whole thing, because I want to learn more about flying."

Loretta smiled. "You want to be a pilot?"

"Well, sort of," he said. He stopped himself before telling her about Javier, the owl, and how he imagined taking flight, and that he wanted to actually fly himself—not in a plane.

Loretta nodded. "You have a vision for yourself—*es bueno*."

"You liked the magazine then?" she said and winked at him.

Francisco smiled. "You put it there?"

She smiled, "*Sí*."

At the store counter, Loretta spoke to a Chinese man wearing wire-rimmed glasses, a cap, and a navy blue shirt. "The usual, Sung," she said.

"You smoke too many cigs, Mrs. Loretta," Sung said. "I heard you coughing outside. You better cut back—they're bad."

"Can't teach an old dog new tricks," Loretta said.

"You're no old dog, Mrs. Loretta. You can do it." He nodded towards Francisco. "Who's this one?"

Loretta put her arm on Francisco's shoulder. "My new friend, Francisco. He's staying at the hotel."

Sung smiled with closed lips.

Loretta pointed to a row of jars in the window. "Francisco—pick out a piece of candy for yourself, then we'll head back."

Francisco quickly turned and surveyed the shelf with a wide sweep then eyed each jar, imagining the delectable treasures inside. He tapped his lips with his finger and raised each lid breathing in the flavors—peppermint, cinnamon, butterscotch, licorice.

He grabbed a fireball and held it up. "This one!"

Sung glanced at Loretta. "Watch out, Mrs. Loretta. He likes the hot ones—he may be a rascal."

Loretta waved her hand. "Oh, Sung. He's no rascal, he's a sweetheart."

Rascal? Francisco thought. He had been called a lot of things but never a rascal, and he liked the freewheeling, wild-sounding part of it. At first, he hadn't liked Loretta's pet names for him, but he was starting to realize that it was just grandma stuff and maybe it wasn't so bad.

On their way back, Francisco popped the fireball into his mouth as Loretta lit a cigarette. When its hot cinnamon flavor rose up through his nostrils and made his eyes water, he blinked and raised his eyebrows. "Yaow!"

Loretta laughed.

Francisco laughed too. He sensed that Loretta saw something special in him. It felt good.

CHAPTER 11

THE INTRODUCTION

Antonia found him behind the hotel under a tin-roofed shed supported with warped timber posts. There was a small wooden table with stained Saturn-like water rings, and a man sat with his back to Antonia. Just beyond the concrete patio, a short Chinese man worked in the sun pinning dingy sheets on a clothesline.

The white man at the table didn't stand when she appeared but took a sip of his beer and held out a hairy freckled arm and pointed toward a stool opposite his chair.

"Sit," he said. He adjusted his horn-rimmed glasses. "Hungry?" He tugged at the bottom of his undersized jacket where the single button that held it closed strained against the pressure of his oversized belly.

"No, thank you," she said.

He had a face that was an assortment of rounded features—a bulbous nose and rubbery thick lips that protruded outward like a blowfish. Curling from underneath his Panama hat, his hair was a mix of red and gray, and he wore a khaki-colored suit with an open white cotton shirt that was grimy at the collar, and splotches of rosacea flared on his neck and cheeks.

"My name's Ray. Yours?"

"Antonia."

"I heard you have a boy. Loretta told me."

"Yes," Antonia said, and she glanced nervously between the man's face and the open door as she waited for Francisco's return.

Bam! There was a loud clatter in the laundry yard. Both she and Ray jumped at the sound of heavy metal hitting paving. "Goddamit! What the hell was that?" Ray bellowed and threw down his napkin.

The Chinese man parted the sheets and peered out. "Sorry, Mister. Dropped my wash basin . . . so sorry."

"That guy . . ." Ray shook his head with a look of disapproval. "He goes by Sam to sound American, but my hunch is he also does it to sound like he's related to Sam Hing, that millionaire who ran a business up on St. Louis Street 'bout twenty years ago. But I know this Sam ain't no relation—he's a peasant smuggled in from Mexico—worked on the railroad then stuck around living in that slum on the northeast side. They call it Chinatown as though it's some grand place, but it's just a pile of busted up building scraps. I'm with our government on this one. Send 'em home. Taking jobs away from others during these hard times."

Antonia bristled at his unkind tone, but she didn't say anything. She needed to hear him out. She needed a job.

"Loretta says Sam's a good worker, but I don't trust him," Ray said.

Antonia sensed a weakness. "You have something to hide?"

He smiled showing his yellowed teeth and raised one eyebrow and stared at her. "Don't we all?"

Just then, a slender young woman with dark straight hair appeared from behind a yellow curtain carrying a steaming plate of beans and rice with strips of gristly beef laying on top. She carefully slid the plate in front of him, reached into her apron, and pulled out a rolled cloth napkin with corn tortillas. When she refilled his beer, he slipped his hand gently under the hem of her skirt and patted her thigh. Her face flushed then she turned and left, and Antonia saw a smile cross her lips.

He looked at his plate and then at Antonia. "Do you mind?" he said.

"Of course not. Go on." She was surprised by his sudden manners.

He speared a chunk of beef and used it to scoop up a heap of beans and then leaned over his plate and shoved the oversized bite in his mouth. He was about to take another when Antonia interrupted and tilted her head toward the waitress.

"Your wife?" Antonia said.

He raised his head, put his fork down, wiped his mouth with his napkin, then stared at her and squinted.

"Are you throwing a stone?" he said.

She didn't respond but stared back at him without a flinch. He chuckled and looked up at the broken fan above like he could use a breath of fresh air.

"Please tell me you're not one of those churchy, overly pious types."

She did not unlock her stare. "That's not why I asked," she said.

He raised his arms and held his palms out in an expression of mock despair.

"Then why, pray tell?" he said.

She did not play into his jocularity but kept her voice measured and clear.

"Your boundaries, I need to know them," she said. "I have a son to care for."

He shook his head, then rocked back in his chair and took another sip of beer before responding with king-like confidence.

"Angelica is my lover," he said. The words rolled off his tongue as if he were describing the sweetness of a luscious peach. Then more curtly he added, "My wife had enough of me years ago."

He cleared his throat. "Enough information then?"

Antonia nodded, knowing that the chess play wasn't over.

"Well, I have a few questions myself," he said. "Where are you from, and what brings you to this dump? I own this hotel, but since you're looking for honesty, let's call a spade a spade."

"Tucson," she said. "Needed a break."

He snickered. "Ah, a break. Excellent choice of words—a response that reveals nothing."

She looked around the terrace rather than making eye contact and didn't respond. Beyond the roof overhang was a gnarled tree trunk and about ten feet up was a deep cavity where the trunk had split. From within, something peered out with slitty eyes.

He noticed her staring at it.

"That damn owl showed up a few days ago. I told Loretta to patch up that hole to get rid of it. I don't need another pest around here. But she wouldn't do it. Said it would keep the pigeons away."

Ray laughed. "And shitfire if she wasn't right. I haven't had a drop of pigeon crap on my table for three days, but I must say, there's something about that thing that gives me the creeps—like he's watching me all the time. *¿Comprende?*"

Antonia raised her eyebrows in a questioning way.

He coughed into his napkin and quickly changed the subject as if Antonia had dug up a weakness. "About the job . . ." he said, "it appears you may be up to the task, and there'll be decent pay to boot. And if you follow my instructions, we will get along fine."

"I will decide that when I hear about the job," she said.

She heard Francisco's voice inside and let out a deep breath then turned her complete attention on Ray. Behind Ray, Angelica watered a pot of yellow and orange marigolds while bending an ear in Ray's direction.

Ray didn't turn to look at her. "Angelica, *vaya por favor*."

Angelica huffed then disappeared behind the kitchen curtain and began clattering dishes in an overtly loud way.

He leaned in and put his elbows on the table. "The job. It has some risks but mostly rewards. It will require a stealthy eye, but I see you have that already. You'll carry things back and forth between El Paso and Juarez—hidden in your clothing."

He picked at his tooth with his long-nailed little finger then sucked in to make sure it was clear while he waited for her to respond.

"Smuggling? I won't be a criminal, if that's what you're asking of me," she said.

He laughed. "Where are you from, sister? The land of the Goody Two-shoes?" He cupped his hand over his mouth and hollered. "Angelica! Bring out the loaves and fishes! We got a damn saint at our table."

"I will not sit here and listen to your fool talk and crass humor."

"Aw, come on now, calm down," he said. "Jesus, you're a touchy one."

He took a deep breath and lowered his voice. "Listen, it's not as bad as you're thinking because this here's the border. You scratch my back, I scratch yours. It's the way things are done. Mexican or American matters not. We all get along like friends, and we all get a little piece of the pie." He rubbed his thumb against his index finger. "People down there want things we have, and we want things they have—but nobody wants to pay customs. Customs money goes back to the feds. We like to keep our business local."

She pushed back her stool and stood up. "I'm not interested."

He laughed. "So quick to be done with me? But you could be good at it, and there will be no harm. And you will have money—for your boy."

"No," she said, and she left the table and walked back to the front desk where Loretta was playing cards with Francisco, and Sam stood looking over Francisco's shoulder.

Francisco pointed to a card and turned his mouth Sam's way. "Should we discard this one? What do you think?"

Sam twisted his mouth then nodded vigorously. "Yes, *eeesh.*"

Loretta looked up and over her glasses. "He's beating me at gin and teaching Sam the game at the same time."

Francisco spoke without taking his eyes off the cards. "And Sam's going to teach me Chinese checkers in return."

Sam looked outside as Ray shifted in his chair. "*Eeesh.* I better get back to work," he said.

Antonia looked at Loretta with an expression of renewed distrust because of the man she had introduced her to. "I'll wash toilets."

Loretta laughed. "He scared you away?" She shook her head. "He is not a bad man, Mrs. Flynn. Besides, I already have a toilet washer," she said. "Angelica."

Antonia pulled at her skirt to straighten it. "I'll find work elsewhere then."

"Easier said than done, *mi amiga.* These are hard times," Loretta said. "You see, we have people like Sam and so many other desperate folks in this town who work for nothing. And even though Sam has done our country a service, now he's looked down upon. He was one of Pershing's Chinese that helped supply the US Army and the general to go south after Pancho Villa. Ray thinks Sam's a liar and made all that up, but I've seen his papers. It doesn't seem to matter though."

Loretta shook her head. "Sam works hard. He's been with us for nearly eight years, and he has a family—a wife and six kids—but they have next to nothing. I've seen the children's sad faces." She took a deep breath and cleared her throat. "The little ones get to me. You understand?"

Antonia lowered her eyes. "I do."

Loretta smiled and chuckled. "And Ray, just when you think he's a bona fide horse's ass, he reveals his soft side. God bless him, he had me wrap and deliver some candy and toys for Sam's kids at Christmas and told me to say it was from me—not him. So, I'm just saying, things aren't always as they seem. Everybody's got their good sides and their bad sides and a lot in between that's soft enough for shaping."

Antonia didn't say anything. The Christmas story did little to alter her impression of Ray.

Loretta's face became serious. "And the hard truth is, there's lots of people here hiding, and looking for work just like you. They make just enough to scrape by and find they can't afford to leave. That's the way it is. Nothing comes easy here, even if you're a blond like you. You should think about Ray's offer."

The fire in Antonia's eyes diminished slightly, and she waved to Francisco. "Come on, Francisco, let's go upstairs."

"Wait, Ma," he said. "We're not finished."

"You can play tomorrow," Antonia said.

"But we're not playing gin tomorrow. Loretta's bored with it—we're playing poker. Loretta says poker's more her style."

Loretta covered her mouth, shrugged, and dramatically tucked her chin as though she had been caught in a most egregious act. Her nails were painted an iridescent blue, and her fingers splayed across her chin and mouth like a peacock in full plumage.

Upstairs, Antonia thought back on her conversation with Loretta. Why was Loretta defending Ray and pushing the job so hard? Why did she care?

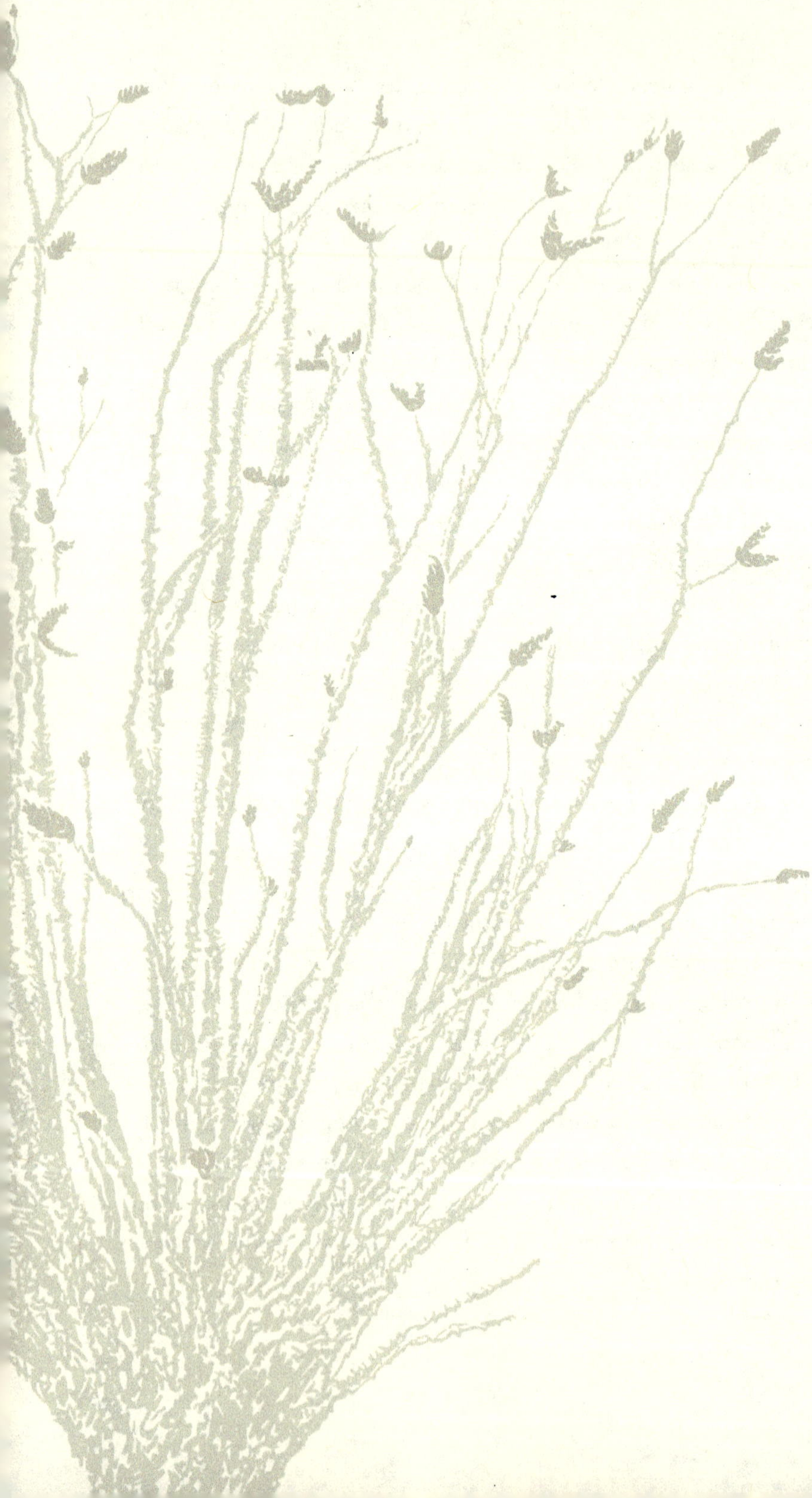

CHAPTER 12

BAD OMENS

For three days, Antonia had beaten the streets looking for work with Francisco by her side. On the third day, she sat on the edge of the bed examining her aching feet where blisters had welled up after walking in high heels. She had applied Vaseline to her sore spots and padded her shoes with toilet paper before putting them on. The birds were chirping outside, and she heard Francisco's stomach growl, but he didn't hop out of bed like he usually did.

"My legs hurt," he said. His voice sounded whiny as a three-year-old. "Do we have to walk a bunch today too?"

"Yes, we have to keep looking," she said, but she didn't tell him that their money was almost used up. She needed to find a job today.

She tried to sound cheerful. "Come on, chop-chop, it's 7:00 a.m. We need to get going."

"Can't I just stay at the hotel and play cards with Mrs. Loretta?"

"No. I know you're tired, but we need to stick together."

Francisco grumbled but slipped on his pants, and when he checked his owl feather, it looked as rumpled and tired as he felt. He blew on it to perk it up, smoothed the down with the tip of his finger, and tucked the feather back in his undershirt.

Downstairs, Paco lay sleeping by the front door, while Loretta cut coupons with a pair of scissors. Her hair was pulled back, but the purple streaks were gone and replaced with pink. As they approached the front desk, Loretta popped what was left of a donut in her mouth then took a slurpy sip of coffee. "Good morning!" she said when she saw Francisco.

Francisco made an exaggerated effort to slump his shoulders. "Goooood morning," he said in a bluesy voice.

Loretta pushed a plate with two powdered sugar donuts toward them. "For you."

Francisco's expression changed from its stormy day appearance to one of bright sunshine. "Thank you," he said.

Antonia touched Francisco's shoulder. "You can have both. I'm not hungry."

Francisco smiled and picked up one in each hand, but before taking a bite, he held them up to his eyes like a pair of glasses. "You like my new spectacles, Mrs. Loretta?" he said.

Loretta laughed as his big bright eyes beamed through the powdery holes. "The latest style in New York, I hear."

Loretta turned her attention to Antonia and raised one eyebrow. "Do you mind if I ask where're you headed today?"

After her strong stance with Ray, Antonia was determined not to appear defeated. She pushed back her shoulders and stood squarely. "North of this neighborhood. A woman told me there were quite a few restaurants and shops up there. I'm sure today will be the day."

Loretta looked down and brushed a few specks of powdered sugar off the desk. "Not trying to tell you what to do, but if it were me, I'd go over to San Antonio Street, a ways past the brickyard. Don't think you'll find much between here and there. The courthouse area and downtown, where the tourists are, is probably your best bet. It's a bit of a walk from this neighborhood, but better fishing I'd say."

A feverish stubbornness reared up in Antonia. Why was she reluctant to take advice from this woman? Was it because the old lady and Francisco had become a bit chummy? Was she jealous? No—she was just being careful. There had to be a motive for Loretta's friendliness. Antonia's stepmother had taught her plenty about that—kindness followed by a slap in the face.

"Okay, we may go that way after we try the other area," Antonia said. "Do you have a map I could look at?"

Loretta put the scissors down and rummaged through a drawer and found a rumpled map. When she tried to smooth it with a whisk of her hand, the scissors slid off the counter and landed on the floor near Antonia's feet.

As Antonia turned to pick them up, Loretta's eyes grew wide, and she grabbed Antonia's wrist. "Don't move!"

"What?" Antonia said as she whipped her head around thinking that a snake might be coiled in a corner or, worse, was about to slither up her leg.

"Stand very still, both of you," Loretta said. She tiptoed around the counter and stomped on the scissors and shouted, "Out, away with you!" Then she put her hand over her heart and looked up towards the ceiling. "*¡Mi Dios!* That was close."

Antonia looked at Loretta with alarm. "What are you talking about?"

Loretta was aghast. "You don't know?"

"Know what?" Antonia said.

"The scissors—if you don't step on them before picking them up, it's bad, very bad." Loretta raised her eyebrows and revealed another layer of color on her lids—a lavender that blended into her blue. "It's a bad omen. Not as bad as a broken mirror but close."

Francisco's eyes were wide with curiosity. "Are there other bad omens?"

Before Loretta could respond, Antonia squelched the drama. "Can't say I'm a believer in such things."

Loretta looked to the side then spoke tersely. "Well, to each his own." She started wiping the counter with an unusually heavy hand like she was trying to remove a stain.

Antonia cleared her throat. "Thank you for the donuts, now come on, Francisco." She turned to go.

Before closing the door behind her, Antonia looked over her shoulder. Loretta had scurried to a vase, selected a plant sprig, and waved it frantically over the place where the scissors had fallen as if she were sweeping something away.

Antonia was alarmed. Was Loretta a complete nut? Though Antonia had come to this hotel specifically to search for Mateo, now she wasn't sure if it was a good idea. It might lead to undesired outcomes.

CHAPTER 13

LORETTA

After Loretta believed she had thoroughly cleansed the place of bad omens, she put her hands on her hips and thought about Antonia—a tough nut to crack—but she wasn't giving up. Maybe the scissors thing had been a bit of an overreaction on her part. She would be careful to hold her tongue in the future about such things. Not everyone had a sense like she did for outside forces—it was a gift but also a curse. Joy mixed with an abundance of hand-wringing.

Outside she heard a noise. What the devil?

She looked out the window. Five or six wrens were flapping their wings and fussing around the crevice where the owl was hiding.

Brave little creatures, she thought. Only half of the owl's head was visible—just two black slits for eyes and pointy ears perfectly camouflaged with the bark of the mesquite.

She had never seen an owl there before and wondered how many days the owl had been there—at least four. By its distinct ears, she knew it was a great horned owl. She knew a little about owls from her cousin Javier. He had a fascination with them and studied their behavior—particularly the one who frequented the church garden and Bell tower at St. Patrick's. And like Javier and others in her family, Loretta shared the belief that owls protected the children in their family. They had heard their great grandmother's story many times and believed.

She was worried about this particular owl and its choice of a roosting spot. For the meantime, she had convinced Ray that having the owl was a good thing—to keep the pests away—but he thought the whole family story was ridiculous.

"That's just a bunch of made-up bullshit," he had said.

He said the owl made him edgy, and she could imagine him going after it with a broom and maybe hurting it. Loretta was concerned. This owl could be the protector of one of her family members, a relative's child. She would make certain that nothing bad happened to it.

CHAPTER 14

DEAD ENDS

While walking down Luna Street, Francisco thought about what he had just witnessed. This whole thing about scissors and bad omens—who was right? His mother or Mrs. Loretta? And why had his mother so abruptly changed the subject—like it was poison.

They took a right on Franklin and walked about thirteen blocks then zigzagged their way toward San Antonio Street. Before them were the mountains just beginning to display the morning light.

Francisco pointed, "Look, Mama. The mountains are blue, purple, and pink. Loretta would love those colors."

Antonia halted instantly and gripped Francisco's shoulders. "Francisco, I don't want you to get too friendly with Mrs. Loretta."

"Why?" he said. "She's been nice to us, but you act like you don't like her."

"Yes, well—" Antonia stopped short.

Francisco had no idea why his mother was so edgy, but he did know that once her mind was made up, she didn't change it. But why did she have to dictate his friends? He had a mind of his own, and despite what his mother said, he wasn't going to stop being friends with Mrs. Loretta.

For now, though, best to change the subject. "Do you know what that tall mountain is called?" he said.

She shook her head.

"North Franklin Peak," he said.

She nodded and smiled. "How'd you know that?"

"My friend Javier told me."

"I've never heard you talk about Javier. A boy from school?"

Francisco was about to tell her more about Javier but decided not to bring up the bell incident again.

"No, just a friend. I wonder how tall that mountain is?" he said, but his mother didn't respond. She had her eye on a building up ahead.

It was a red brick building with a sign outside: Cotton St. Cleaning and Dye Works. The shop, with its large plate glass windows and a lace curtain fringe hanging above, had a handwritten sign in the corner near the door that said, "Not hiring" like it was a frequent question.

Next door was an open-air market, The Renaldo Fruitery, with racks of postcards and magazines and metal Coca-Cola coolers with sliding lids near the street curb. When Francisco saw the Coke bins, he looked up hopefully.

"Can I get one? I'm kind of thirsty from the donuts."

"Too early, we'll find a water fountain," she said. "Maybe later when we need a pick-me-up."

Antonia entered the store, perused the fruit bins, and picked out two apples hoping that a purchase might have a positive influence on the shop clerk. "Looking to hire?" she asked.

A middle-aged lady with weary eyes looked up over her glasses and shook her head like it was too much energy to speak.

"Know of anywhere else around here?" Antonia asked as she paid for the apples.

The woman's head kept wagging. She reminded Francisco of a bobble head doll set into motion, and he wondered how long she would keep going.

Down another two blocks, they came to Ackerman's Pharmacy. Inside, the smell of aged wood, rubbing alcohol, and other medicinal scents filled the air. In the long high-ceilinged room, light fixtures of varying styles and lengths hung on long chains from the tin-clad ceiling. In the middle aisle was a table of neatly stacked newspapers and a calendar with giant-sized letters that shouted the date: "December 3."

While Francisco eyed the eight-foot-high shelves with hundreds of bottles of all shapes and sizes—some blue, some clear, most auburn tinted, he imagined the potions that might lie within. Maybe something to make you sleepy or another to make you laugh hilariously or fall in love.

He liked the order in the shop—a medicinal library. He could visualize his mother saying, "Good day, ma'am," when the door opened, and the shop bell rang. He could help stock the shelves and maybe carry peoples' packages while the pharmacist mixed concoctions in the back.

Antonia rang the bell on the glass top cabinet, and a clean-shaven man in a white jacket appeared.

"May I help you?" he said.

"I'm looking for a job," she said. "I can do anything you need."

He gave her a look-over and rubbed his hands together like he was washing them with soap.

"I can't afford a full-time position but maybe one day a week for a few hours of cleaning and dusting. It won't be much . . . say thirty cents an hour?"

Antonia took a deep breath and replied, "Thank you, perhaps we'll come back later."

The man responded. "You won't find much, I'm afraid. Sorry, it's the times."

CHAPTER 15

STUPID PRIDE

Antonia felt both discouraged and increasingly desperate. Four days of fruitless searching had passed with no better job offer than the pharmacy.

Not even a family of mice could live on what the pharmacist offered. She sat in bed wearing her coat over her gown with her knees pulled up to her chest to keep the room's chill at bay.

In the distance, she heard a train whistle. Even though Francisco was right beside her, curled up and sleeping, a loneliness settled in that made her legs go limp. She looked down at her hands and rubbed them together trying to generate warmth, but the cold remained. No longer were her hands smooth from the creams she had applied when living with Elton. Now, they were chapped from the wind and sun, and both hers and Francisco's faces were a baked brown, and a weariness had settled over both of them.

Before going to bed, Francisco didn't read his magazine, and he didn't say anything about what he had been so chatty about the days before—stories from his magazine about dinosaurs, bears in the wild, arrowhead hunting—instead he just drifted off like a fading star.

As Francisco slept, she picked up a newspaper that she had dug out of a trashcan in the park. On the front page were photographs of worn-looking bodies waiting in food lines in New York, Chicago, Los Angeles, and in her mind, she transferred her own face and Francisco's onto the printed page and was overwhelmed with anxiety. Dropping the paper in her lap, she pressed her fingers against her temples and concentrated on holding back tears. She repeated her mantra: "Be strong, Antonia. Be strong. You must be strong."

Three dollars was all she had left, and that meager amount had to cover food and board. Raising the paper again, she turned to the employment section but found only one job listing:

Dog Race Park; part-time ticket-taker; age 18+.

She knew Francisco would never be allowed, and she couldn't leave him at the hotel. If Elton showed, anything could happen. She imagined Elton questioning Loretta, and what would Loretta do? She might tell Elton everything—particularly if Elton pushed a few bills her way.

She cast the paper aside and fell back onto the bed. The mattress felt hard as stone, and the room's structure felt like it was about to cave in on her. She noticed every detail with duress—peeling wallpaper, water-stained plaster, spots of black mold. A room decomposing before her very eyes.

Maybe she had made a mistake. Maybe she should have taken the money in the mason jar back in Tucson to give her more time. *Stupid Pride.*

She didn't know what time it was when she fell asleep, but in a dream, she saw Elton's face. He called to her, "Come home, I promise . . ." Everything was blurry as if he were in a cloud, and she squinted to see more clearly if perhaps something had changed. Maybe he did love her, maybe he cared, maybe things could be different.

She was reaching out, maybe to touch his hand or caress his cheek, when she suddenly awoke to shrill screaming—angry words, foul words, a thud against a wall, then a man's booming voice.

"Bitch!"

The yelling continued and Antonia covered her ears. "No!" she said aloud to convince herself. "I did *not* make a mistake."

Next to her Francisco awoke in a panic. "Make them stop!" he said. He covered his head with his pillow and jerked restlessly with every shout. She held him tight for several minutes until she couldn't take his pain any longer.

With a blanket wrapped around her, she stomped down the hall and banged on the door with the flat of her palm. "For God's sake, I have a child trying to sleep."

There was quiet for a moment, then a woman's voice shouted, "Shut your fat mouth, Pete!" But the pause in their argument didn't last.

The next morning, she spoke to Loretta about the noise while Francisco was still upstairs sleeping.

"I can't do much," Loretta said. "I understand, but it's business. Having a child in this hotel is unusual," then her voice dropped, "I'm sorry."

Antonia sighed. "I know it's a lot to ask, but do you think you could give us a room free of charge for just another night or two? I'll pay you back after I find work."

Loretta held up her palm. "Just one night," she sighed. "That's all I can do without getting Ray riled up. Perhaps you should reconsider his offer."

Antonia dropped her head. Every ounce of fight had drained from her body. For a few moments, she said nothing, but in the tension of the silence, she remembered Loretta's words about Ray: "He is not a bad man," and then her own: "I will do whatever it takes."

The options at this point were grim. If she didn't accept Ray's offer, they'd be forced to beg. Even then, her worst nightmare might come true—returning home to Elton, or to her parents, with her hand out facing her stepmother's vicious stare. The shame would be too much to bear. No.

Antonia raised her chin and looked at Loretta. "Okay," she said.

Antonia was expecting Loretta to be calmly empathetic—maybe a head nod and a look of understanding or a pat on the hand like everything's going to be okay.

Instead, Loretta rubbed her hands together and grinned so broadly that Antonia could see every tooth in her head—like she had just won a bucket of money. Why was she so exuberant, Antonia wondered. Was it because she truly cared, or was it something else?

When Antonia stepped onto the covered patio at 11:15 a.m., Ray was sitting at the table with his chair facing her direction. His plate was scraped clean except for a smear of refried beans, and his paper napkin was bunched up on top. Three empty beer bottles were scattered around, and he held another loosely in his right hand. When he saw her, he tipped his Panama hat, and since humiliation was not his intent, he only raised his eyebrows in question.

She nodded.

His serious expression disappeared, and he broke into a wide smile, and his face turned a flushed red.

He raised his arm and pointed a finger upward. "Angelica, bring this lady a tequila! A toast!"

Antonia stared at him squarely. "I don't drink," she said.

He threw his head back and laughed. "*Gawwwd damn!* Even better!"

He flashed her a rascally smile and whispered, "Souses make rotten smugglers." He doubled over laughing then reared back so hard against his chair that his jacket button popped free and revealed his tight shirt, swelled stomach, and a pink belly button at his parted shirttails.

Antonia recoiled at the spoken word—*smuggler*. Was she really going to do this? Break the law? Settle, she thought—one step at a time. You're not committed yet.

Ray looked down and gave his bulge a hearty rub with both hands and chuckled. "Well shit! Too many beers." He waved at her. "Come, sit. It's time to celebrate. We'll talk business tomorrow."

Francisco appeared at the doorway as Angelica plopped down a bottle of tequila and a single glass in front of Ray.

"Francisco, *muchacho*! Come outside and tell me about your day and what you learned about our beautiful oasis of a town."

Francisco's lids were heavy from lack of sleep. He looked at his shoes and didn't say anything.

Ray shifted heavily and the wooden legs creaked like they were about to split under his weight. "Shy fella are you?" he said. "Well, Loretta says you're a good reader. We'll have to get you some more magazines and books. My own children are grown, and they could care less about their poor Papa, so you and I will become friends. What do you say?"

"Maybe," Francisco said.

Ray roared another laugh with his mouth wide open like a lion. "*Gawwwwd almighty*! Wary as a coyote at daybreak. Just like your mama!"

"Sit down," Ray said, and he patted the seat next to him. "You like Cokes?"

"Yes," Francisco said.

"How about a plate of enchiladas too?"

Francisco was starving so he didn't say no. "Please, yes."

Ray waved at Angelica. "Plate of enchiladas for the boy and his mom."

Over Ray's shoulder, Francisco spotted a slight movement in the tree cavity beyond the porch. He knew immediately it was an owl even though the patterning of its feathers were almost indistinguishable from the tree bark, a blend of dark and light gray.

At first, the owl's eyes were closed, but a moment later, as if the owl could feel Francisco's presence, it blinked, opening its eyes wide. Francisco blinked back. The owl blinked again.

Francisco kept quiet for fear that this loud man might do something to scare it away. He wondered, was this Javier's friend or another? He knew an owl's territory could be twenty miles or more and the church was just a few miles away. Had Javier's owl followed him?

To not draw attention, Francisco quickly diverted his eyes away from the owl and toward the woman with the long dark hair who handed him a Coke. He took a sip.

"There'll be a Coke for you every day if you're a good kid, and lunch for you and your mom, and you can stay at the hotel as long as you like." Ray clapped Francisco so hard on the back that Francisco spewed a bit of soda.

Ray chuckled. "Sorry, little cowboy. Just wait, you'll get used to me."

Francisco wasn't so sure.

CHAPTER 16

THE OWL

Back in the room after a full plate of food, Francisco felt better. He had noticed that his mother only picked at her plate.

"How come you weren't hungry?" he asked.

She touched his hair with a weary expression. "No reason in particular."

He hopped onto the bed then flopped down, stretched out, and lay on his stomach. "But you always eat everything on your plate."

She gave a slight smile. "You're right. I usually do. I guess I'm just a little nervous about the new job. That's all."

"Well, at least you got one, and we don't have to walk anymore," Francisco said. "And now, we can stay at the hotel and eat here too. I like enchiladas and Coke."

"Yes," she said, "that part's good. I'm glad you're happy about that."

Francisco knew what he was about to say might irritate Antonia, but he said it anyway. "And I'll get to play cards with Mrs. Loretta a lot more."

Antonia sighed.

"Come on, Ma. She's nice," Francisco said. "Give her a chance, you'll like her."

He turned his head slightly. "What do you say?"

Antonia smiled. "Yeah, okay," she said. "Maybe you're right."

He rolled over and looked at the ceiling then kicked his legs in a bicycle motion as though he was enjoying the moment.

"Guess what?" he said.

"What?"

"I saw an owl outside—just beyond the patio in the mesquite tree. Did you see it?"

"Not today, but Ray mentioned it yesterday."

Francisco kept spinning his legs. "It was a great horned owl. I could tell by its ears and the V-shaped brown feathers between its eyes that dip down to its beak. They're fierce hunters; I know about them."

"I'm not surprised that you do. Tell me more."

His mother seemed truly interested.

"They're my favorite bird. Their soft feathers help them fly really quietly so they can sneak up on their prey. And they have amazing night vision, and their call sounds like this." He made a circle with his lips. "*Hoo, hoo . . . hoo, hoo*—soft sounding. Not shrieky like a screech owl."

Antonia smiled, looked upward, then closed her eyes. "Now that you mention it, I remember that sound. I heard it once when I was with your father. In our family barn one evening—it was the first time we met. He was brushing one of our horses, and an owl called in the distance. He pointed it out to me. And like you, he knew it was a great horned owl."

"Really?" Francisco said. "He knew about owls like me?"

"Yes," Antonia said. She leaned back on the bed next to him

and put her head under her hands and gazed upwards as though the ceiling had disappeared and the night sky was revealed.

To Francisco, she looked relaxed and peaceful.

"I'm glad you told me that," he said. "So, he's like me?"

"Very much," Antonia whispered. "Very much."

Francisco grew quiet and thoughtful. He couldn't remember ever having a conversation like this with his mother. It was as if they had turned a page and a whole new chapter lay before them. He felt a fullness in his chest like he had learned something deep and important that would change him forever.

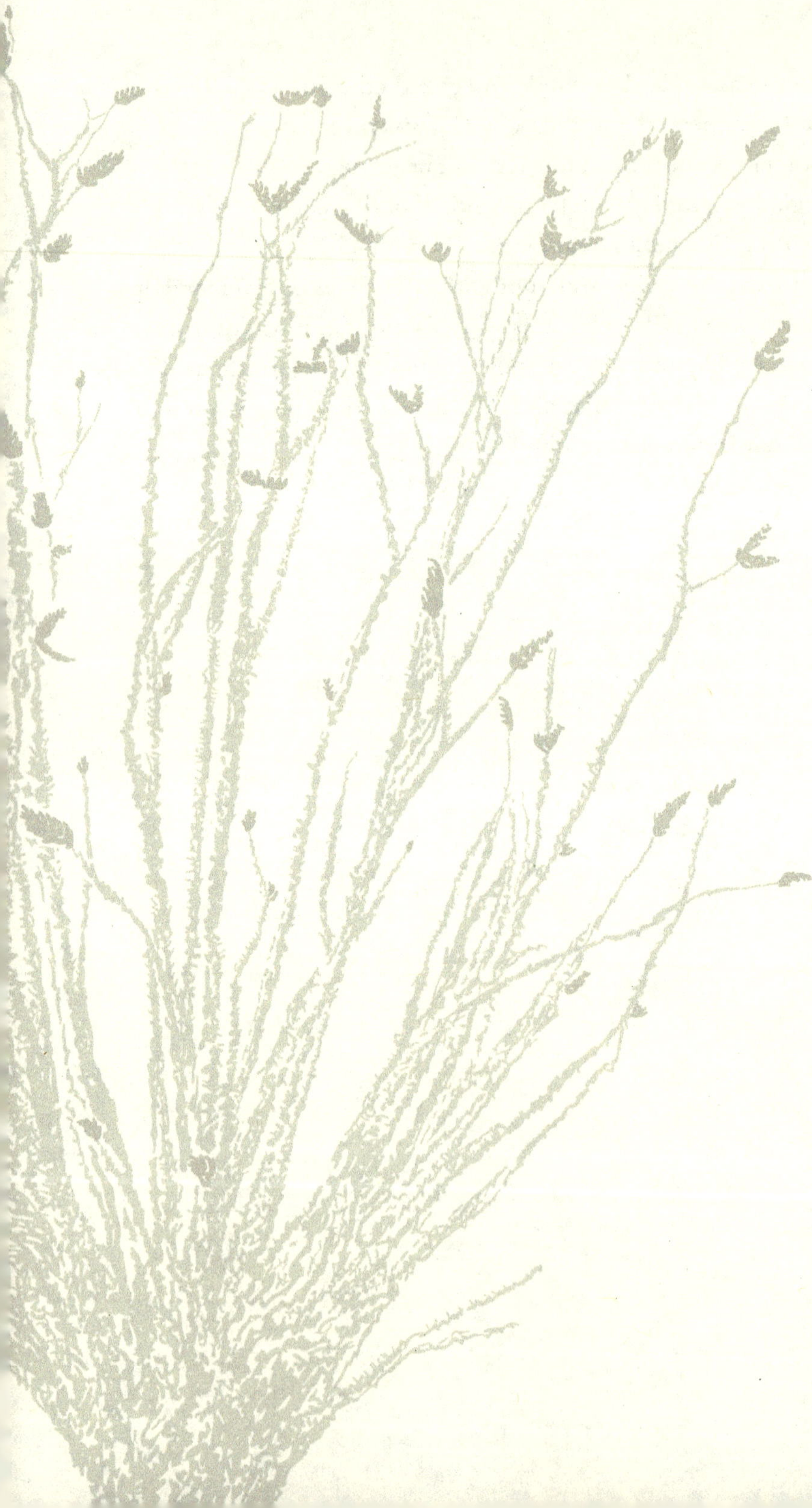

CHAPTER 17

THE DEAL

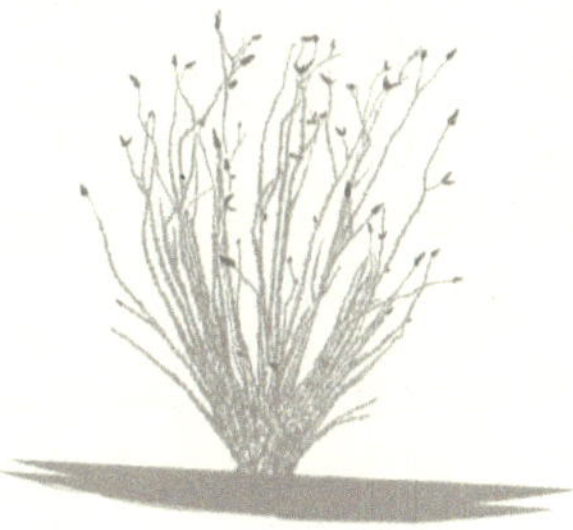

The next morning, when Antonia met Ray on the patio, he wasn't drinking beer or eating, but was chewing on a fat cigar and wearing a serious expression. He pointed to the chair. As Antonia pulled it out, it scraped loudly against the concrete.

Ray winced and clutched his temples between his fingers. "That doesn't help my headache," he said.

"Sorry," Antonia said, but she had no real sympathy. Because of Elton, she knew a hangover when she saw one—bloodshot eyes, sharp tongue.

After she sat, he took a deep breath. "Look, as long as you're working for me, you and Francisco will be taken care of. This hotel's mine, and like I said yesterday, this will be your home."

She flinched at the implied ownership and suddenly felt a tinge of fear.

"We'll stay here for now," she said, "but we'll consider other options later."

He spoke tersely. "Tomorrow is scouting day at the Stevenson bridge. Watch and listen. Get used to the noises and what's going on—the cars, the people, the trolley. Take the boy too. He needs to feel comfortable as well."

"Of course, I'm taking Francisco, I wouldn't—" she said.

Ray threw his hand up to silence her and frowned. "Christ, you're touchy," he said. "Just like my ex-wife. Couldn't get a word out without her bustin' my chops."

Antonia stopped talking, but her face reddened and inside she stewed.

He slid a five-dollar bill her way. "Here's an advance. Buy Francisco a new shirt and let him pick out something else he wants—a toy or something."

He put his elbows on the table and leaned toward her as the rancid smell of cigar breath leaked from his mouth. "You're big on honesty, right?" he said.

She nodded, but by his annoyed expression, she knew his words weren't going to be pleasant.

"Well, here it is. The dress you're wearing makes you look like a peasant. And when you pull your hair back in a bun, as it is now, you look like you've been milking cows all morning. Wear it down, over your shoulders. And buy yourself a new dress and an umbrella."

Her voice was bitter. "Why an umbrella?"

"Your skin's too dark from walking around town. You need to look pale like you're living a rich woman's life."

Antonia didn't like the playacting—being someone that she wasn't. And she hated having to kowtow to his demands, but she didn't interrupt him.

Ray leaned back in his chair, took a long tug on his cigar, and blew a plume of smoke toward the shed's rafters.

"It will be a breeze to get through the Mexican side because of your blond hair," he said. "On the American side, see what it's like. Be friendly, but don't talk too much. Better to be on the shy side—your boy shouldn't ask a lot of questions either. When you're done, meet me back here for lunch. Then, I'll give you more instructions."

Antonia nodded.

"And don't forget, I like you and your boy, but this is business. Got it?"

She gave him her fake smile then quickly turned and left. Anger, humiliation—it tore at her insides. She was succumbing to her lowest self.

CHAPTER 18

LORETTA

After Antonia went upstairs, Ray appeared in the doorway, and Loretta stomped toward him and whispered fiercely, "You called her a peasant? Are you out of your mind?"

Ray held up a palm. "Whoa . . . whoa. I said, she *looks* like a peasant. I didn't call her a peasant."

"Don't be such a hard-ass, Ray. I know that's difficult for you. You probably scared her off again."

Ray rolled his eyes. "She needs to know this ain't play shit."

Loretta shook her head. "She's not an idiot—she gets the picture. It's okay for us to play a little good-cop-bad-cop, but don't overdo it."

Ray nodded, but she could tell he was half listening and probably thinking about rolling in the hay with Angelica.

Loretta took a deep breath to calm down. "Okay. I was a little too happy when she said she'd talk to you. My mistake. But now I'm going to turn on my subtle charm."

"I didn't know you had any of that," Ray said. "Did you make a recent purchase at the department store?"

"Shut up, Ray," Loretta said with a sly smile.

He chuckled. "Okay, okay. You do your job, I'll do mine."

Ray called to Angelica and waved as he walked out the door. "Later, sweetheart. Ain't got it in me today."

After he was gone, Loretta was still nervous. Had Ray blown it?

She scrambled to the office, opened a drawer then grabbed her tarot cards. Slowly and carefully, she laid one card down at a time with a snap. She pushed her rhinestone glasses up against her nose and whispered, "The Sun . . . the Magician . . . the Wheel of Fortune . . . good . . . good." She took a deep breath and stared at the cards intently. "Speak to me." Warily, she snapped the last card down. "THE FOOL AND THE FORTUNE?" She gasped. "*¡Dios mío!*"

Suddenly, Antonia popped her head in the office door. Loretta jumped then scooped the cards up and with a swift whisk, shoved them into the drawer.

"Solitaire. Lost again," she said, then she clicked her newly painted fingernails nervously on the desk. "How can I help you?"

"We're out of toilet tissue," Antonia said.

"Oh my!" Loretta said. "Now there's a crisis!"

Loretta pointed to a shelf. "Right there. Grab some." She raised her hand and wiggled her fingers showing off her nails. "How do you like my new color?"

Antonia remembered Francisco's words—give Loretta a chance. "It's nice," she said, "and I'm sorry if I've been short with you. You've been helpful—thank you."

"Listen, doll. Don't worry," Loretta said. "And remember what I told you about Ray not being all bad. You'll see."

Antonia gave her a weak smile.

"When you feel like it, come back down, and I'll paint your nails pink too. It'll make you feel happier."

"Maybe I will, thank you," Antonia said, and as she turned to walk away, Loretta hollered after her.

"Oh, and listen. I'll ask Ray if we can do a few things to brighten your room. Maybe fix that window, pick out some curtains, and get another lamp so Francisco can see better while he reads. That should cheer things up a bit. Don't you think?"

"Yes, thank you," Antonia said.

Antonia was halfway up the first flight of stairs when she came to a stop and rested her hands on the balustrade.

"Do you have children, Loretta?"

"No," Loretta said. "We couldn't," and though she tried to smile, she knew her feelings were written all over her face. "But Charlie and I made the best of our life . . ." then her voice trailed off.

"I'm sorry," Antonia said.

"Yeah, well . . ." Loretta responded.

Antonia hesitated but spoke. "Your husband? Is he . . .?"

"Heart attack, ten years ago." Loretta said. "I'm surprised I didn't go first after all my slaving at this hotel and his lazing around the house. The cuss." She waved her hand like she was pushing something away. "Ah, I shouldn't speak poorly of him. He was a decent man—I miss him. Living by myself gets lonely."

Then Loretta smiled. "That's why I enjoy your boy so much. Gives me something to look forward to in the morning. Francisco's my companion now—not just the flies circling my head."

"He's fond of you," Antonia said. "And just so you know, I've thought about it, and I'm going to do it—I have to."

Loretta tilted her head to the side and nodded sympathetically. "I understand. Sometimes we have to make hard decisions." It took every ounce of her control to squelch an ear-to-ear smile.

Antonia turned to leave but stopped.

"You need something else?" Loretta asked.

"Well, I did have something I wanted to ask," Antonia said. "I had a friend who stayed at your hotel probably fifteen years or so ago. That's how I knew about your place because he mentioned the mural outside, and I wondered if you remembered someone with the last name Garcia. He would have been maybe fourteen years old and worked at the rodeo?"

Loretta laughed. "You're certainly taxing my brain. I did work here back then, but we had all kinds of rodeo people come and go, and Garcia's a common name around here. It's like my last name—Jones. My Charlie was American, you see. Jones and Garcias—we're like rabbits."

"Well, if it helps, his first name was Mateo."

Loretta shook her head. "Doesn't help much—lots of Mateos too. And let's face it. My memory's pretty shot at my age. I'm seventy-two now. But at least your friend had good taste picking our establishment." She laughed at her own sarcasm.

Antonia pulled at her blouse sleeve. "I just thought I'd ask."

"Does this person mean something special to you?"

Antonia's face turned pink.

"Ohhh," Loretta said and pushed her hair away from her glasses to get a better look. "A love interest some time ago—*¿un Romeo?*"

Antonia smoothed her skirt and looked at her feet but didn't respond.

Loretta smiled. "In that case, let me think on it," she said. "I'll ask around—lots of family here."

"Thank you," Antonia said. "I knew it was a long shot."

Loretta smiled. "A long shot for love is worth it. I'm quite the matchmaker, you know. If you ever need help that is." Loretta paused. "But you're married?"

"Yes, but . . ."

"I see," Loretta said. "I've had some experience with such things as well." She took off her glasses and pointed to a scar above her eyebrow. "Not from my Charlie, mind you, someone before him. I try to hide it with the glasses, but I'll never be able to erase it from my mind."

"How did you know?" Antonia said.

"I had a hunch by the look in your eyes—sadness and determination."

Antonia smiled uncomfortably. "I better get back upstairs."

After Antonia left, Loretta couldn't hold back her jubilation. She sashayed toward the front door with her blue and purple skirt swishing around her knees then grabbed a broom from the hall closet, stepped outside into the midday sun, and began sweeping and singing like a chirping bird—her strokes kept time with chorus of her tune.

Este que tiene de "aguila los ojos
y que dio medida en dondequiera . . ."

To her surprise, Ray rounded the corner and tapped a fresh pack of cigarettes on his wrist.

"Why're you so happy?" he asked.

She leaned in. "She's gonna do it for sure. She told me."

Loretta laughed and did a little jig around her broom, kicking up her bright pink, fuzzy slippers. Suddenly, the broom became her tango partner. She turned her head dramatically and let her pink streak of hair cover one eye before she took three broad steps down the cobble sidewalk.

"I gotta hand it to you, Loretta," Ray said. "You still got the moves, girl. I get what Charlie saw in you."

Loretta swooned and spun around with her arms out wide. "I can almost feel the fire opal in my hand—its glistening warmth and infinite beauty!"

CHAPTER 19

MEXICO

It was Monday, and there was a brisk wind out of the northwest as Antonia and Francisco walked down Texas Street in the direction of downtown. In the dawn light, they moved at a clip to stay warm but mostly to keep pace with the town's early morning bustle. The streets were already filled with honking horns, delivery trucks, and quick-stepping men in dark suits and ladies with tight-fitting hip lines and flared skirts.

Antonia was focused on getting to the bridge, and even though this was only a scouting run, anxiety about what she was going to do later made her edgy.

Beside her, Francisco was a chatterbox.

"Look, there's a movie theatre," he said. "We should go sometime. Oh, and over there, they have horses and carriages. Maybe we could do that too."

Antonia didn't respond.

They passed bank buildings, churches, and gleaming theatres toward Hotel Paso del Norte with its white terracotta trimmings that stood out against a crisp blue sky.

As they approached the hotel, a doorman pushed open a wide swinging portal and a gust of warm air that smelled of coffee and toasted bread emerged along with a young man in a gray overcoat and bowler hat who was linked arm-in-arm with a glamourous-looking woman wearing a feathered cap. They stepped into the chilly air with a jocularity that oozed money.

"Something smells good," Francisco said. "Can we stop?"

"Not there, we'll find a place over in Mexico." She could easily have been a customer at that hotel when she was married to Elton but no longer. The divide between herself and those people now felt as wide as the Rio Grande.

"I like that woman's feather on her hat—it's from a pheasant," Francisco said.

"Yes," Antonia said.

"Bet you didn't know that they like to take dust baths—spreading their wings and sweeping dirt into their feathers. Funny, huh?"

Antonia looked at him and smiled for a split second before returning her attention south.

Down Stanton Street, toward the international bridge, the wide street began to narrow. A collection of low buildings with tile roofs framed the bridge entry, and an American flag atop a tall pole whipped and snapped, warning those who passed to pay attention. Remembering Ray's instructions, Antonia glanced from side to side trying to take in every detail. Ahead was a wooden A-framed shed where car engines sputtered and emitted black fumes from tail pipes.

As they neared, Antonia suddenly felt a tension rise that made her limbs feel like taut ropes.

"Is that it?" Francisco said. "Mexico?" Without waiting for an answer, he said, "¡*Hoooola, Mexico*!"

A smaller shed covered a divided walkway with metal pipe railings and turnstiles, and white metal signs with boldfaced black lettering were nailed into the wood siding—Keep to Left, *Tome Su Izquierda.* To Antonia, the signs seemed to come alive, barking orders with watchful eyes as if awaiting to avenge any misstep.

Her legs were shaky. Relax . . . breathe, she thought.

As they approached the shed, several paces ahead of them, a tall lanky man in a dark suit pressed his hand on the top of his hat to keep it from blowing off his head and kicked at the pigeons that blocked his path.

"Bloody pests!" he yelled, and the pigeons once again fluttered and dispersed.

A voice inside the shed called out, "Good morning, sir," but the lanky man didn't return the friendly greeting and gruffly responded.

"What's good about it?" He pushed the turnstile with such force that it spun several times in his wake.

"Why's that man mad?" Francisco said.

"Shhh," Antonia said. "Just stay close to me."

"I am close to you."

Antonia leaned down and whispered, "Francisco, you are trying my patience. You must listen and do as I say."

A man dressed in a green uniform, shiny black shoes, and an officer's billed hat stepped outside as they neared the turnstile. His face was stern and stoney. He squinted and stared upriver into the distance until they toed-up in front of him. As Antonia handed him their passports, her hand quivered and he noticed.

"Your reason for entering?" he said in a dull tone.

She pushed back her scarf slightly to reveal strands of blond hair. "Just shopping," she said, and she tried to smile but knew that it looked forced.

He didn't bother to open her passport but instead turned his head to the side and looked her over.

"Your boy?" he said without taking his eyes off her.

Antonia nodded.

The man handed the passports back and waved them on speaking flatly. "Go on, have a good day."

Antonia breathed deeply as though she had just resurfaced from being underwater. This wasn't going to be easy—she was not a good liar. And most of all, the shaking had to stop.

Once on the bridge, they walked past a gauntlet of hunched-over bodies as they waited in line for entry into the United States. When the bridge's steel framing began to shudder under foot, Francisco looked over his shoulder as a red-and-white southbound trolley rumbled past with its brass bell clanging.

"Can we take the trolley sometime?" he said.

"Maybe," Antonia said. She noticed that the trolley was mostly empty and wondered when the tourists would begin to cross.

At the middle of the bridge, a chilling gust of wind barreled down behind them, and Antonia buttoned her coat tight and retied her scarf, while Francisco spread his coat wide and let the wind fill his jacket and push him forward like a sail.

He began to run ahead of her and shouted, "Look, I'm flying!" He circled back and swooped past her several times before running to the bridge railing where he stepped onto the bottom rail and peered over the edge to the river below.

"Francisco!" Antonia yelled. "Be careful."

When she grabbed his coat collar and held on tight, he scanned the edges of the weaving brown rivulets then pointed to a cluster of gray long-legged birds under the bridge near the southern shore. Though the morning light had not yet penetrated the riverbed, their blood-red crests and long, sharp beaks stood out. "Look, sandhill cranes!"

"What?" Antonia said.

"Sandhill cranes. I read about them. They stay here in the winter and fly north in the spring. Listen. Can you hear their call?"

Antonia cocked her ear. "I can't hear it," she said and turned away. "Come on, Francisco, we must go."

Francisco didn't budge. There was a creature winding through the carrizo cane, and he watched as it crept along the riverbank towards the group of cranes. When a gust of wind parted the cane, the creature's furry tail and pointed snout became visible.

Cupping his hands around his mouth, Francisco called, "*Kar-r-r-r- o-o-o.*" He waited, but when nothing happened, he tried again and this time, raised his chin, pursed his lips, and released a shriller warning, "*Kar-r-r-r- o-o-o . . . Kar-r-r-r- o-o-o.*" He paused, waiting for his voice to reach them. Then, in a sudden flourish, the entire grouping of birds turned their heads in his direction, raised their long necks, opened their beaks, and let out a chorus: "*Kar-r-r-r- o-o-o . . . Kar-r-r-r- o-o-o . . . Kar-r-r-r- o-o-o.*" The birds took off in urgent flight in a rush of flapping wings.

He ran to catch up with Antonia. "Did you see that? I saved them! One of them was about to get eaten."

Antonia wasn't interested in what was happening along the river below. She was too busy looking ahead toward the edge of the bridge where the road grew narrower and was densely lined with ramshackle buildings. The scene was a tangle of wind-beaten signs beckoning tourists—O'Brien's Pub, Kentucky Bar, Jockey Club—as if Boston, New York, or Louisville had spread tendrils southward like an invasive plant species. It was too early for this part of town to come alive. Like a ghost town, it made Antonia uneasy.

She pulled Francisco close as they walked on the western side of the street to stay in the light instead of shadow. With every step, she listened and observed. She watched as sleepy-eyed boys filled newspaper bins in front of the Black Cat Café. Across the street, a woman with a shawl over her head and mouth swept hopelessly in the midst of swirling dust near Levy's store—a place that touted Veracruz cigars, *zarapes*, and gemstones.

This part of town was not the place to linger, Ray had told her—"pickpockets, prostitutes, any kind of scammer you can think of." He had warned her and said, "With your blond hair, you'll be target *número uno* in that devil's den. Keep walking south."

Before Antonia could blink, they were surrounded by a pack of children, each jostling to get in close, holding out their hands for money. A little girl with wide eyes and a dirty face walked backwards and tugged on Antonia's skirt and said, "*Centavos please, Señora.*" Antonia diverted into the street, but like a flock of ducklings, the children followed behind, and Francisco was carried along in their midst as though he were one of them.

"I'm sorry," Antonia kept saying. "So sorry." And when she turned around, she couldn't find Francisco.

A shout of desperation—like a wounded animal—came from the portico of a bar, and the tall lanky man they had seen earlier burst onto the sidewalk with a rotund man in an apron trailing frantically behind. The lanky man clenched his hat in his fist, and his curly red hair spiraled outward in disarray.

With arms raised, the rotund man pleaded, "*Please, Señor. Mañana. I get you the money, mañana*!" But the tall man moved forward with long determined strides, then abruptly spun around.

"Too late!"

His voice reverberated like cannon fire, and the children with legs and arms flying dispersed into the street's hidden recesses.

Francisco was left standing alone.

Alone. He heard his mother's voice: "Hurry, let's go." But he didn't move right away. He looked around with wide eyes.

Mexico—he was actually here. He remembered the movies where

vaqueros and *bandidos* like the great Pancho Villa roamed the streets with their pistols strapped at their hips. There was something wild here. It scared him and made his heart beat quickly with excitement.

Alive one minute, a quick draw, *POW!* dead the next.

Loretta had shown Francisco a newspaper clipping with a picture of Villa, on horseback, with his broad-brimmed hat, drooping mustache, and his signature double-breasted bandoliers. She had raised her eyebrows when she said, "He's been in the movies too."

"Did you ever meet him?" Francisco asked, but when she answered, no, and saw his face drop with disappointment, she snapped her gum then pointed to the horse in the clipping. "But I did see his horse once—*Siete Leguas*—tied to a rail in Juarez."

"Really?"

She didn't answer his question directly or meet his eyes but added, "Word has it, he was a hero among horses for running seven leagues in a single day, leaving other exhausted horses behind."

"Was Pancho a hero?" Francisco said.

"Some say yes, some say no."

"I want to be a hero," Francisco had said.

She shook her head. "Being a hero isn't all it's cracked up to be. It's all in the eyes of the beholder. But being heroic is different. That's about you and only you. Doing what you believe is right. You'll find your purpose."

"His purpose?" He had never thought of it that way.

He had looked more closely at the rings on her fingers and pointed. "The blue ones, what are they?"

"Turquoise. Those were my mother's." She pointed to another smaller stone on her pinky. "This green one is jade. My husband gave it to me when we were married, and these orange and purple ones aren't real gemstones, they're glass and set in copper, but I still like them."

"Which is your favorite?" he had asked.

She smiled and dreamily looked out the window. "My birth stone—an opal. And my favorite is the fire opal. In it, you can see worlds beyond—in blues, yellows, oranges, purples, and any color you can imagine. The longer you look, the deeper you see."

Francisco had nodded as he tried to envision what Loretta was describing. "And then infinity?" he asked.

Loretta smiled. "You are a smart one, aren't you." She rubbed her hands together and said, "I don't have one, but I *want* one. They say its energy rays fill you with strength and joy."

"Where can you find them?" Francisco had asked.

"Mexico," she said. "They are formed in the depths of ancient volcanoes."

Here in the middle of the street, in Mexico, Francisco stood in wonder. Volcanoes, *bandidos*, fire opals. He felt an energy here—something mystical, powerful, and invigorating.

CHAPTER 20

THE MERCADO

Though Ray had told her to look for a large stucco building with terracotta arches, Antonia didn't need to read the words on the parapet—*Mercado Cuauhtemoc*—to know that she was there. The cars parked out front and people spilling into the streets in clumps of busied motion was enough to signal their arrival. To Antonia, the mood was overbearing. Dogs wrestled and barked within a grove of Anaqua trees; chickens pecked for worms in a flattened dirt patch that appeared completely wormless; a mother held a crying baby; and men with wide-brimmed hats huddled in groups running their fingers over their beards and nodding like they were sharing secrets.

"Shop there. Get to know the place. In the early morning, it will be mostly locals," Ray had said.

Inside, the market was an even greater burst of energy and bright colors. There were tables layered with plantains, red peppers, prickly pears, and mangos. And from a spiderweb of scaffolding hung an array of Mexican flags with their red, white, and green vertical stripes and pinatas of all colors, shapes, and sizes.

A mariachi band in a far corner filled the space with a cacophony of tuning instruments, and a piercing noise squealed through the rafters as one of the musicians gave the microphone a test with an exuberant "*Buenos días*!"

Lining every aisle were stalls filled with all things imaginable—*maracas*, rainbow-colored ukuleles, dresses, sombreros, jewelry, brass lanterns, and shiny metal trinkets. Goods were stacked to the ceiling in mountains of boxes. Antonia took a deep breath. The clutter was closing in on her, but when she looked at Francisco, his face was like a shining sun. He searched the spaces around him with an expression of wonder.

She wanted to feel happy like he did, but she felt nothing but wariness. "Come, Francisco, I need to look for a dress."

Near a line of windows, Antonia found a table stacked with women's blouses, and behind it, were racks of cotton dresses with colorfully embroidered necklines and hems. She found one that was a pale blue, more fitted and less billowy than most of the selection. She held it up under her chin and smoothed the skirt with her hand to check the length.

"Mirror?" A woman asked and pointed. "*Allí*!"

"*Gracias*," Antonia said and walked over to look at herself. She held the dress up and turned her hips.

"Do you like it, Francisco?"

"It's pretty," he said, "but when do I get to shop?"

"In a minute," she said. "Help me find an umbrella first."

They walked around, weaving through clumps of shoppers and merchants organizing their displays, until they came upon a flower stand filled with exotic scents, blown glass ornaments, and brass windchimes that tinkled in front of a whirring electric fan.

Francisco pointed to a bin in the corner full of umbrellas with carved wooden handles.

"Over here," he said. "I'll pick one out for you."

He selected a rainbow-colored one and had it halfway open when the woman who had showed Antonia the mirror rushed toward him, grabbed it, and shut the umbrella with a snap then shook her head with a panicked expression.

"No, no, no," she said. "*¡Mala suerte!*" She pointed to a sign: "*No abra los paraguas en el interior.*" Then below it in English: "Do not open umbrellas inside."

Francisco turned quickly towards Antonia. "Why?"

Antonia sighed and wondered if superstition was not just a Loretta thing but rampant. "Bad luck," she said. "That's what some people believe."

The woman seemed to pick up on Antonia's dismissing tone and wore a worried expression like Antonia's naivete would lead to a world of misfortune.

Just beyond the umbrella stand, something else caught Francisco's eye. He poked Antonia in the arm. "That's what I want," he said and pointed to a bin full of y-shaped wood with thick rubber bands.

"A slingshot?" Antonia said.

"Yes, I'll use it to slay the one-eyed pirates, or the hairy barbarians who come at us with their clubs. I'll nail them between the eyes!"

Antonia tried to laugh and share his joy, but she couldn't muster it. Instead, it came out like an unpleasant cough.

Francisco finished off a cinnamon bun that he had picked out among rows of crimped pies and sugar-coated treats as Antonia stood in line at the checkout counter. He thought about how he had felt earlier when he was standing in the street.

In this place, this land, something came alive in him. Why? He had no idea, but it felt instinctive.

His mother seemed just the opposite with her rushed movements, head jerks at loud noises, and the way she pushed him with a heavy hand through the crowds. She was uncomfortable. Was she afraid of something?

He thought about the umbrella incident and Loretta and the new language he was learning: scissors (bad unless you stepped on them when they fell), horseshoes (good—lucky), owls (good—courageous protectors), umbrellas (bad inside but okay outside). He wanted to know more, as if this new language could shape a person's destiny.

He pulled the slingshot out from under his belt and ran his fingers over the curves of its smooth wooden handle. He held it up and stretched the thick rubber band as far as it would go then released it and imagined a stone flying with the speed of a comet. *Phooosh!*

Suddenly, he was ripped away from his dreaming when a thunderous noise came from outside. Francisco stretched his neck and peered through the terracotta portal to catch a glimpse of the commotion.

"You son of a bitch!" A man hurled his fist into the face of another man wearing a wide-brimmed hat. The hat sailed in the air, and the man to fell to the ground with his arms and legs splayed like a discarded rag doll. Francisco squinted and stared into the bright sunlight and recognized the man's tall lanky form. Red-faced and fuming, the man stood over the splayed figure. To Francisco, it looked like his head was about to blast off his body and reel skyward. Three times he had seen this man. Three times this man had been consumed with anger. And once, he had used his fists.

Who was he? Francisco wondered. And why wasn't anyone helping the knocked-out man?

Hearing the loud skirmish outside, seeing the prostrate body, the bloody face, expressions of fear in the crowd, Antonia felt the sudden instinct to flee.

Outside the building, she dragged Francisco by the hand through the crowd then hurriedly headed up the street—northward. The wind had picked up, so she leaned forward to maintain momentum.

Ahead of them, more and more Americans trickled in. Some hung from the trolley with dresses and coattails flapping in the wind. Others paraded gayly with heads thrown back in brash laughter, pointing, smoking, patting children on the head, and handing out coins with expressions of superiority as though Juarez and its citizens were merely a source of entertainment—a cheap carnival—nothing more.

Antonia knew the likes of these people and their haughtiness, just as her stepmother had been about Mateo.

But who was she to judge? With Elton, she had chosen the same: money, clothes, a house, a car. Look at yourself in the mirror, she thought.

And now, what was she becoming? Something worse—a smuggler. A criminal. She doubted herself all over again. Maybe it was all too dangerous. Maybe she was putting their lives at risk.

It was almost noon when they approached the Mexican customs booth, and Antonia recognized the same officers she had seen coming in. One impatiently tapped his watch and called to someone inside. "*Cinco minutos.*"

"Okay, okay, go, but don't forget to bring me . . ." He cut his sentence short and put his hand near his mouth and tipped it back like he was holding a drink.

The other officer gave him a thumbs up. "*Coca-cola, ¿sí?*"

The other man nodded.

But before passing, Antonia got a good look at both of their faces. They had almost identical dark mustaches that were neatly clipped, and both men were of almost equal height. In their uniforms, they looked remarkably similar, but she could tell them apart by the shape of their noses and a mole on one of the officer's forehead.

The one with the mole and bulbous nose was nonchalant, smiled and waved them on without looking in their bags or giving any special attention to either her or Francisco. The one with the sharp nose eyed them like a fox but didn't stop them.

Antonia would mention this man to Ray. He had led her to believe that there would be no problem, but this man's look was unnerving.

CHAPTER 21

ELTON

When Antonia and Francisco approached the hotel, the foul exhaust from the downriver smelter stacks filled the air with an acrid smell that burned their eyes and nose. Inside the foyer, three women in brightly colored dresses huddled next to the door chatting and smoking cigarettes. As Antonia and Francisco weaved through them, they leaned against the walls and blinked lazily with their pencil-thin eyebrows and eyelashes thick with mascara.

"You the new girl?" one asked after exhaling a stream of smoke. Though the woman smiled, Antonia couldn't tell if it was genuine or mocking. In either case, she didn't like the sound of it—as if she were a showgirl or, worse, a prostitute.

"We are staying at the hotel, yes," Antonia said.

The tallest woman wore a loose-fitting jacket, a vivid green like a spring leaf. She blew smoke rings that ascended from her rose-colored lips as though she were a beautiful flower releasing pollen.

Francisco stuck his finger through one of them as it floated by.

"You like my rings?" she said and shimmied her shoulders.

Francisco nodded and blushed at the sudden attention from the women.

"You must be Francisco," she said. "Loretta tells us you are not only beautiful on the outside but also within."

Francisco's face turned a more full-bodied red as Antonia put her hand on his shoulder and ushered him toward the front door. When he turned to look back, all three women were waving their fingers at him and smiling.

He ducked his chin and offered up an embarrassed grin in return.

Inside the lobby, Loretta was dusting a table but jerked around when she heard them enter. Her eyes met Antonia's with an expression of suppressed alarm. "You're back . . . well . . ." she said, then quickly turned to Francisco. "I have a surprise for you. I put another *Boys' Life* magazine by your bed. And Ray brought you three books—cowboy stories, I think. Go check it out, I need to visit with your mama—about girl stuff."

Wide-eyed and eager, Francisco bolted up the stairway, and when he got to the landing, he turned back and shouted, "Thank you!" over his shoulder. "Oh, and look what I got." He held up the slingshot triumphantly.

Loretta smiled. "Very nice. You'll have to show me how to use it."

After Francisco had disappeared, Loretta waved for Antonia to enter the office. Closing the door behind them, she cleared her throat and touched her hair nervously. "A good morning across the river? You're back sooner than I expected."

Antonia dismissed the question then stared at Loretta. "What's wrong? Did something happen while we were away?"

Loretta leaned against the desk and raised an eyebrow. "A man came around."

Antonia took a deep breath and tried to remain calm. "He asked if there was a woman with a boy here. He showed me a picture."

Antonia swallowed hard. "What did he look like?"

"Medium height, brown hair, wore a plaid jacket and was whiskery and red-eyed like he hadn't slept. He asked if there was a room. I said, 'No.'"

Antonia closed her eyes and tilted her head upward. "Thank God," she said.

"You're welcome, but he did ask if there was another hotel nearby. I said 'no' again, only downtown, but I'm not sure he believed me. There was something about the way he looked at me—like he thought I was lying."

"Were you lying?"

Loretta shifted her eyes. "It seemed worth the risk."

"Where did he go?"

Loretta moved behind the desk and sat down. "I sent Sam to follow him for a few blocks to make sure he didn't find the hotel around the corner, but Sam took it on himself to follow him all the way to Main Street and watched as he entered the Hotel Encino."

"Where is that?"

"About a mile from here."

Antonia covered her mouth then pulled it away trying to regain her composure. "Thank you, Loretta. Thank you," she said. "And please, please don't tell Francisco about *any* of this."

"Why would I do that?" Loretta said. "I will do what I can for you because I've already said I like you and your boy."

Antonia lowered her head. "It was my husband."

Loretta held up her palm and turned her head to the side. "Don't tell me anymore," she said. "It's better that way—in case there are questions. I know enough by your expression that you're afraid, and because of it, I don't like him."

Loretta drummed her fingers on the desk and shook her head. "I knew it, I just knew it. When the wind changed directions and blew the smelter smoke our way, something was . . ."

"Was what?" Antonia said.

"Never mind," Loretta said. She paused and met Antonia eye to eye.

"Listen. I have a plan, but you'll need to cooperate. I'll let Ray know too. He has his ways."

"His ways?" Antonia said. "That's *not* what I want."

"We'll see what you want if or when things get worse—if the foul air continues."

Antonia suddenly looked wild-eyed, and a surge of adrenaline rushed through her body. It was the same panic she had felt when Elton circled the room before knocking her to the floor.

Loretta whispered. "Meet me upstairs—room 210—in an hour," she said. "I've sent Sam for some supplies. Bring Francisco too and the things you purchased today." Then she looked at Antonia with a serious expression.

"Ray's not stupid, you know? He will manage it for you and Francisco."

Antonia's body recoiled like a cornered cat. Indebtedness. Beholden.

She walked briskly toward the stairs and whispered defiantly to herself, "I won't let it happen again—never—it's time to leave."

Francisco lay cross-legged twirling his stockinged foot while he read when Antonia opened the door and spoke in a rapid staccato. "Francisco, pack your things, we're leaving. I've heard of another job elsewhere—better pay—in Del Rio. We need to go right away."

Francisco was too absorbed in his reading to fully listen. "Says here, it takes five gallons of water to grow a walnut," he said.

"That's a lot of water for such a small . . ." Then he stopped. "Wait, what? We're leaving?" He dropped his magazine. "Why?" he said. "I like it here. Everyone's so nice."

"Things will be better, I promise."

"I don't need it to be better. I like it."

"Francisco, get a move on. Pack your things."

He sat up straight and wrapped his arms around his legs. "But wait, Sam said he'd teach me how to play Chinese checkers tomorrow. He's bringing his board from home to show me."

She scurried around the room grabbing her brush, comb, and hair ties. "I'm sorry, but you'll have to learn from someone else."

Francisco frowned and kicked at the covers. "But I don't have any other friends who are Chinese to teach me."

"Francisco, please. I'm doing this for us," Antonia said, as she stepped into the closet and started taking clothes off hangers and throwing things in her satchel.

Francisco knew something was wrong. He had witnessed enough of her panics before, and he instinctively grabbed a pillow and hugged it tight for a few moments then sheepishly said, "Why do we have to rush? Has something bad happened?"

"No," she said. "We just need to go. That's all."

He hugged the pillow tighter when he heard footsteps in the hallway and narrowed his eyes when he saw movement through the keyhole.

She turned and glanced at him impatiently. "Come on now, we'll get lunch on the train. Maybe they'll have milkshakes or Coke-floats, and peanut butter sandwiches, your favorite, then we'll be in Del Rio before you know it. We'll find a nicer hotel, then we'll get settled. Things will be fine."

As she babbled on, Francisco kept his eye on the keyhole and touched his owl feather.

CHAPTER 22

LORETTA

Ray was at his lunch table, gazing down on a steaming plate of tamales, when Loretta whisked up behind him and grabbed his shoulder and squeezed hard.

"Ouch, what the?" Ray said turning her way.

"They're leaving," she said. "I overheard her talking to Francisco in the room."

"What?" Ray said. "Didn't you tell her about the plan—room 210? You tried to convince her to stay, right?"

Loretta pulled out a chair and sat with a huff. "Yes, but I could see by her panic that she didn't trust us. Anyone."

"Oh, for God's sake!" Ray threw down his napkin. "I told you she was that type. Skittish as a beaten dog."

Loretta pushed her hair behind her ear. "Can you blame her?"

"No," Ray said, drumming his plump fingers on the table. His blue eyes were like ice. "You need to *make* her stay," he said.

Loretta leaned close to his ear and whispered. "I told her you would take care of the guy, if need be."

Ray clenched his jaw, looked from side to side and spoke through his teeth. "You told her I would kill him?"

Loretta took a deep breath. "No, Jesus, Ray, do you think I'm stupid? I said you had 'your ways.' I was just trying to get her to stay."

He threw his hands up. "Well, that sure as hell didn't work."

"You got any brighter ideas, Mr. Genius?"

He raised his fork and shoved a bite of tamale in his mouth.

Loretta kicked his chair. "How can you eat at a time like this?"

"Settle down. I'm thinking," Ray said. "Ideas sometimes come while I'm eating."

When he didn't say anything, Loretta said, "We *need* her; she's *the one*!"

For a few moments, Ray and Loretta sat elbow to elbow without saying a word. Loretta tapped his arm.

"I'll go up and tell her that he's back—that he's talking to you right now, and I saw him slip you a twenty-dollar bill and overheard him say that there would be more money if Ray helped find you and the boy."

She stared intently at Ray to see what he thought. Ray took two more mouthfuls and chewed rapidly, but he didn't say anything, so she continued.

"That will at least give us some time, and I'll convince her that her best protection is here with us and with my disguises." Loretta started speaking like she was practicing her lines for the theatre. She turned her head to the side and put her best grandmotherly face on. "We will look after you and Francisco. You have my word. And once your husband sees that you're not here, he'll leave—and all will be fine. But if you go now, he may follow, and there would be no one to help. How will you survive with no money? Here you will have money and safety."

Loretta looked at Ray with raised eyebrows. "How does that sound?"

"Good," he said. "And if she still wants to leave after a few days, after we've secured the stone, then it doesn't matter whether she goes or stays." He grabbed Loretta's arm. "Go do it, hurry!"

Loretta pushed her chair back abruptly, quickly turned then hesitated when she felt a flutter in her heart. She touched Ray's shoulder gently this time. "I must say, if they were to go, I would miss Francisco."

Antonia and Francisco were two steps into the hallway holding their bags when Loretta appeared and held up both hands like a traffic cop at an intersection.

"Wait," she said in a gentle voice. "Please hear me out."

Antonia took two more steps forward. "You can't stop us."

Loretta dropped her hands. "I'm not going to stop you. I'm just asking you to listen."

Antonia looked back. "Come on, Francisco."

Francisco held firm in his still stance. "I know it was Elton, Ma. You can't hide it from me. I'm not a little kid anymore."

Antonia turned, dropped her bag, and knelt in front of him then combed her fingers through his hair. "I'm just trying to do what's best for us."

He jerked his head away. "Maybe what's best for us is here. You haven't heard what Mrs. Loretta has to say."

Antonia's expression turned angry. "Francisco, you listen to me now. I'm your mother, and you will do as I say."

Francisco raised his arms and shouted. "It's not just about you, Ma. It's about me too!"

Tears collected at the corner of his eyes, but he brushed them away defiantly and gripped his fists at his side. "You think you've been protecting me all this time. But the truth is, I've been protecting us too. I'm the one who threw water in his face to keep him from hitting you; I'm the one who was outside in the bushes ready to save you if he came back angry; I'm the one who . . ." His voice became shaky. He looked at his feet, then stared straight into Antonia's eyes.

"I'm part of this, and I want to listen to what Mrs. Loretta has to say."

Antonia closed her eyes for a moment but then nodded.

Loretta was flabbergasted—this little boy believed in her. Her chest felt full with warmth, and she blinked, breathed deeply, then paused before snapping back to reality. Focus on the plan.

Loretta whisked them back into their room, closed the door, locked it, and patted the bed for them to sit. Though Antonia slumped heavily with exhaustion, Francisco sat erect as though he was receiving a top-secret message from a spy.

Loretta clasped her hands, leaned toward them, and whispered.

"Okay. The problem is this. If you leave and go elsewhere, he might follow. Then you'll always be looking over your shoulder, but if you consider my plan, you'll be rid of him for good. Okay?"

As Antonia took a deep breath, Francisco nodded energetically.

Loretta pushed her shoulders back with confidence. "So, here's the plan. I'm going to disguise you."

Antonia shook her head. "Wait, what?"

"Ma, please, just listen," Francisco said.

Antonia nervously balled up the blanket with her fists. Francisco scooched closer to hear Loretta's words.

"In case he comes around again, I'll disguise you for a few days, so he won't recognize you. I have *everything* to make it convincing—trust me. Clothes, makeup, wigs, you'll see. Then when he thinks you've left, he'll be gone for good." She clapped her hands together in summation. "So you see? All will be fine."

Antonia held her head in her hands and shook her head. "I don't believe this."

Loretta added, "And, you'll be making money the whole time." She looked at Antonia but not at Francisco. "With you know . . . the trips."

Francisco stood up abruptly. "Let's do it!"

He glanced at his mother and turned to Loretta with a beaming expression. "What about chaps, a leather vest, a broad-brimmed hat, and a knife strapped to my belt like Pancho Villa?"

Loretta smiled and nodded. "That's good, yes, very good. We can try several things." She rubbed her hands together and grinned. When Francisco beamed, Loretta felt a prick of guilt. She knew exactly what she was doing—helping Antonia and Francisco but mostly for her and Ray's benefit. Was she a bad person?

In response to Loretta's kindness, Francisco felt a strange sensation—like he was close to tears but closer to feeling happiness. Loretta and Sam were his friends. Even though he was a little scared of Ray, Ray was nice enough to give him some books on cowboys.

It was all so different than what he had experienced from his real family—a father long gone, grandparents who were alive but that he only knew from pictures, and a stepfather who was cruel.

Finally, they weren't alone. Finally, someone was going to help them. Finally, someone cared.

Was this what real family was supposed to feel like?

CHAPTER 23

ROOM 210

Room 210 was like a department store showroom. Racks of ladies' dresses of all colors and sizes were lined up on one side of the room, and on the other were shelves filled with neat stacks of lingerie. Above the lingerie were assorted metal stands with wigs in various styles, ranging from long to short and in all colorations from salt-and-pepper gray to copper red to chestnut brown, platinum blond, and mousy blond. In the far corner of the room was a full-length mirror and next to it an upright rack where women's hats and ornamental jewelry hung like decorations on a Christmas tree.

"Welcome to my shop," Loretta said with a proud-looking and slightly mischievous grin. "And you thought I just worked the desk." She held her arms out and turned in a circle. My real passion lies here. You wouldn't guess it by my desk clothes, but I have a real knack for style—putting things together, you know. Just ask those pretty ladies out front. They *love* Loretta's Lounge. They slip out of their grocery store or maids' uniforms and into my 'glad rags' and feel dolled up and special."

She pointed to a rack of dresses to her left and smiled. "This is my fall collection, navies, buffs, emerald greens, and wine reds. I like to mix colors too. Blouses and skirts that is—in the same color range but in a slightly different hue."

As Loretta spoke, Antonia noticed that none of the dresses were new. Most had hem and sleeve adjustments, and the colors were slightly faded and many had stains around the necklines.

Loretta lowered her head and peered over her glasses. "And of course, I consult the latest fashions. I peruse *Ladies' Home Journal* and *Vogue*. Sung, Sam's brother, lets me flip through the magazines at his market so long as I don't block customers or tatter the corners of the pages. His wife is a seamstress and does sewing repairs for me, and of course I pay her for her excellent work, but I also let her borrow a few things every now and then."

Taking a few steps towards a window Loretta pointed. "And spring is over here—my favorite time of year—pinks, purples, and, of course, yellow— bright as the daffodils in my yard. I get my hints from nature. The subtleties provide endless inspiration for mixing colors—if you know what I mean?"

Antonia didn't exactly, but she nodded anyway. Since Loretta was coming to their aid, Antonia added, "You do have a flair."

Loretta pushed back her hair and adjusted her rhinestone glasses as if she were primping for a photography shoot. "Really? You think so?"

Francisco broke in. "I like the way your hair color and eyeshadow match."

When Loretta dipped her chin with delight, two additional chins were revealed. "Such a charmer, Francisco. The girls better watch out."

Losing patience with the fashion discussion and fearing that Elton might return at any moment, Antonia interrupted. "What next?"

Francisco looked around. "All I see is ladies' clothes. I'm not going to be a girl, am I?"

Loretta immediately chimed in. "Of course not. I've sent Angelica shopping for you. She'll be back with something perfect. You're going to love it."

Francisco scratched his head. "Okay, but what about Ma? Who is she going to look like?"

Loretta smiled playfully. "Your mother will look like your *abuela*."

"*Abuela*?" Antonia said in a slightly put-off tone. "You mean I'm going to look like an old—"

Francisco interjected. "I know that word," he said. "Javier taught me. It means grandmother, right?"

"From Javier?" Loretta said.

"Yes. My friend, the bell ringer at the church."

Loretta jerked her head back with surprise. "I didn't know you two had met. Javier's my cousin."

"Then you must know the man who sells the empanadas too?" Francisco said.

"Of course, that's Gabriel, my second cousin on my father's side." She tapped her finger on her chin. "Or maybe he's my second cousin once removed—not sure exactly." She looked at Antonia and lowered her glasses. "See, Ma'am, we are a very close-knit community. A beautiful woven basket of many colors, you might say. We know each other, we help each other."

Antonia pursed her lips with a touch of suspicion and anxiety. The trip to Juarez had been unsettling—the angry man, the fistfight—but maybe those were exceptions.

She still needed money, and for now, there was no other option. The plan made some sense. And maybe it was the better of bad ideas, but there was still something about Loretta's tone that felt like a sales job.

Be careful, she thought. Don't lose your footing in slippery territory.

CHAPTER 24

DISGUISED

His disguise? It wasn't exactly as he had hoped, but it wasn't *that* bad. That afternoon, Loretta had secured a long black wig to his head then braided the hair on both sides. He was disappointed that Angelica hadn't brought him a broad-brimmed hat, but the little bowler was growing on him. And he wasn't fond of the glasses at all. They made him look even more bookish than he already was. But he did get a vest. It wasn't leather but at least it was tan-colored, so it looked close to the real thing.

"Sorry about the glasses, but we need to hide your eyes," Loretta had said. "They are too distinctive. Too beautiful."

The most disappointing revelation was that his outfit didn't include a knife, so he took his slingshot and stuffed it in his waistline where he could whip it out at any moment and load the rock that he kept in his pocket.

His mother's outfit was astonishing. With a gray wig curled up and pinned into a bun, thick spectacles, a frumpy black dress, an overstuffed girdle, cane, and lots of makeup, Loretta had turned Antonia into the grandmother he had never known.

And Loretta had even asked for his advice. "This hat or that one?" she had said with a smile. "Which one makes her look older?"

Francisco had pursed his lips then pointed to one with black netting that would turn down over Antonia's eyes. "That one makes you look like someone died."

"Good idea," Loretta had said. "No one will mess with a widow."

"You have to walk all hunched over," Francisco told his mother. "Like your back is killing you . . . and maybe a limp . . ."

Loretta nodded but tilted her head to the side then added, "But we don't want to overdo it, Francisco. The limp may be a bit much. After all, we don't want anyone calling *la ambulancia*." She nudged him playfully with her fist, and they both broke out laughing.

When Francisco looked up at his mother, she wasn't smiling. He knew the burn of teasing, so he reached for her hand and could feel a chill in her fingers, the same chill he had felt during one of Elton's rages. And for the first time, he recognized what it was—fear.

"You look great, Ma," he said. "There's no way Elton will know it's you."

When they descended the rickety steps fully disguised, Loretta clapped her hands in self-recognition of her achievements. "Don't you two look wonderful!"

After adjusting Francisco's collar a smidge, she said, "Now as I said earlier, go three blocks north on Luna, and it's on the right. Ana's tamale house. You can't miss it. My niece Ana will be waiting for you—I called her. It's usually a lunch place, but Ana will let you in—best tamales in town. Go, have a nice meal, and relax. This one's on me."

"Thank you," Antonia said as she leaned her cane against a chair and tugged on her dress, still getting used to the pillows under her girdle.

"Pillows moving on you?" Loretta said. "You gotta cinch that girdle tight." She turned her attention to Francisco. "And remember what I said, hold onto your braids when you take off your hat, so your wig doesn't come loose."

"Okay," Francisco said.

As they were leaving, Loretta called after them. "Have a lovely dinner with your granny, Jesse!" Her mouth curled into a wicked smile, and she giggled.

Jesse was Francisco's self-selected new first name, and he liked it. It sounded tough and western-like. Antonia was now Alma—which he also picked out—because Alma sounded like a grandma. They had all agreed that Smith would be a good last name because it was easy to remember.

It was a little after six p.m., and completely dark outside, when Francisco and Antonia left. The neighborhood was mostly quiet except for the buzz of the streetlights that cast pools of light onto a sidewalk exposing rivulets of cracks and occasional sunken spots where it looked as though a cannonball had made a direct hit.

Once outside, Antonia groused, "Loretta's getting on my nerves with her not-so-funny comments. She seems to enjoy making me look like a decrepit old bag."

"I think you look . . . you know . . ." Francisco searched for the word, " . . . sweet."

"Hardly," Antonia said with a huff. "I feel like I'm looking into a mirror at my unfortunate future. But I must agree with you, it seems convincing."

Francisco was suddenly aware that his mother was listening to him more and more, so he tried to sound supportive. "Yes. We'll just need to do this for a while then . . ." He stopped mid-sentence when he saw a man cross under a streetlight about fifteen feet ahead and stride toward them, swerving slightly, with heavy clomping steps. At first, the man appeared blurry through Francisco's glasses, but when he peered over the top and narrowed his focus, he knew immediately by the man's gait, tan overcoat, worn-looking fedora, and brown, red, and orange plaid scarf that it was Elton.

He grabbed Antonia's elbow, pushed her along, and said in a false voice, "This way, Grandma."

Passing within five feet of each other, Elton slowed and gave them a hard stare but then moved on and turned the corner.

After he was well out of sight, Antonia whispered breathily, "Was it him?"

Francisco nodded. "Yes, but it worked. Come on, we're almost to Ana's."

CHAPTER 25

LORETTA

When the hotel's front door opened and slammed against the wall, Loretta jumped and stared into the dark entry foyer with a startled expression. Elton strode toward the front desk with a fierceness in his step.

He pointed a finger at Loretta. "You lied to me. They *were* here."

Loretta could smell whiskey on his breath and opened the top drawer below the desk and laid her hand on her loaded revolver then straightened her back. "I don't know what you're talking about, mister, and I don't like your tone or the accusation."

He leaned toward her, and his scarf raked the counter. "I showed the same picture I showed you to an old man selling empanadas in the park. He said he couldn't be sure it was them, but he did remember seeing a woman and boy around here one day."

Loretta pushed her hair back behind her ear and rolled her eyes at the gaudy combination of colors on his scarf. She summed up his character. Bad man—terrible taste.

"What old man are you talking about?" she said.

Elton banged his fist on the counter. "I don't know his name, but it was the guy with the horseshoe on his cart."

Loretta let out a long laugh and shook her head but gripped the pistol tighter. "Ohhh, Gabriel, my cousin. Well, you'll have to excuse him. He's old and gets confused sometimes." She did her best to force a look of well-intentioned concern. "You didn't waste money on him for information, did you? He means well but is not always . . . you know . . . reliable."

Elton huffed. "Like I said, I showed him the picture, and he said he saw them outside a nearby hotel. And *you* told me this was the *only* hotel in this area."

Loretta softened her expression and nodded. "Ahhhh. You must understand that Gabriel is all over town selling empanadas and can easily be confused about where he is and what he remembers. The word 'nearby' is where you may have been misled. Perhaps, you should have been more precise with your questioning?"

Elton closed his eyes, threw back his head, and sighed with frustration. "What do you mean?"

Loretta extended her hand and casually examined her nails as she crafted her drawn-out explanation to give Antonia and Francisco more time to get to Ana's.

"You see, nearby could mean lots of hotels in our town. From a local's perspective, like Gabriel, everything is nearby—our town may *seem* big to others, but to us, it's small." She gave him an empathetic look and rambled on.

"It's confusing, I know. For example, if you were to ask someone where the train station is, one of our citizens might point and say, 'just down there,' and you might interpret that as a few blocks away, but in reality, it might be a few miles away. We have a small-town way of speaking."

She paused and examined him. "Perhaps where you're from

you speak differently?" She waited for a response, but he had none, so she continued.

"Well, here, we have a lot of flexibility in our language." She pulled on a rubber band around her wrist and smiled. "Stretch, you might say. But we all understand each other, so it doesn't really matter. *¿Comprendes?*"

Elton looked confused. "*Comprendes* what?" he said, and he pulled a bottle from his hip pocket and took a long slug. His eyes glazed over, and he glanced upwards as if he had forgotten his line of questioning.

Loretta shrugged and pointed to his bottle. "Surely, as a gentleman you know that it's not polite to drink and not offer to share?" She clicked a long blue fingernail on the edge of a teacup near her ledger. "Just a touch in here?"

As she pushed the cup and saucer toward him, he frowned but poured a little in.

She took a sip then put the cup back down. "Thank you. Your harsh words are forgiven now." Leaning toward him, and with a conspiratorial expression, she said, "I sense that you have good reason for searching." She paused. "Maybe you were cheated upon or have a vendetta?" She raised her eyebrows and long lines of wrinkles scrunched up on her forehead.

He looked at her flatly, opened his mouth, but his thought had drifted away like exhaled smoke.

She raised a finger. "Ah, I see then. Just the opposite. You love her, you're lonely, and you want her back."

The bottle went to his lips again, and she noticed the tension on his face relax slightly after he took a swig. "Yeah, well, it's complicated."

Loretta pooched out her lips and nodded in agreement. "Life is complicated, most certainly." She paused again to assess Elton's changing mood.

"Look, it's none of my business . . ." she said, ". . . but if I were you, I wouldn't give up. Call me a romantic, but true love never dies. My Charlie died a few years ago, and I haven't gotten over it. I would have walked to the end of the earth for him. And I feel a bit bad for you. If you wait here, I'll call Gabriel and ask him exactly what he meant because I sense your desire." Then she winked at him. "And, I love a happy ending."

He put his elbows on the counter. "Now, we're getting somewhere."

Loretta disappeared into the office and pretended to make a call. "Operator? Yes, GL-26530. Thank you." Pause. "Hello, Marna, *esta Gabriel alli*?" Pause. "*Sí,* please?"

She looked at her watch and waited for the second hand to tick off a full minute. "Oh, Gabriel, sorry to bother you." Pause. "*Sí, sí,* of course, but there's a man here at the hotel who's looking for a woman and boy." Pause. "Yes, that's right, he had a picture. Well, no one here at Hotel Luna fits his description, so he was confused by your answer the other day when you saw him. *Sí,* yes, I know."

She looked at her watch again . . . *tick tick tick* . . . for fifteen seconds.

"Well, perhaps another hotel?" Pause. "Are you sure . . . with bags?" Pause. "Ah, a taxi?" Pause. "Oh, Manuel, *sí*. Okay then. I will tell him. He is very concerned about their safety and whereabouts, and I'm just trying to help." Pause. "Yes, thank you, Gabriel. Go back to bed now. Goodnight, dear."

She put the receiver down—*click*—then walked back to the desk, took a deep breath, and looked at Elton over her bejeweled rhinestone glasses. "He was a bit ornery, because I woke him, but lucky for you, he had some more information. He said, when he was talking later that day with Manuel, our grandnephew, a taxi driver, that they were in front of the Chesapeake Hotel—close to downtown—and he drove them to the station to meet the 2:00 p.m. Argonaut, so they must be headed to Del Rio or somewhere further because that's where the two o'clock goes—east."

He put both hands flat on the counter and looked her in the eye. "Are you sure?"

"As sure as I can be. Manuel is young, he would remember the details."

"Well, then," Elton said, and turned to walk away, but Loretta reached out and tugged on his shirt sleeve then pointed to her cup.

"*¿Uno más?*"

Elton gave her a foxlike grin then poured with a slightly heavier hand than before.

Loretta raised her cup and smiled. "To you and your happy ending!"

Loretta leaned against the doorframe and bit her lip nervously as she watched Elton walk away. When he didn't turn at the corner but instead walked straight in the direction of Ana's café, her mind began to race.

From one of the street light posts, something suddenly swooped downward then there was a shrieking howl.

"Shit . . . goddammit . . . get off of me!" Elton yelled. He bent over and covered his head with his arms as a creature hovered over him and thrashed around with broad flapping wings. Elton started running and the creature chased after him, dipping, diving, and attacking him three times before it flew off into the night.

Loretta covered her mouth in astonishment. She knew exactly what it was.

Rushing back inside, Loretta grabbed the phone and with shaking hands dialed the café. "Ana, I need your help right away!

There's a man outside your café in a fedora and ugly scarf who's drunk and yelling. Hide the old lady and boy in case he tries to come in. I'll tell you more later. *Adiós*."

CHAPTER 26

ANA'S TAMALE HOUSE

Ana dashed toward the café's front door, locked it, switched off the Ana's Tamale House neon sign and put a red and white closed sign on the windowsill between the lace curtains and windowpane.

She scurried to the back of the café where Antonia and Francisco sat in a booth eating. "Loretta called. Hide in the bathroom, quick! Lock it."

"What's going on?" Antonia said.

"No time to explain. Just go," Ana said.

"Where is it?" Antonia said.

"Down the hall on your right. Hurry."

As Antonia and Francisco bolted in that direction, there was banging on the door and then Elton's voice.

"Let me in, dammit!"

Ana shouted from within, "Sorry, closed!"

Elton banged harder. "Open up!"

Ana wrung her hands on her apron then took slow steps toward the door and spoke again. "We're closed, I said. Open at 7:00 a.m. tomorrow."

Standing outside, Elton's face was twisted with pain, and his jacket sleeve was ripped off and dangling. "I've been attacked. It was a fucking owl! Just let me in—it might come back."

Ana parted the lace curtain and spoke through the window glass. "I'm so sorry, but we have no medical supplies here. I can call a taxi to take you to the hospital. Just wait outside."

"Outside? Are you nuts? It might come back." He started kicking at the door frame.

Ana held up her palms. "Okay, okay. Calm down and stop banging and kicking. You're gonna break the door glass." She looked over her shoulder at her cook—a thick bruiser of a man—who stood near the stove.

The cook picked up a butcher knife and gave Ana a nod. "I'll handle it if he causes trouble," he said.

Slowly, Ana released the door chain, opened up, then stared at Elton's blood-soaked sleeve and the deep scratch on his face. "My goodness. What happened?"

Elton leaned into the door then gave her the up and down. "How many times do I have to tell you? It was a fucking owl, out of nowhere, just swooped down and attacked me."

The cook turned and walked towards Elton while gripping the knife. "Hey, watch your mouth. She's trying to help."

Elton stumbled toward the café counter and threw himself down on a stool.

Ana took a rag from her apron pocket and handed it to him. "Hold it tight against your arm. Like I said, I'll call a taxi to take you to the hospital. You might need stitches."

She picked up the phone, dialed, then spoke. "Manuel, can you come by the café? There's a man here who needs to go to the hospital.

He's not dying but hurry as fast as you can."

Elton rolled up his sleeve, and when he saw the blood oozing from his cut, he tied the rag around his arm, closed his eyes, put his head on the counter, and groaned.

"Just relax," Ana said. "While you wait, I'll get you a cup of coffee."

The cook returned to the stove but kept his eye on Elton and held the knife in one hand as he pushed grease with a spatula into a metal slot.

Ana returned with a steaming cup of coffee and slid it in front of Elton.

"Thanks," Elton said gruffly then he touched his cheek. When he saw a blood splotch on the tip of his finger he said, "You got a bathroom with a mirror?"

Ana reached for her purse. "I have a compact with a mirror, you can take a look with that." She looked at the cook with wide eyes.

He nodded as he walked down the hall toward the bathroom.

As Ana unloaded and dug through all the pockets in her purse, she moved with a deliberate slowness. "I thought I had my compact . . . but maybe . . . perhaps, I left it at home. Oh no, wait, it's in my cosmetic bag—hold on." She walked over to the sink, bent over, opened a cabinet, and pulled out another bag and started rooting through it.

Elton sighed. "Don't you have a mirror in the bathroom? I gotta take a leak too."

"It's out of order," she said.

"Oh, for Christ's sake," Elton said. "I don't care. I have to go."

Inside the bathroom, Antonia heard everything, and when there was a tap on the door, she stepped backwards and gripped the sink and stood in front of Francisco. This was it, she thought. It's all over—he's going to see us up close and figure it out.

"It's me, the cook. This way," a gravelly voice whispered.

Antonia cracked the door and saw the cook's stubble-covered face and greasy apron then put her hands on Francisco's shoulders and followed the cook's thudding footsteps a few steps down the dark hall.

He pointed towards a closet and whispered. "In there. Lock it."

The closet had an unbearable stench. Smelly mops and washcloths hung from hooks next to a bag of trash that reeked of discarded rotten meat.

"Ick!" Francisco whispered. Antonia poked him and gave him a quiet shush. She handed him a handkerchief to cover his nose and held her own with pinched fingers.

Both flinched when they heard footsteps and the door handle jiggle.

"Not that one," Ana called. "On your right."

"What a dump," Elton grumbled as his shoes stuck to the floor near the bathroom.

The passing minutes seemed like forever to Antonia as they waited then heard a flush and Elton's sticky footsteps going back to the dining area.

"I think I'm gonna throw up," Francisco said. His shoulders rolled forward as he gagged.

Antonia put her arm around him. "Hang on, a little longer," she whispered as she felt beads of sweat forming on his neck.

Outside a horn honked loudly and Antonia released a sigh. "Thank God," she whispered.

She heard Ana speak. "I hope you feel better. Come again."

Elton grumbled loudly. "Right . . ."

Antonia recognized his sarcasm but didn't dare assume that they were safe. They had dodged a bullet thanks to Loretta.

Back at the hotel, Loretta was waiting for them in the doorway. In their frenzied return, the pillow that was supposed to be on Antonia's rump had slid to her side creating a giant bulge like an enormous growth. Wide eyed and flustered, Antonia held her cane like she was ready to take a swing at someone.

Meanwhile, Francisco was ghostly pale from the stomach trauma.

Loretta gasped. "I heard it was close." She gently lifted off Francisco's hat and bent down and hugged him tight. "Are you alright?"

He swallowed hard. "Yes, but I thought I was going to throw up in the cleaning closet."

Loretta fanned him with his hat and whispered, "You poor thing." She looked up at Antonia. "Thank God for Ana's cook and his quick thinking."

"You heard already?" Antonia said.

"Of course," Loretta said, "Ana just phoned and told me *everything*." She put her hand over her heart. "My disguises are good, but I was still a wreck."

Antonia flopped down in a chair and sighed deeply, then she dabbed her forehead with her hanky while waving her hand under her chin like a fan.

Loretta blinked and beamed. "Oh my, Mrs. Smith! You deserve an award for that performance just now—gesturing and fanning yourself like a grand dame in the 'talkies.' You're growing into your role like a professional!"

Loretta was surprised when Antonia smiled and chuckled. Maybe Antonia was becoming more comfortable and trusting now that the plan had worked.

"Let's go to bed, Francisco," Antonia said, and when she reached the top of the landing, she added, "Thank you, Loretta. For everything."

Loretta watched Francisco as he headed toward the stairs. For a moment, he paused and cocked his ear. "I'll be up in a minute, Ma," he said, then he ran to the window that overlooked the porch and rubbed his palm against the frost covered glass.

"What is it?" Loretta said.

"I thought I heard a hoot," he said.

He peered out the window in the direction of the crevice in the twisted tree.

"I can't see it though. It's too dark."

Then suddenly, he took a hop backwards.

"What?" Loretta said.

"It's the owl," Francisco said. "It's right here on the window ledge. Its eyes are like tiny yellow moons." Francisco touched the glass as if reaching out to a friend and made a circle with his lips and blew—*Hoo-h'HOO-hoo-hoo.*

Hoo-h'HOO-hoo-hoo, the owl trilled back.

Francisco turned and looked at Loretta. "It was Javier's owl, wasn't it—that beat up on Elton?"

Loretta gently touched Francisco's head. "You have a friend," she said, and she looked at him and smiled.

"Javier gave me one of the owl's feathers," he said, and he pulled it out from his shirt to show her. "See? I keep it around my neck, so I won't lose it."

"It's beautiful, and you're smart to do that," Loretta said.

Francisco was quiet for a moment. "That bad man's not my real father, you know? Ma says my real father was kind."

"Knowing you, I expected that," Loretta said.

"My real father is named Mateo, but we don't know where he is."

Loretta nodded and whispered to herself, "I thought so." She hesitated then asked quietly, "Did you ever know him?"

"No," Francisco said. "But Ma says he's in my heart and that's what matters. But I still wish I could meet him—so I can know who I am."

Loretta gazed at him then tilted her head to the side. "You are very special, Francisco. You know that, right?"

Francisco shook his head and looked at his feet.

"Trust me, you are," she said and reached out with her palm upwards. He placed his hand on top of hers, and she could feel a warmth flow through her hand up her arm and into her chest and wrap around her heart like a warm blanket. Her breath caught in her throat, and she couldn't speak for a moment.

After he let his hand drop, Francisco leapt up the stairs two at a time and spread his arms wide.

"I'm flying, see, Loretta? Like the great horned owl in the night—fierce, brave, and strong."

"You are, my sweet," Loretta whispered as Francisco disappeared down the second-story hallway.

She stood alone in amazement. After Francisco mentioned meeting Javier at the bell tower, Loretta, Javier, and Gabriel had talked. Javier had told her of his hunch, and Gabriel had agreed—such relationships with owls were only borne out through family. She shuddered with joy at what that might mean—but who was Francisco?

She would go to see Javier in the church garden at first light.

That night in his dream, Francisco flew up to the mountain peak with the great horned owl by his side. He waved to Javier as he swooped past the bell tower then down the street and through the park where Gabriel stood gazing up at him against a star-speckled sky. Gabriel shouted, "¡*Muy fuerte*!" and pumped his arm as Francisco glided past then out over the Rio Grande, where he dipped low over the wetlands where the sandhill cranes followed his ascent into the sky with their raised beaks. "*I'm freeeeee*," he shouted, and the sound of his voice dispersed and swirled around him, like stardust, in an atmospheric wind.

CHAPTER 27

FIRST LIGHT

Loretta was already dressed when she heard the bell just four blocks away from her apartment on Lido Street. She buttoned her coat and headed into the early light with quick steps and a heart full of anticipation.

With the deep purple eastern skies behind her, the mountains to the north were mostly in shadow, but Mount Franklin, at the very tip, was covered in pink light like a cheerful cap.

She found Javier in the garden pruning a broken tree limb.

When he saw her walking toward him at a quick pace, he lowered the handsaw to his side. "What's wrong?" he said.

Loretta put on a wide smile. "Nothing's wrong, Javier. Nothing at all." She took a deep breath and clasped her hands together. "I think you're right!"

Javier stepped toward her and held her shoulders gently with his outstretched hands and looked into her eyes. "What happened?" he said.

"The owl came, it attacked a bad man who was looking for them."

Then she flailed her arms, reenacting the moment. "He tried to protect himself, but the owl came at him three times before it flew away. He had cuts all over his face and arms."

Javier's eyes grew wide, and the green became as brilliant as the open sea. "What happened with the boy and his mother?" Javier said.

"They were inside the café with Ana. Ana hid them when the man came asking for help. Ana was so *aterrado*—so scared." Loretta took a deep breath and looked up. "*Gracias a Dios*. The bad man left and didn't find them."

"But where did the—" Javier said, but before he could finish, Loretta interrupted with a breathy voice and grabbed Javier's arm and held it tight.

"And there's more. Back at the hotel, the owl landed on the windowsill right in front of Francisco and . . ." Then she hopped on her toes as if she were an excited child.

"*¿Qué, qué?*" Javier said. "Tell me!"

"They spoke!"

Javier looked toward the edge of the garden where a wooden bench was partially lit by a sunray. He walked over with wobbly legs then sat and put his head in his hands. "I knew it," he said.

Loretta sat beside him. "Aren't you happy?" she said.

Javier looked up with a wide grin and laughed. "Do I look happy?"

She held both of his hands in hers. "Do you know who he is?" she said.

He shook his head. "No, but he's definitely one of us—family."

"His mother was asking questions too—when Francisco wasn't there. She asked if I knew a Mateo Garcia from about fifteen years back. I got the sense that they were more than friends," she said. "Do you know of him?"

Javier shrugged. "Lots of Garcias."

"Then how will we find out?" Loretta said.

Javier ran a hand over the nape of his neck then tapped the tips of his fingers together. "The owl will give us clues. We must be patient, watch, and listen. But most importantly, we cannot let the boy and his mother leave the circle, or we will never know."

Loretta nodded rapidly in agreement. "Yes, yes, of course," she said. "*The circle.*" She knew what he meant—only the circle of their family could see and learn who he was—only her blood relations, no one else.

Javier turned his face towards hers. "It wasn't just me, Gabriel felt something too." He smiled. "He has returned to us like a gift," Javier said.

Loretta nodded and smiled, but suddenly an intense shiver spiraled down her spine.

"I have to go. I must speak to Ray, now!"

CHAPTER 28

LORETTA

When Ray entered the hotel that morning, with coffee and a donut in hand, Loretta was waiting. Leaping up from her stool, she grabbed his elbow and pushed him toward the office.

"Hey, hey!" he said. "You're gonna spill my coffee. What's the damned emergency?"

She closed the door and stood straight as a rod. "We can't do it," she said.

Ray took a bite of his donut, and sugar sprinkles dusted his black shirt where his belly protruded. "Do what?" He slurped his coffee.

Loretta stared at him and stamped her foot. "It!"

Ray shoved the rest of the donut in his mouth and looked at Loretta incredulously.

"I mean . . . I won't do it," she said.

"Why, for God's sake?" Ray asked.

Loretta paced nervously for a moment and slapped the desk with the palm of her hand. "It's too risky."

Ray chuckled uncomfortably then nodded and responded in a

voice that rolled up then down like a roller-coaster ride. "Ohhhhh, I get it. The boy has gotten under your skin."

Loretta sighed and pulled at her shirttail. "Yes, I guess so."

Ray stopped his chuckling abruptly. "Well, it's too late. Everything's lined up."

Loretta looked fiercely into his eyes. "Un-line it then!" she said.

Ray now wore a condescending expression. "Oh, Loretta, come on, you're acting like a doting grandmother. Everything will be fine. He's the perfect one to do it. It will be sewn into his cuffs, and he and no one else will ever know—not Rico, not Hector, not the customs officers—trust me, they won't stop and search a boy."

Loretta shook her head with ferocity like it would fly off at any moment.

"Come on, Loretta. It's what we've been waiting for. The red beauty will finally be in our hands—and don't forget the big payday. A new house, a car perhaps? You can retire and won't have to work in this dump anymore."

He burped, adding emphasis to his point.

She looked down at her feet. "I've started to enjoy working in this dump. I have my girls to care for, and now Francisco is here."

Ray dropped his head. "How can you be so shortsighted? It's not like Francisco will stay forever. They'll be gone before you know it. Look at how restless his mother is. And if we don't do it now, we'll have missed our chance."

"I don't care!" she snapped.

Ray stiffened and pulled at his belt to lift his pants. "You seem to forget who's in charge," he said.

"That's where you're wrong," she said. "You'd have none of this without me. I do *everything*, know *everyone*, and arrange *everything*. All you do is sit on that porch, get fat from my food, and go on about how Angelica is your lover, and get all smoochy with her like you're some Don Juan."

Ray threw his hat on the floor. "Those are low blows." He pointed a finger at her. "In case you've forgotten, we are partners, and I do plenty. Without this hotel, there wouldn't have been loans, and without the loans, this business of ours would never have thrived."

Loretta nudged his hat with her foot. "I don't need the fire opal anymore to be happy," she said. "We'll just go about business as usual."

He dropped his shoulders and spoke softly. "What's gotten into you?" he said.

She shook her head. "You won't understand."

"It's not your stupid tarot card shit, is it?"

She shook her head again. "They're not stupid. I've learned a lot from those cards, but that's not it."

"Then what?"

She didn't say anything.

"Oh, for God's sake," he said. "You've been talking to Javier, haven't you? The owls have been speaking to him again?"

He took a deep breath and shook his head. "You and your cousins and your owl talk—it's ridiculous," he said. He looked out the window at the owl in the crevice. "It's not enough that I have that thing out there looking at me all day—with those slitty eyes."

Ray clutched his temples between his fingers. "Okay then. But promise me you'll think about it. I'll call it off for tomorrow, but Antonia and Francisco will still do their first run, then perhaps, you'll see how smoothly it goes and reconsider."

Loretta's hands were shaking slightly when she lit a cigarette, took a long tug, and shook her head. "I doubt it," she said.

Ray lowered his eyes towards hers and raised her chin with his finger. "Still friends?"

Loretta paused and moved her mouth from side to side. "Hardly," she said, then she handed him the cigarette. "You're my brother. More than friends."

Ray took a tug. "That's right," he said, and he laid his hand on her shoulder. "I was the Irish bastard, but your father took me in anyway—*and* loved me."

"Yes," she said and smiled. "Francisco doesn't have that, you know. He doesn't have a father that he knows—he doesn't have someone to love and guide him. You should get it more than anyone."

"You can't protect him forever," Ray said. "He's not yours."

"I know," Loretta said and looked at her feet. She didn't tell Ray anymore. He wouldn't understand.

CHAPTER 29

THE CROSSING

Francisco was dressed in his disguise and ready at 7:15 a.m. as Antonia secured her wig with bobby pins.

He looked at his watch and tapped his foot. "We need to get going, so I can be back in time to play checkers with Sam."

"Hold your horses. This outfit takes time to get on," Antonia said.

When they finally got downstairs, a plate of corn muffins awaited them on a table near the window along with a pitcher of water and two drinking glasses. Sam was mopping the cracked linoleum floor as though there was hope for its appearance, with a detergent that smelled sour like vinegar, and backing his way out toward the patio leaving a slick surface in his wake.

He pointed to Francisco. "Little Fran, I brought checkerboard. We play later. Mrs. Loretta say okay. Before Mr. Ray come." Sam shook his head up and down with his mouth wide and teeth showing.

Francisco beamed, "Okay!"

Loretta was in the office speaking loudly on the phone. "*Sí*, Eva, *¿puede oírme?* Okay good. An old lady—*una vieja, sí*—black dress, lace hat—Mrs. Smith and *un niño* with *dos trenzas* and a bowler. *Sí*, that's right. *Se llama,* Jesse."

An old man with a bristly beard sat slumped in a dingy yellow lounge chair, snoring, with an empty whiskey bottle balanced on his belly that rose and fell with every breath like it was floating on sea swells.

Francisco walked around the counter and stood in the office doorway, filling only a third of it, and grinned. When Loretta saw him, she quickly hung up. "*Adiós*, Eva. Gotta go," she said.

"Who's that old man?" Francisco whispered.

"Oh, that's Uncle Buzz. He likes to drop by and chat early in the morning," Loretta said. "And sometimes he takes a little snooze before he goes home." She turned her head sideways and looked at the old man. "His wife died a year ago. He gets lonely."

Francisco thought the name suited him—like he was a giant bumble bee perched on a bright yellow sunflower.

When Sam gently adjusted the pillow under the old man's neck and gave him a pat on the shoulder, the old man snorted loudly then smacked his lips. Loretta smiled. "Must be dreaming about chocolate meringue pie, his favorite dessert and mine too."

"Guess what?" Francisco said. "It's mine also!"

Loretta tapped her chin and shook her head with yet another look of astonishment. "Imagine that . . ."

Antonia appeared behind Francisco with her glasses hanging on a string at her neckline. "I can't see a darn thing in these glasses," she said. "I'm only going to wear them around here. Once we cross over, I'm taking them off, so I don't break my neck."

"I don't think you'll need to wear them much longer," Loretta said. "I feel certain that wretched man isn't coming back, but let's give it some time just to be sure." Loretta herded them into the lobby and pointed to the table. "Ana made those for you, enjoy as many as you like now, and grab a napkin from the kitchen to put some in your purse for later."

"Thank you," Antonia said, then she ran her hand over her back-end with the pillows and oversized girdle. "This thing is so bulky. I keep knocking things off tables."

Loretta laughed. "Well, at least you can take it off at night, sweetie. Mine is permanent."

Francisco was surprised that Antonia smiled in return. Maybe his mother had finally accepted that Loretta was a nice person. And with all of the attention Francisco was getting from Loretta, Ana, and now Sam, he felt wanted—like this place was a home.

Loretta reached out and buttoned Francisco's topcoat button. "It's going to be chilly on the bridge today—the wind is coming from the north. So, stay buttoned up, we don't want you catching a cold," she said and winked at him.

Then she reached out for Antonia's shoulders. "Feeling good?"

Antonia nodded.

"Don't worry . . . everything will go smooth as silk," Loretta said.

Antonia nodded.

What's to worry about, Francisco thought. We're just going to Mexico again.

Loretta could hear the ladies in the hallway upstairs chatting and waiting for her to attend to their outfits for the day. Tuesdays and Thursdays were busy. All the girls went over in the early morning and returned around noon so they could take a nap and get ready for the night shifts at their regular jobs.

Before heading up, she pulled a thumbtack from the bulletin board to adjust a poster that was announcing "Freddy the Fury" bull coming to the rodeo. The tack was set hard, and when she tried to pull it out, the tip of her fingernail broke off.

"No, not today!" she said shrilly. "*Dios mío*—my nerves."

She darted over to her collection of crystalline stones that lay on a small round table by the window and reviewed the procedure in her mind. Then she precisely implemented it as though she were following a meticulous family recipe:

1. Raise the window

2. Remove the sage incense stick from the jar

3. Immediately resecure the lid so as not to release too much magic

4. Strike a match and light the incense

5. Wave the stick in seven counterclockwise circles around the crystals until a small cloud forms

6. Take a deep breath then blow out with all your might!

Loretta blew and the small cloud disappeared through the screen, and she quickly shut the window and locked the latch then put her hands on her hips. "Phew!"

She smiled as she glanced at Uncle Buzz who had missed it all.

"Rest easy, Uncle," she said, then she removed her shawl from her shoulders and placed it over his arms and chest. "Everything should be okay now."

Antonia sat on the trolley with her gloved hands in her lap and Francisco by her side. Loretta had insisted that they take the trolley, "since Antonia was an old lady and all," Loretta had said. "And you must wear gloves, because your hands are pretty and smooth," Loretta had added. "They'll give you away if you don't."

Antonia was starting to change her feeling about Loretta. Ever since Loretta had orchestrated the disguises and managed the situation with Elton, Antonia was more trusting. But she also was crystal clear that today would be different than yesterday. Scouting was one thing, smuggling was another. But oddly, she felt a sense of confidence—like she could do this.

When they slowed at the customs house, and the driver rang the bell, Francisco looked up and smiled. Antonia gave him a quick smile back but then eyed the officers. The one they had seen yesterday—with the foxlike stare—was there again, but when they passed through, he didn't even look at them.

On the bridge, Francisco sat upright then cupped his ear. "They're out there. I can hear the cranes again. Can you?"

Antonia shook her head. "I'm afraid my ears aren't as good as yours."

"Sometimes I think I can hear things that others can't," Francisco said. "Animals mostly—it's hard to explain."

Antonia stared through the trolley windshield.

Francisco nudged her arm. "How long will we be over there? We *have* to be back before Mr. Ray comes for lunch. Loretta said Mr. Ray won't like it if Sam's playing games instead of working." Francisco paused and looked toward the river. "I think Mr. Ray doesn't like Sam—why?"

"I don't know," Antonia said. "Maybe because Sam's different—different country, different culture."

"Why does that matter?"

"It shouldn't," she said.

"Is that why the kids at my school didn't like me? Cause I was different looking than them?"

She put her arm around him. "They just didn't know how special you are."

"So, special's good but different's bad?"

"Neither are bad." Antonia said. "Sometimes kids can be mean—just like grown-ups."

"I'm tired of being special and different," Francisco said. "I just want to fit in."

She squeezed his hand. "Let's talk about today," Antonia said. "First, we'll go in the market, meet a friend of Loretta's. She's making a dress for me, then we'll go to a café and meet another person. He's going to give me some things to bring back, and that will be it."

"What kind of things?"

Antonia hesitated. She hated lying to Francisco, but she had to. The less he knew the better. "Clothes and jewelry for her collection and for a friend who has a shop in Albuquerque." The enormity of the lie that flowed so easily from her lips appalled her.

CHAPTER 30

EVA'S PLACE

The trolley didn't stop just across the bridge. Instead, it took them directly to the market. When they arrived a young man in a pin-striped suit reached for Antonia's hand and helped her down the steps and onto a dusty patch half a block from the *mercado*.

Though Antonia was trying to be mindful of her grandmotherly role, for a moment she forgot and descended nimbly down the steps as the young man glanced at her with raised eyebrows and an expression of admiration.

He tipped his hat and smiled. "*Ten un buen día,*" he said, then strode in front of them toward the market's wide open wooden doors where the dogs that had been tussling the day before were sprawled lazily in the morning sunshine. There was no crying baby either, only the sound of wind chimes tinkling in the breeze as men leaned leisurely against their cars with their hats tipped back and legs crossed.

To Antonia, the whole morning felt more relaxed than the day before. The tension that the tall, lanky man had created with his harsh words and yelling was gone. Though the air was chilly, it felt fresh with the scent of dried eucalyptus leaves mixed with the tangy fragrance of juniper trees. And Francisco's mood had also seemed to take a turn for the better. After their trolley conversation, he had grown quiet, but now he seemed joyful as he trotted in front of her with a skip in his step. Maybe Loretta had been right. Maybe things would go more smoothly today.

Inside the *mercado*, Antonia did exactly as Ray had directed. Find the clothing stall with a sign that said Eva's Place.

A hand on her shoulder alerted Antonia to the presence of a middle-aged dark-haired woman wearing a loose white dress and a close-lipped smile.

"*Señora, ¿Cómo está? ¿Bien?* It's me *Eeeeeeva*," she said. Then she spelled it out and raised her eyebrows. "E-V-A, remember?"

"Of course," Antonia said.

Eva turned to Francisco. "Little Jesse?" She pinched Francisco's cheek. "Aren't you a cute one," she said with an exaggerated smile.

Francisco rubbed his cheek with his sleeve.

Abruptly, Eva turned to Antonia and held out her arm. "Come with me, my dear, I'll show you my best dresses—especially for you, Missus." She waved to a lady at another booth and smiled. "*Hola, Reina.*" She whispered in Antonia's ear, "Reina's dresses are cheap. Cotton's too thin. I have a special one for you."

Eva led Antonia and Francisco up a short flight of stairs to a low-ceilinged room where three women were hunched over sewing machines feeding cloth toward tapping needles with arhythmic surges. Every square inch of the room, except for the middle where the women worked, was stacked with bolts of mostly white cloth that muffled the market noise and made the mariachi band sound like it was miles away.

To Antonia, it called up images of a padded room in an asylum.

"Looks like heaven," Francisco said.

Eva smirked. "Hardly." Then she waved her arm. "Here is where you'll find what you want. Only for special customers—the cotton is thick and soft," she said in an overly loud voice. She closed the door behind them.

Eva bent over and spoke to Francisco. "What size do you wear, *mi pequeño*?"

Francisco blinked. He didn't understand the meaning of *pequeño* but felt certain, by her high-pitched sing-songy tone, that she considered him younger than he was.

He pushed back his shoulders and said, "I wear an extra small." He didn't bother to tell her how old he was. He was done with that.

"Ah *sííííí*," she said and patted him on the head like he was a puppy. "We have something perfect for you." She nodded toward a youngster who wore a felt hat, tan pants, and boots and sat at a table in the corner carefully cutting strips of cloth with a pair of scissors.

"Maria, take this handsome *muchacho* to get a Coke and sit outside the door."

As Francisco turned to go, Antonia whispered to Eva. "But I don't want him to be out of my sight."

Eva's expression instantly changed from a smile to a frown, and she whispered back, "Do you want to work with me or no? I don't have time for divas. The boy will be fine—right outside the door."

Thrown aback by Eva's sudden sternness, Antonia felt a chill.

There were two short wooden stools by the door where they sat. The girl reached into a bucket and pulled out two Cokes, opened one, and handed it to Francisco. After taking off her hat, she opened the other, tilted her head back, and took a long slug, finishing off more than half of the bottle.

After saying nothing for a while, Maria let out a loud burp, and Francisco looked at her with an amused expression.

"What?" she said. "Never heard a girl burp?"

"I guess so but not loud like that," he said.

She kicked the floor with the toe of her boot. "Well, I got news for you. I can burp, fart, and cuss better than any boy. Wanna learn some cuss words in Spanish?"

Francisco shrugged. "I guess."

"What letter of the alphabet do you want to start with? I know them all."

Before responding, Francisco gave her a look over. Her skin was dark and smooth, and her shoulder-length brown hair hung around her face like curtains.

He squinted. "T," he said.

She blew out air and shook her head as though she couldn't believe it. "That's easy," she said, then she bared her pearl-colored teeth behind flattened lips. "¡*Eres un tramposo*!"

"What does that mean?" he said.

She raised her chin as if she had won a heated argument with a fitting summation. "It means 'you're a liar and a cheat!'"

Francisco felt a sudden surge of admiration and smiled. "How old are you?" he said.

"Fourteen," she said, quickly adjusting her sitting position so that she was facing him. "Let me guess how old you are."

Francisco had dreaded her response and was certain she would think he was younger than he was and braced himself for yet another demeaning, awkward moment.

She rubbed her chin, eyed him from head to toe, and squinted. "You're twelve," she said crisply.

Francisco raised his head abruptly like he was thrown off guard.

She cuffed her knee with the palm of her hand. "Well, am I right?"

"Yes," he said, "How'd you guess?"

She laughed and drained the last of her Coke then spun the bottle on the wooden floorboards.

"It's your eyes. They make you look wiser—older. They're intense—kind of wild—like you know things."

He wasn't sure if it was a compliment or not, and she could tell. "Smart, I mean, in a good way, not beady like a rat. More like an owl."

He remembered his owl feather. "I like owls. A friend gave me this. His name's Javier—do you know him?"

She laughed. "Probably, but I know lots of Javiers—Javier Rodriguez, Javier Ramirez, Javier Sanchez, Javier Gonzales. I could go on for days."

He held the feather up for her to see. "Well, my Javier said owls are good protectors, so I wear it around my neck for that reason."

"Yeah, I know about that too," she said. "My grandparents tell me the same thing."

Francisco glanced downward with a look of disappointment and changed the subject. "How do you know English so well?"

"My grandfather taught me. He said it's good to know what people on the other side are thinking and saying. That way you know whether to trust them or not."

Francisco leaned over, put his finger to the floor, and let a pill bug crawl onto his fingernail. "Other side?"

"Yeah. He works over there—across the river."

The pill bug crawled toward his knuckle as he watched it creep. "What's the big deal with this side and that side? Seems all the same to me. I'm a kid, you're older but still a kid, but we're not *that* different."

"But you got more money," she said, "that's the difference."

He shook his head. "Not really. We used to have some, but we left it all behind."

She looked at him sideways, and her shiny dark hair fell over most of her face until she flicked it back over her shoulder. "Sorry, but that sounds stupid."

"Depends," he said. "You can have money but still be scared and mad all the time. Or you can be happier with less—like I am now."

"Easy for you to say," she said. "I'll bet all of your friends have enough money for shoes."

"Well yes . . ." he said, ". . . but I don't really have any friends my age." He blushed at the admission then stared at his feet.

She gave him a long questioning look and gently yanked on one of his braids.

"Well, you got me, now," she said.

He cleared his throat and covered his mouth with his hand to hide his smile.

She reached into her pocket and pulled out a tin of snuff and held it out. "Want some?"

"No thanks," he said. "Last time I had some, I threw up. My stepfather made me try it."

"It takes some getting used to," she said. "It's no big deal to throw up. I've done that too." She put her hat back on, leaned against the wall, and used her Coke bottle for spitting.

"So, how'd you learn to cuss like that?" Francisco said.

"My cousins taught me." She pointed her thumb in the direction of the closed door. "My aunt Eva's sons—one of them is a Javier too. They're jerks, but sometimes you can learn stuff from jerks."

"Hmmm," Francisco said. "I'll remember that." He was about to ask her what other things she had learned from her jerk cousins, but the mariachi band cranked up full throttle, filling the market with harmonic voices, blaring trumpets, and quick strumming guitars.

As they listened, Francisco tapped his foot to the music. He liked having a friend almost his age, even if it was only for a few minutes.

Inside the sewing room, Eva pointed towards a young birdish-looking girl who was barefooted and head-down over her machine. Her clothes were dirty and tattered, and her hair looked like a pilfered wren's nest.

"That *nina's* my best seamstress. Not a pretty face, but who cares," Eva said. "She works harder than anyone else and doesn't give me any . . . how do you say?" She rolled her eyes upwards then blurted out, "Sass! *¿Comprendes?*"

Though Antonia didn't like Eva's harsh assessment of the young lady, she didn't say anything. It was clear that Eva was a force to be reckoned with, and she didn't want to cross her—not now. Too much was at stake.

"She's almost finished with your dress," Eva said. "Loretta gave me the measurements, so it'll fit. It'll be big on you 'cause its gotta hold the cargo." She squinted and looked at Antonia as though she were considering the load capacity of a donkey. "When the girl's done, put the dress in your bag, take it back, and wear it next time." Suddenly, a sideways grin appeared on Eva's face like she was about to enjoy her next thought. "Ray said you needed to look high-class, not worn like a dirty tub brush."

Antonia endured this insult by turning her back to Eva. She examined a bolt of pink linen before approaching the skinny seamstress.

Her soon-to-be new dress was midnight blue with white and orange embroidery running down the long sleeves and circling the mid-calf hemline. She reached out to touch the fabric and rubbed it between her fingers as the young girl cut a thread from the needle and tied it off.

"It's nice," Antonia said.

"*Gracias*," the girl whispered without raising her head.

Eva's voice remained stern as she pointed to a pile of pants and shirts. "While you're waiting, pick from those for your boy. Those are for when you've ditched that old lady outfit and he's back to himself."

Antonia walked over to the pile and sorted through a stack of crisp white shirts and pin-striped trousers. Antonia could feel Eva standing close behind her.

"You won't leave the way you came in," Eva said and nodded toward a small door in the corner. "That's your exit—through an underground tunnel that takes you to the bathroom of the restaurant across the street."

"A tunnel?" Antonia said.

Eva ignored her question. "Knock on the sink pipes three times with the wood handle of the plunger and flush the toilet twice. Then he will come."

"Who is he?"

"No names. No more questions. Just do as I say." She leaned in close to Antonia's ear, and Antonia could smell the strong odor of garlic on her breath.

"Here's a tip for our relationship—business only. *No me caes bien.* And in case you don't speak Spanish that means, I don't like you." Then she pointed to her chest. "Me? I'm just a poor dressmaker for all of Ray's and Loretta's girls—I starve, the rest of you get rich. *¿Comprendes?*"

Antonia looked down not knowing where else to cast her eyes.

Eva snapped her gum loudly emphasizing her next point. "You *gringos* think you're special—like you can just push us around. And Loretta, she thinks she is too. She was poor like me until she married that white man, Charlie. My husband was her cousin, but my *familia* doesn't matter to her anymore. Now she treats me like *una sirvienta.* When she needs me, she says, 'Oh, Eva, you're *marvilloso'* but when she doesn't, she treats me like *basura*—garbage."

Eva thumped her chest with her fist. "My husband, Tomas, fought with the *revolucionarios.* He was a warrior for his people like Pancho Villa, but Loretta married a *gringo* who doesn't give a damn about us. Do you know what happened when your army came after Pancho into our country, our home, our land?" She squinched her mouth like she was going to spit. "Your *gringo* soldiers hung my Tomas."

Antonia cleared her throat and lowered her head. "I'm sorry, I have no ill intent, I only . . ."

Eva shook her head, then walked to the door, opened it, and forced a smile Francisco's way. "Come in, and go with *su madre.* Next time, Maria will take you for candy. You like *caramelo*?"

Francisco smiled. "I like Cokes better."

Eva's fake smile suddenly flattened. "Well, we'll see . . ." she said. She ruffled his hair with a little too much force and mumbled, "*Malcriado.*"

Maria leaned against a post. "*Adiós, amigo.* And next time let's skip the Coke and have a beer!"

Eva glared at Maria.

Antonia was shocked.

Francisco shuffled his feet nervously but grinned.

CHAPTER 31

THE TUNNEL

The tunnel was narrow, about five feet high, and dimly lit. Water droplets leaked from above through cracks in the wooden framing that held the earth back on all sides. The ground felt squishy underfoot, and a rivulet of water trickled down the middle of the path. About thirty feet ahead, a wall-mounted blue light cast a seawater-colored reflection on a wooden door. Moldy greenish splotches were splayed across the wood like underwater creatures.

"Why are we going this way?" Francisco said. "It smells bad, like rotten eggs."

"It's a shortcut, that's all. To meet the guy Loretta wants me to talk to."

"Couldn't we just walk there from outside?"

"Francisco, please. Don't ask so many questions—not now. I'm just following directions."

Once they reached the door, Antonia pushed it open and peered inside. There was a sink with rust-colored stains at the drain, a light bulb dangling from a wire, a cracked mirror, and a toilet with the lid closed. The smell of sulfur was overwhelming.

"Seems like we're always in smelly places," Francisco whispered.

"Stay here for a second," Antonia said. "I have to use the bathroom." She stepped inside, found the plunger but decided to use her cane instead, since God only knows what was on the plunger's rubber end, and she'd be damned if she'd touch it. She made a mental note to bring the cane with her next time too.

Tap Tap. She flushed the toilet, waited for the bowl to refill then flushed again. Looking in the mirror, she straightened her hat then pulled on her dress to make sure her pillows were in the right place.

There were heavy footsteps, a tap on the opposite door, then a man's low voice. "This way."

As Francisco and Antonia followed a short fat man down a dark hall into a crowded restaurant, the man didn't speak to either of them. He pointed toward a dimly lit corner table where a dark figure sat reading the newspaper and smoking a cigar.

Without lowering his paper, the man said, "Rico, take the boy to the bar and get him a drink."

The fat man rubbed his stubbly beard, displaying a large silver ring with a black stone on his pinky finger. He cupped the back of Francisco's neck with a clammy hand and guided him past a busboy with a tray piled high with greasy plates and empty beer mugs and through a maze of tables towards a corner seat at the bar. The restaurant was packed with slumped over men in rumpled suits with cigarettes hanging from the corners of their mouths. Women with bleary eyes leaned over glasses of champagne as their long-beaded necklaces draped onto checkered tablecloths.

To Francisco, everyone looked like they had just crawled out of bed and were still half asleep. At the bar, Francisco climbed up onto a stool, and a bartender with a handlebar mustache as thick as rope wiped off the counter and looked at him with a serious expression. "What'll you have? *Cerveza*, Tequila?"

The fat man, Rico, chuckled then gently punched Francisco in the arm. "You heard the man. What'll you have?"

Francisco had never sat at a bar before, so he surveyed the bottles at the base of a giant mirror but saw nothing resembling the shape of a Coke bottle.

"Got any Cokes?" he said.

The bartender disappeared behind two swinging doors.

Out of the corner of his eye, Francisco examined the man named Rico. A mat of curly black chest hair spilled from his white shirt at the neckline.

"*Muchacho*, what's your name?" Rico said.

"Fra—I mean Jesse." Francisco said.

"Jesse, eh?" Rico said. "A little outlaw?" He threw back his head and laughed displaying crooked rows of stained teeth then elbowed Francisco with a force that almost knocked Francisco off his stool.

When the bartender came back and pushed a Coke Francisco's way, Rico nodded toward the liquor shelf. "Double tequila." He reached into his inside jacket pocket and pulled out a deck of cards. He held them up for Francisco to see then shuffled them with thick, short fingers that, to Francisco, looked like a row of suckling piglets.

"Loretta tells me you're good at poker," he said. "And I want to find out just how good."

"I'm okay," Francisco said, but he knew that wasn't true. He was probably better than okay, because he had mastered the recognition of a bluff from Loretta's teaching.

Over the past few days, he and Loretta had easily played thirty hands—Texas Hold'em, blackjack, seven-card stud.

He thought about one of their games just yesterday. Francisco had shuffled the cards. "Five-card stud," he announced.

As he dealt, Loretta had gazed at him. "Your eyes . . ." she said, ". . . they are your allure. They'll be your secret weapon in poker."

He looked up. "Allure?"

"Yes. They're like the fire opals I love. Unexplored planets, wild looking, endless, enticing." She had wiggled her fingers like a sorceress casting a spell and sung her words. "Meet your opponent eye to eye. Draw them in. Observe. Watch as they lose themselves into the depths of your being and without knowing it, reveal their secrets."

Though Francisco had squirmed in his chair with a bit of uneasiness, he was also intrigued. "You really think so?"

She slapped her hand on the counter. "Of course, I think so! You, Francisco, will be like a spider—the moth will flounder in your web then you will *pounce*!"

When she had shouted the word "pounce" and grabbed his sides and tickled him, he almost jumped out of his skin. She laughed and gave him an affectionate pinch. "Trust your auntie Loretta. You will see that I'm right."

And surprisingly, Maria had mentioned it earlier. Maybe his eyes were the thing that set him apart—in a good way.

He snapped back to the moment when Rico pushed the cards his direction and bellowed, "Dealer's choice!"

Suddenly, as though a shot had been fired, everyone in the restaurant became silent and turned their heads in Rico's direction.

A blond-headed fellow at a corner table cupped his hands over his mouth and shouted, "Don't lose your *camisa*, Rico—to that baby shark!" The whole restaurant turned into a roil of raucous laughter as Francisco shuffled the cards.

"Seven-card stud," Francisco said confidently. He stared at the cards then at Rico. Observe, then pounce!

Antonia stood and waited for the man to lower his newspaper. When he finally did, she saw that his hair was black as ink, slicked down, and parted in the middle. He wore a gray vest over a black shirt and a paisley tie that was snug against his bulging Adam's apple.

Unlike Rico, he had a well-groomed appearance with his steely gray eyes, thin lips, and clean-shaven face, but his tidy appearance was overwhelmed by an overabundance of cheap-smelling cologne.

Instead of a cigar, he now had a toothpick clinched between his teeth, and when he uttered his first words, "Sit and listen," his voice was quiet but clear like a low-volume radio.

He didn't tell her his name, and he didn't smile as a waiter slid a cup of coffee in front of Antonia then walked away without apologizing for the slosh that created a pool in her saucer.

"Your job is simple," he said. "You dress like Loretta says. You'll pack several layers of silks—like stockings, ties, and lingerie—under your dress and tucked into the lining of your coat. You'll walk across with your boy from the American side and go directly to the *mercado*. Like today, go to Eva's stall. She'll fit you in a different dress for going back."

"Why do I have to change again?"

He paused. "Don't ask questions."

She straightened her back. "I *will* ask questions if I think they're important."

He acted as if he didn't hear her. "Always take the tunnel and use the same code as today unless Eva tells you otherwise. Then come directly to my table—your boy will sit with me while Rico, my restaurant manager, stocks you up."

He shifted his eyes and waited for the momentary silence in the restaurant to return to its usual clamor. "He'll fill your pockets and the lining of your coat with bladders."

She shook her head and knew immediately what he meant. "Hold on. Ray didn't say anything about tequila. I thought it was just silks."

He cut her off. "Ray's an idiot. If there's any question, you do as I say, not Ray."

She looked around then whispered, "But what if—"

"You won't get caught if you follow my directions. The customs' officers—I know their shifts." He tapped the tips of his fingers together then stared at her. "Get it?"

She nodded.

"And besides, nobody gives a shit about tequila or silks going back and forth. There might as well be a pipeline because of prohibition. So, you see, just like I said. It's simple. Silks this way, tequila that way."

"What questions will they ask?"

"If they ask any, they'll ask what's in the bag. They don't want you carrying out stuff that's tariff worthy. Go ahead and show them. Rico will fill your bag with a few cheap items like blouses or crappy jewelry. If they ask what they're for, tell them you're visiting a friend in El Paso for a few days, and they're gifts for folks back home. That's all you have to say."

She gritted her teeth. "I still don't like the tequila part."

He chuckled. "Ray told me about you." Then he abruptly stopped laughing and sneered. "Get over it!"

He took a slurp of his coffee and stretched his neck from side to side wearing an expression of tried patience.

Antonia despised his tone, but she held her tongue and stared straight into his eyes to remind him of her steel.

He clicked his fingernails on the table. "Today, stay in that old lady outfit. Your load will be light so you can get used to the weight. Then you'll do another run on Thursday with a heavier load and one on

Saturday and Sunday when the tourists are flocking the area. It'll be easy to get lost in the crowd those days."

"When do I get paid?"

"Ray will take care of that."

The man cleared his throat with a low growling noise and glanced in Rico's direction. Without a word, Rico responded like an obedient dog, shoved his stool back, and tugged on Francisco's shirtsleeve to follow. The man pointed with his thumb toward the back of the restaurant then pointed his index finger at a chair for Francisco to sit.

Antonia tried to keep her voice steady. "I'll be right back," she said. "Stay here with Mr. . . . ?"

"Mister," the man said as he raised the newspaper and paid no attention to Francisco.

Antonia looked at Francisco and gave him a tight smile, then Rico reached into his back pocket, pulled out a folded magazine, slid it across the table, and winked—*Boys' Life*. "Loretta said you like it."

Francisco wasn't sure if he should speak in the presence of this "Mister," so he stayed quiet.

When Mister wasn't looking, Francisco peered over the top of his magazine. Mister's head was bent over a ledger and the slick shininess of his black hair reminded Francisco of a dung beetle's shell. What was it about this man that made Francisco uneasy? Was it his dung beetle hair, his close-set eyes, or his possum-like nose—not that Francisco had a thing against possums, but they weren't the most beautiful of earth's creatures.

But he didn't linger on the thought and instead reached in his pocket and jingled the coins he had won. Loretta's advice had worked like a charm. When Francisco drew his third ace, he looked up at Rico with a flat expression and drilled his gaze into Rico's eyes. He waited a minute then pushed the five coins Rico had loaned him across the bar.

Rico scratched his head, cleared his throat, then slid eight coins toward the pot. "Call," he had said, and a smile of confidence crossed his face.

Francisco kept his gaze steady on Rico then turned over his three aces. Did he celebrate? No. Loretta had said celebrating would take the power from his magic, so he scooped up the coin pile and immediately started to shuffle.

Rico had reached out and smothered Francisco's hand with his piglet fingers.

"Hold on, little fella," he said, "five of those are mine. I can be nice but not that nice."

Francisco looked up to see if he was kidding, but when Rico grabbed five coins, he was surprised. Loretta had always let him keep the loan, but this game was the real deal—and Francisco liked it.

Francisco repeated Rico's words in his head: "I can be nice, but not that nice." He made a mental note. Keep an eye on this guy, he thought—even if he is friends with Loretta.

CHAPTER 32

THE BACK ROOM

Antonia followed him as he waddled past open storage areas spilling with cleaning supplies and stacked baskets of dirty napkins and tablecloths. When they approached a back room with a closed door, much to her surprise, he opened it for her and allowed her to enter first. He extended his arm and held out his palm.

"Hand me your coat then have a seat in my guest chair. Put your feet up. Rest a minute."

The chair was rust-colored leather with worn spots on the arm and a split in the seat cushion, but the leather felt soft and comfortable.

Rico hung her coat on a rack then with his back to her, began to run his hands over the inner lining.

"Loretta did a good job on that old lady outfit. I would swear you just left the mortuary and walked over here after crying over your dead husband. Loretta has a knack."

Antonia didn't laugh.

"Nervous?" he asked, but he didn't turn around.

"Not really," she said.

He chuckled, and she could tell that he didn't believe her.

"Well, a little," Antonia said.

"First time is always nerve-wracking—seen it a million times. You don't need to worry though. Just say to yourself, 'it's nothing more than a regular shopping day.'"

He pointed to a basket containing a jumble of blouses, scarves, and embroidered belts. "Put a couple of those in that paper sack. Find a few you think Loretta might like with lots of color. She gets mad if I give her drab stuff."

Antonia nodded and began to sort through the goods as Rico chatted on.

"Loretta and I have known each other since we were kids. Our mothers were close—cousins several times removed but still blood."

"Is Loretta related to everyone?"

Rico gave a snortish laugh. "Yeah, it can be good and bad. Everyone knows the clean and the dirty laundry."

"So does that mean you're related to Eva too?"

"No, Eva comes from another branch. The mean, always pissed-off branch."

"I could tell," Antonia said.

"Don't pay attention to her. She's got bad feelings toward *gringos*."

"Sounds like she might have good reason."

"Maybe, maybe not. Things are complicated here. Many have lingering memories and attitudes from the Revolution. This part of Mexico was like a hornet's nest—the *federales* and *yanquis* threatening each other, the *revolutionaires* fighting the *federales*—somebody was always poking the nest and making it more dangerous. Meanwhile, most of us were just trying to keep our heads down and feed our families. But when you lose a loved one like she did, then anger festers."

Antonia looked outside through a dirty window towards a twiggy tree. "So, you've been in this business for some time?"

"Been running this restaurant for twenty years. This tequila stuff isn't mine. That's Mr. Cox's business—the man you just talked to. I just fill the pouches and get a few *pesos* for it."

Antonia wasn't sure she believed him, but she didn't press him. "You speak English well, like Loretta."

"You must if you want to make money. These tourists want to come to Mexico, but they only want to speak English when they get here. You get tipped like a peasant if you don't speak good English."

He took a bottle of hay-colored liquor from a cabinet stacked with boxes and pulled out the cork with his teeth while gripping a leather bladder in his other hand. He walked over to where she was seated and pulled up a chair next to her.

"Hold this open while I pour it in," he said. The smell of peppery spices mixed with earthy-scented alcohol made her eyes water. When she winced and pulled away, he laughed. "Good stuff, eh?"

"I wouldn't know," Antonia said.

He tightened the cap on the bladder and kept talking.

"I'm going to put one and a half liters on each side to balance you out. Should be about six pounds overall—in the inner pockets of your coat. Tell me on Thursday how that feels. You look pretty strong and have a sturdy figure. I think you could easily handle two to three liters on each side."

Once again, the pack-mule reference, Antonia thought. It was insulting, but at least this Rico fellow gave a damn about what she thought.

He walked to his desk, pulled a key from his pocket, opened a lower drawer, and laid two burlap bags wrapped and tied with string on the desktop. "You have a girdle on, right?"

Put off by the intimacy of the question, Antonia lowered her voice. "Yes," but then added, "and two pillows under it."

"Eva likes to make pretty girls like you suffer in undersized girdles.

Let's just say, I've heard every cuss word in the book directed at Eva."

"Glad I'm not the only one," Antonia said.

He held out the two bags. "Put these in your girdle and remove one of those pillows. I'll turn my back. Don't worry. Some of Loretta's girls like me to peek, but I can tell that's not your style."

Antonia turned away then rolled her eyes. "No," she said.

"If I forget to pack those cigars, there's hell to pay. I don't get my money from Mr. Cox, and I get a verbal blistering too."

"Why cigars? Thought they were legal?"

He shuffled through some papers while Antonia hitched her dress up and stuffed the cigars in at both hips and retied the laces on the girdle.

"These are Cubans," Rico said. "The owner of the hotel Paso del Norte in El Paso has a thing for Cuban cigars, and he's willing to pay a pretty penny. He likes to hand them out to his best customers to keep them coming back. But he doesn't like to pay the customs at the border. That's why you're carrying them."

After she was done, Rico moved to the chair behind his desk, reached into a top drawer and pulled out a sewing needle from a tomato-shaped pincushion then sorted through a few spools of thread, holding each up to the tan lining of Antonia's coat to match the color. He cut off a long piece of thread, licked the tip, held the needle up to the light, and pushed the thread through the hole.

She adjusted her girdle because the burlap bags felt scratchy against her skin then fluffed her dress to make sure there were no revealing bulges. When Antonia turned around, he was sewing her coat pockets shut with carefully spaced stitching.

"Never seen a man sew," she said.

"Have to make sure it looks like a real seamstress's work to be extra safe. Don't want the patrol to get suspicious—sloppy work gets people in trouble."

He hummed a tune that Antonia didn't know for a minute then stopped. "I may look tough, but I was a mama's boy. She taught me to sew—said it would come in handy someday. And damned if she wasn't right."

Antonia gave a slight smile and watched while he worked.

"I like your boy," he said as he tied off a knot. "Loretta talks about him a lot. Francisco this, Francisco that. She says there's something about him that's special. I agree. He reminds me of a kid I used to play with when I was little—it's the eyes. His were so wide and bright, just like your boy's."

Antonia's head jolted his way as though she had been pricked with a straight pin, but she tried to settle. Stay calm, she thought.

"What was your friend's name?" she said, trying to sound nonchalant.

Rico threw his head back and looked up at the ceiling like he was searching his mind. "He went by Pepe—that's all I can remember."

Rico leaned over and cut the thread with his teeth then raised his head and thought for a moment. "I don't know what happened to him. Never saw him again after grade school."

"But he lived in Juarez?" she asked.

Rico looked sideways at her. "What's it to you?"

Antonia opened her mouth then snapped it shut. Stop, she thought. You're about to smuggle illegal goods across the border—keep your mind on the business at hand.

"Nothing, just making conversation," she said.

After he was finished with his stitching, he stood up and held the coat up to a desk lamp and examined his handiwork.

"This should do. What do you think?"

Antonia leaned over, ran her finger over the seams, and carefully examined each pouch pocket, but when her hand trembled slightly, she quickly pulled back. "Looks professional to me."

"Good," he said. "I need you ladies to feel confident."

"Now, one last thing," he said. He took the half-filled tequila bottle and poured some in a shot glass. "Take a swig. It'll settle your nerves."

She shook her head.

"Okay, you're missing out on the finest tequila in Mexico! Smooth as silk."

"No thanks," she said.

"That's good," he said. "You passed the test. Ray said you were a teetotaler, and because of it, he's sure you'll be our most reliable. We've had a few who liked to dip in the goods somewhere between here and El Paso. 'I just took a smidge,' they'd say."

Rico slapped his knee with his thick hand. "But Ray knew how to deal with it. He'd put on a stern face and say, 'If you do it again, I'm docking your pay for that smidge—that smidge is worth more than you make in a single crossing,' and that usually took care of the problem."

He handed her the coat, and she slipped it on and took a few steps around the room to get used to the weight. The bags were filled to the brim so they didn't slosh, but she could feel their weight pulling on her shoulders.

"Keep your shoulders straight," he said. "And walk with your weight firmly on your ass—don't try to carry it with your back. That cane should help you this time."

He strode around the room as if in a fashion parade with his hands on his hips, chin raised, shoulders back, and butt tucked in.

Antonia had to smile. "You do that well."

"I was the baby—the only boy with five sisters. They used to dress me up, so I guess I had my fair share of practice."

Antonia started to feel her guard slipping and she stiffened. "Are we done?" she said.

Rico stopped abruptly and nodded like she had thrown a cold bucket of water on a budding relationship.

He buttoned his top button and tucked in his shirttail. "Let's go," he said without smiling.

Antonia let out a sigh of relief when she and Francisco stepped out of the dark restaurant and into the sunlight. Cox's clipped tone and cold stare mixed with Rico's attempts to make friendly conversation made her unsure if either were trustworthy.

As they neared the bridge, a cold sweat began to form at the back of her neck. Damn these burlap bags, she thought. They're slipping down in the girdle and the pillow's sliding again.

As they neared a shop left of the bridge, she said, "Francisco, I need to step inside for a moment. Come with me."

Inside, the store was bright and filled with tourist trinkets and bins of stones with labels above—lapis, turquoise, emeralds, sapphires. Antonia knew none of the gemstones were real, but Francisco appeared charmed by the heaping displays of color that sparkled in the morning sunrays.

When Antonia approached the checkout counter with nothing in her hand to buy, an old woman sitting on a stool pointed to a sign. "*No baño.*"

"For my grandson? Please?"

The lady showed no expression, just pointed to the sign again.

"We'll buy something," Antonia said.

The old woman raised a crooked finger and pointed toward a door that looked like someone had knocked out the lower panel with their foot.

The door squeaked when she opened it, and when they passed through, it slammed behind them on spring hinges. Once again, they were in a dark hallway.

"Wait here, Francisco," Antonia said.

"Can't I look around outside?" he said.

"No, I'll be just a minute."

Light from the missing panel illuminated the first couple of feet, but after a few steps in, she had to feel her way along a corridor of rough adobe walls. After about ten steps, Antonia's fingers grazed over a wooden frame with an open door. She stepped inside and felt around with her hands until her fingers touched the cold surface of a porcelain sink.

"Please tell me there's a light in here," she said, then she raised her arms, waved them around, and with her wrist, swatted a bulb hanging from a wire. Once it stopped swinging, she turned a switch and the light flickered on for few seconds then off. She tried to screw the bulb in tighter, but it continued to blink.

"Ugg!" she said.

"You, okay?" Francisco called.

She groaned. "Yes, but the darn light flickers, and I can't see a blasted thing."

She took off her coat, hung it on the doorknob, then raised her dress and fumbled with the ties on her girdle but couldn't loosen the knot where she had cinched it tight. She tried pulling at it with her fingernails then out of frustration gave the ties a hard yank.

Suddenly, the girdle loosened, the pillow slipped, and there was a *splash*.

"Dammit!" she groaned.

In the on-off light, she made out a large mop tub filled to the brim with something floating at the surface. It wasn't the pillow.

"Jesus, no!" she said, then the light flicked off for good.

"What happened?" Francisco said.

"I dropped something, but I can't see to find it. Can you come fix this light?"

"Coming," he said.

Reaching the bathroom, he searched with his hands for something to stand on while Antonia swirled her hand in the tub frantically trying to snag the burlap bags among slimy mop strings. At the bottom of the tub, she found them. Yanking them out, she tossed them on the floor and wiped her hands on her skirt.

"Disgusting," she said.

"I got it!" Francisco said. The light flickered on. He was standing on the sink.

Antonia's shoulders dropped when she saw the sopping mess at her feet. She untied the string around the bags and pulled out two soggy cardboard boxes. After raising the lid, she tried to dab the cigars with the hem of her dress, but it was useless. They were soaked.

"What's that?" Francisco said.

"Cigars," she said.

"You bought cigars?"

"No . . . I mean yes," she said. "They're for Ray."

When she tried to pick one up, the brown leaves peeled back and what was inside wasn't brown like tobacco—it was white and clumpy like wet powder.

At first, she could only stare with astonishment, then her chest tightened, and she could hardly breathe.

"You go on back, now," she said trying to sound calm. "I'm gonna clean this mess up and get my outfit back on." She cleared her throat, but her voice was weak. "Go look around the store, I'll be there in a minute."

After he was gone, she frantically whipped her head from side to side, then in a sudden impulse threw the entire contents of both boxes into the toilet—*flush*. Her hands were shaking, and like a frantic clawing animal, she ripped open the seams in her coat, yanked out the bladders and dumped the contents—*Flush.*

When Antonia emerged, Francisco was at the cashier. A crystal lay on the counter, and he slid a coin toward the old lady.

Antonia tapped him on the shoulder, and when he turned around, his mother's face scared him.

"You look white!"

She held her hand over her mouth and gagged. "I feel sick. We need to get back to the hotel right away."

Francisco looked at her with wide eyes. "Want to take the trolley? Probably faster."

"Yes!"

CHAPTER 33

NO CIGARS

When she crossed the threshold of Hotel Luna, her vision was telescopic. Everything at the edges was fuzzy but the focus of her attention—the back of Ray's bald head—was sharp and clear. She knew Francisco was behind her, but she didn't know how far. She whisked past the front desk, not caring if Loretta was there or not, and almost ran over Sam, who was on his knees wiping up a spill.

As Antonia blew past, Loretta's newspaper insert fluttered in her wake. Loretta put down her scissors and coupons and called out to Antonia's back.

"How was it?"

When Antonia didn't respond, Loretta looked at Francisco and whispered, "What's wrong?"

"She's sick, I think."

Loretta reached into her candy drawer. "Here, honey. Go upstairs for a few minutes, then I'll come get you, and we can play some cards."

"I won three centavos off Mr. Rico today! And can I play checkers with Sam now?" Francisco asked.

"Yes. Do that!" Loretta burst out. She nodded at Sam with wide eyes. "Go play on the table in my lounge."

Sam got up quickly. "*Essh*, let's go little Fran—I'll teach you."

Loretta bolted outside onto the patio just in time to hear Antonia let out a shouty whisper. "You son of a bitch!"

Ray turned his head slowly in her direction and took a long slug of his beer. Then he calmly said, "What?"

Antonia ripped off her hat, threw it on the ground, then pulled at her wig. "Ohh, you know what. You lied to me!"

"Huh?" Ray said. "Calm down, for Christ's sake."

She waved a fist at him. "Those cigars . . ."

"Hey, hey," he said. "Keep it down."

Antonia spun around in a furious circle.

Ray held up his palms. "What's the problem with bringing a few cigars? Yeah, I didn't tell you about that, but who cares? Cigars are nothing."

She moved toward him like a hawk swooping down on its prey then clinched the edges of the table and put her nose two inches from his.

"Nothing? You call that nothing?" she snarled. "Those weren't cigars."

Ray lowered his chin and tilted his head back as if her breath were hot as fire. "What the fuck are you talking about? My girls deliver cigars every trip, for that hoity-toity owner of the hotel."

Antonia started shaking her head, and her hair came loose from her bun and hung in strings around her face. "Either you're a liar or the biggest dumbass I've ever met. Which is it, Ray?"

Loretta, who had watched with wide eyes, reached out and touched her arm. "Settle down. Tell us what happened."

Antonia glared at Loretta then slammed her fist on the table. "I'll tell you what the hell happened. Both of you must take me for an idiot. You think I can't tell the difference between tobacco and cocaine?"

Loretta took a step back. "Cocaine?"

"Co-co-co-c-cai—?" Ray started to stutter, but Antonia cut him off.

"Listen up, you two. I made my boundaries very clear."

Loretta looked at Ray in disbelief, and her lip began to quiver with rage. "You did that?"

Ray threw his hands up and his face was flushed red. "No, for Christ's sake. I don't know what she's talking about."

Antonia's face was wrenched and wild looking. "And you know what I did? I flushed all of it. That and the tequila."

Ray shook his head like he hadn't heard right. "You flushed my tequila down the toilet?"

"Shut up, Ray," Loretta snapped. She tried to muster a calm expression then looked directly into Antonia's eyes. "Tell me *exactly* what happened?"

Antonia fell into a chair and buried her face in her hands. She told Loretta about the store, the bathroom, the girdle, the splash, the soggy cigars, and when she got to the part about the crumbly white stuff, Loretta covered her mouth with her hands and glared at Ray.

Ray's eyes grew narrow with rage. "Why didn't you just hide it? You had to flush it away?" His expression suddenly changed to wide-eyed fear.

Ray shook his head and looked at Loretta. "I promise . . . I didn't know."

Loretta bared her teeth. "You've never said anything about cigars! This is some heavy shit, Ray! Maybe you should put that pea brain of yours to work and think about what's gonna happen when *he* finds out!"

This time Ray covered his mouth, as all the possibilities ran through his mind, and he gasped. "We've got to figure out a plan . . . I don't know . . ."

Loretta glared. "We nothing. You're on your own, Ray! I only have *one* thing on my mind. I need to talk to Javier, immediately!"

She tried to speak calmly to Antonia. "Go upstairs," she said. "I'll send Angelica up with some tea. I'll be back in an hour. I'll take care of this, I promise." Then she ran back into the hotel, jerked her arms in her coat, and rushed out the door with her long scarf flying like a cape behind her.

CHAPTER 34

THE GARDEN

The clouds had moved out, and the garden was filled with bright sunshine. Javier was standing on a wood box and cleaning a stained-glass window with a white rag. Loretta could smell the strong scent of vinegar as she approached.

He held his hand over his eyes to shade the sun and was immediately taken aback by her pale face and frightened expression. He stepped down off the box. "*¿Qué ha pasado*? What's wrong?"

Loretta tried to speak, but nothing came out.

Javier held her shoulders with both his hands. "It's okay, just tell me."

Loretta's head swayed back and forth in disbelief at her own words, "It's Francisco and his mother—they're in danger."

"Why?"

Loretta held Javier in a desperate embrace and whispered the whole story into his ear. "Drugs . . . Cox . . . someone's going to pay . . . Francisco, Antonia . . . we have to do something now!"

She dropped down and sat on the box with her head in her

hands as Javier looked at his feet. "*Esto es muy malo*," he mumbled. "*Muy muy malo*."

Loretta nodded, and her eyes were wet. "We have to hide them. Somewhere but where? Cox has his ways. He'll find them, and then they'll both be . . ." She let out a high-pitched whimper and covered her mouth.

Javier frowned, and his usual soft eyes turned hard. "What does Ray say?"

"He says he didn't know about it, but I don't care what Ray says. He got them into this mess, and I don't trust him to fix it."

Javier paced in a circle. "Perhaps he could speak to Cox and make something up?"

Loretta shook her head. "You know Ray, he can't lie his way out of a paper bag. He'll get sweaty and start stuttering, then make things worse and maybe end up dead while trying. He's already shaking in his boots."

Her mind was racing. "Maybe we should put them on a train."

Javier held up his palm. "No. Not a good idea. He'll go after them and find them. Nothing stops *Escorpión*."

"*¿Escorpión?*" Loretta gasped. "You think he's involved?"

Javier wagged his head. "I don't know, but it's possible."

Loretta looked at Javier with pleading eyes. "We can't lose Francisco—we can't."

Javier rubbed his gray stubble with his thick fingers and turned his back to her. When he turned around his eyes were an intense green like emeralds.

"Santiago," he said.

Loretta stared at him. "You think that'll work?"

For a minute, Javier didn't say a word but stood looking upward towards the bell tower, then he lowered his head. "Go back to the hotel, get the boy and his mother. Bring them here. I will hide them in the church until dark. Manuel can pick us up in his taxi. Then we'll go."

"The desert?" Loretta said.

"Yes."

"You know how to get there?"

"No, but we'll figure it out."

Javier and Loretta stood silently and listened to the wind stirring in the juniper tree as its needles raked against the small window where Francisco had first come eye to eye with the owl. Javier shifted his gaze upward and scanned the shadows of the bell tower where the owl sometimes roosted, then he looked skyward and spoke in a whisper, "Great grandmother, another of your children is among us. Help us, and the owl protect him."

Loretta nodded, draped the scarf over her head, wheeled around, and disappeared through the wrought iron gate.

CHAPTER 35

THE PLAN

It was early afternoon when Loretta whisked past Paco as he lazily stretched his scrawny canine limbs at the threshold of Hotel Luna. Sam was outside pinning up sheets on the clothesline, and two men in cowboy hats sat on the back patio with their faces buried in plates of steaming food.

Loretta walked past them and forced a smile in their direction. "*¿Está bueno?*"

One man nodded and the other grunted, "*Sí.*"

Behind the blue curtain, Loretta found Angelica drying beer glasses. She tried to speak calmly. "I need you to look after the front desk this evening. I have an errand to run and won't be back until the morning. I'll pay you double for it."

Angelica raised her eyebrows. "Double? You never pay double for anything."

"Yes, well it's important, and I need to know I can count on you. I will ask Sam to manage the kitchen."

"Okay," Angelica said in a groan.

Loretta then moved swiftly to where Sam was folding pillowcases.

"Sam, please help Angelica with the kitchen. And later, I may need your help with something else." She leaned in and whispered, "We might have trouble. Keep watch for people who come and go, and when I come back, report to me on who they are, what they look like, and what they said. It's very important, you understand?"

Sam pushed his glasses up on his nose. "Yes, Mrs. Loretta. You can count on Sam."

Loretta touched his shoulder. "Thank you."

He looked into her eyes. "Is there trouble with the lady and the boy?"

"Why do you ask?" Loretta said.

He tugged on her dress and waved her inside the laundry room where the air was thick with the smell of sour towels. "There are rumors in our part of town. Our families work in places where we hear things."

"What do you hear?"

"At the downtown hotel, in the office on the third floor, there was a fight—*eeesh*, a big fight around noon—behind closed doors where my brother Sung's son cleans. Mr. Ray's name came up, and there was talk of a blond-headed woman and a boy."

Loretta gasped. "¡*Dios mío*!"

Sam rubbed his hands together. "Not good, Mrs. Loretta—the talk was very angry. I told Mr. Ray, and he left right away without even taking his hat."

"Did he tell you where he was going?"

"No, he just left."

"¡*Dios mío!*" Loretta said again.

Sam leaned in close to Loretta's ear and whispered, "Friends and family will listen closely for any new tips. You have been good to us when others have not. I *want* to help."

Loretta met his gaze, held both his hands in hers, and gripped them tightly with unspoken commitment. She had always defended Sam when Ray blustered, but she had never touched him or held his hand. His palms were rough from all of the cleaning, but the tops were soft like silk.

"I must go speak to Antonia," she said.

Sam nodded.

Upstairs, Loretta tapped on Antonia's room door. "Everything okay? Feeling better now?"

Francisco opened the door. The *Boys' Life* magazine lay open on the bed, and he was wearing an undershirt, pants, and socks.

"How is she?" Loretta said.

"Better, I think," Francisco said. "She's down the hall, freshening up, she said."

"I will check on her then," Loretta said, but before turning away, she looked at Francisco and smiled. "How was checkers?"

"Good, we played three games. I think I got the hang of it."

"You're a quick learner," she said. "Reading anything interesting?"

"Yes! I read about smoke signals and what they mean and other kinds of signs that soldiers use to communicate. Maybe I'll show them to you later when we're playing cards."

Loretta touched his face gently with the tips of her fingers. "Of course."

Francisco laughed. "And the bad guys won't know what we mean."

Loretta smiled again then closed the door and walked down the hall to the bathroom, stepped inside, and locked the door behind. The window was wide open, and the cold gave Loretta a shiver.

Antonia was standing in front of the mirror staring at herself with a blank expression.

"You okay?" Loretta said.

Antonia's voice was as blunt as a dull knife. "How could I possibly be okay?"

"I have a plan," Loretta said. "You and Francisco must pack all your things immediately. My nephew Manuel will pick you up out front and taxi you to the train station. You will get out, walk inside, then go out the back door where Manuel will be waiting for you. Get back in the car, and he'll drive you to the church. My cousin Javier will hide you in the church offices until dark, and I will meet you there. Then Manuel will pick us back up and we'll go—"

Antonia interrupted, "Where, Loretta? Where will we go?" She gripped the sink edge and grit her teeth. "I'm not ignorant. Maybe you should drive me straight to the cemetery and purchase my gravesite?"

She didn't look at Loretta but stared into the mirror like she was talking to herself. Her face and eyes were puffy, then she turned abruptly towards Loretta with a look of desperation.

"Throw me to the wolves—I don't care. Save him."

Loretta swallowed hard. "You're both going to be fine. You're going to stay with my cousin Santiago in the desert for a while—until it's safe and enough time has passed. They'll think you're long gone. No one will know. We'll take care of you." She looked up and crossed her heart. "I promise."

Antonia shook her head, turned on the faucet, splashed water on her face, then stared fiercely at Loretta as water dripped from her nose and chin. "And I promise, too, if something goes wrong, I will take out *anyone* in my way to save Francisco." She grabbed a towel from the countertop to wipe off her face. Underneath was the pearl-handled pistol.

Loretta's eyes grew wide.

Francisco was leaning against the headboard, with his legs stretched out across the bed, looking at his magazine and waving his arm in a circle above his head, when Antonia entered the room.

"Guess what this means?" he said.

She looked at him but then glanced away.

"I'm practicing my military hand signals," he said and continued to circle his arm.

"Hmm." Antonia said. "Does it mean, 'Let's get going?'"

Francisco threw his head back and laughed. "No, just the opposite. It means assemble. Everybody's supposed to stop what they're doing and come over."

He tried another and raked his hand across his throat and Antonia's eyes grew wide.

"I'm not good at this game," she snapped.

"It means, be quiet, stop talking. That's all," he said. "Did you think it meant something else?" He wiggled his toes and laughed. "You'd make a terrible soldier."

"Okay, got it," Antonia said as she turned to the closet and began stuffing clothes into her satchel.

"What are you doing?" Francisco said. His face suddenly turned from cheerful to serious.

"I'm packing up 'cause we're going on a trip."

Francisco frowned. "I thought we weren't going to leave. Why?"

"Well, Mrs. Loretta has an uncle who needs some help. He's getting old, you see, and can't get around well anymore. She can't go and stay with him 'cause she's too busy running the hotel, so she asked if I would help. She's going to pay me to cook for him and things like that."

Francisco rolled on his side and rested his head on his elbow. "Where does he live?"

"A ways out of town—in the country. Not sure exactly. It'll be . . . you know . . . a nice change."

He rubbed the blanket with his palm. He needed to touch something comforting. "But I don't want a change, remember? We talked about this."

Antonia kept her head down. "Yeah, but we'll be doing Loretta a favor. You should feel good about that. And in the country, there'll be new places to explore. You know, country stuff."

He scratched his head. "You mean like horses, cowboys, roping calves, and telling stories by the campfire?"

Antonia's voice rolled on her tongue. "Maaaaybeeee . . ."

"Hmm," Francisco said. "I guess that sounds alright for a little while."

He scooched to the edge of the bed. "Will we still get to see Mrs. Loretta?"

"Probably not as often, because she has to work."

Francisco interrupted. "But I was going to teach her about the hand signals. I promised her."

"You can still do that—when she visits."

It was Francisco's turn to sigh. "Okaaaaaay." He sat for a minute then grinned. "Do I get to wear some new clothes this time too? Like boots, a cowboy hat?"

"We'll see, Francisco, I don't know."

Francisco twisted his lips with a look of disappointment. "Yeah, I guess you're right. There's no cowboy stuff in Mrs. Loretta's lounge. But maybe we can buy . . . ?" His voice trailed off because he could tell that his mother was starting to grow impatient.

"At least I have my slingshot. It will be perfect for shooting snakes and rats and—"

Antonia threw her head back. "Oh God, Francisco—your mind. It just goes and goes."

"What's wrong with that?"

She shook her head and tried to smile. "Nothing. But for now, put your mind to packing up."

She glanced over her shoulder. "Oh by the way, we need to drop by the train station first. I want to grab a schedule in case we need to catch the train back to town sometime. Then we're going to go to the church for a little bit and wait for Loretta and her cousin who will take us."

"Mr. Javier, my friend?"

"Yes."

Francisco hopped up and started packing then checked to make sure that the string that held his owl feather was secure around his neck.

"This does sound fun," he chirped.

With his bag fully packed and his book strap over his shoulder, Francisco bolted downstairs. Behind the desk, Angelica was painting her nails with Loretta's polish, and Sam was outside clearing the lunch dishes.

"Where's Loretta?" he said.

Angelica didn't look up but nodded toward the front door.

When he approached her, Loretta was looking nervously both ways down the street. She glanced at her watch then restlessly folded and unfolded her arms.

Francisco tugged on her cotton dress. "What are you doing?" he said.

Loretta turned abruptly, put both hands on his shoulders, spun him around, and pushed him inside toward the chair by the window. "You wait here," she said. "Is your mother ready?"

"Almost," Francisco said. He noticed that Loretta's eyes were wet, and she was wiping her nose. "Are you crying?" he said.

She covered her mouth with a handkerchief then cleared her throat and coughed. "Something must be in the air," she said. "It's making my eyes water and nose run. You stay here, I'll be outside."

"But I want to show you the signs before we leave."

Loretta looked towards the front door then back at Francisco. "Okay, quickly," she said.

Francisco stood up and thrust his arm into a stiff L-shape and tightened his fist. "When you're marching and you want your troops to stop, this means *freeze*!"

He looked into her eyes to make sure she understood. She nodded but then absent-mindedly looked back towards the door. "I need to go outside, Francisco."

"Wait, one more," he said, then he straightened out his arm and waved and flapped it up and down like a wing. "This means *take cover* . . . and hold on, the last one . . . I showed this one to Mama . . ." And he raked his hand across his neck again. "Guess what this means?"

Loretta's eyes grew wide, and she gasped. "Gotta go," she said, then dashed outside.

Francisco sat in the straight-back wooden chair and swung his legs and looked around the hotel lobby. Everyone was acting so strangely—his mother suddenly telling him to pack; Loretta skittish as a cornered cat, pushing him about, not smiling or teasing with him; Angelica doing Loretta's job; and Sam doing Angelica's job. What was going on?

He looked through the open window toward the cavity in the mesquite tree where the owl roosted. It wasn't there. He twiddled his thumbs and tried to remember other signals.

Something rustling outside startled him, and then there was a whooshing sound. When he followed the sound with his eyes, he saw it. The owl had landed on the neighboring rooftop and gripped the edge of the gutter with its talons. They stared at each other with piercing eyes as if some source of energy were passing between them. When Francisco blinked, the owl spread its wings and flew.

You're leaving? Moving during daylight? What are you trying to tell me?

CHAPTER 36

RICO'S RESTAURANT

When Ray entered Rico's in Juarez, he didn't bother to take off his overcoat nor did he wait in line behind a cluster of tourists who stood at the head waiter's desk, tugging on cigarettes with squinty eyes and flicking ashes into a brass spittoon on the windowsill. Instead, he strode straight to the bar where Rico was hunched over an expense log and chewing on a pencil eraser.

Ray clamped his thick hand on Rico's shoulder and squeezed with a vice-like grip.

Rico tried to shrug free. "*¡Ay! ¿Qué pasó?*"

Ray snarled, "Where's Cox?" and glanced toward the back corner where Cox usually sat. The table was empty except for a crumpled napkin and dirty dishes. Ray didn't loosen his grip on Rico's shoulder.

Rico winced. "For Christ sakes, Ray, let go!"

"I ain't letting go 'til you tell me where *he* is!"

"What the hell's gotten into you, Ray?"

Ray glared at Rico and bared his yellowed teeth. "Don't tell me you don't know what I'm talking about." A few people in the restaurant turned their gaze in the direction of the bar.

Rico whispered, "You're making a scene, goddammit. And for the record, I have no idea what you're talking about." He pointed his thumb toward the back of the restaurant. "He's in the office."

Ray didn't say sorry or thank you. Instead, he marched toward the back, roughly elbowing a busboy along his way, then turned the office door handle and shoved it open without knocking.

Inside, Cox was sitting in a chair with his feet propped up on the desk smoking a cigar. His vest was unbuttoned, his tie loose, but his hair was still immaculately combed.

"There you are, Ray. You got my call. I left a message with your girl, and I guess she told you," Cox said.

"No, I didn't get your message," Ray growled.

"Mr. Eliot's secretary, from Hotel Paso, called early this morning. No cigars delivered. On their way I presume?"

Ray clinched his fists at his sides, and his neck veins bulged. "You fucking screwed me!"

Cox raised his palms and chuckled. "You need to get control of that mick temper, Ray. You're going to have a heart attack."

"We had an agreement—you said it was *just* cigars. Don't play coy with me."

Cox lowered his feet from the desk, took another puff from his cigar, and blew smoke in Ray's direction then shrugged. "Cigars are cigars."

"Bullshit!" Ray shouted. "You know what I'm talking about. I found out."

Cox said nothing.

"You put my girls in jeopardy!"

Cox clucked and shook his head. "I like that about you, Ray. Sticking up for your girls. *Es muy macho, cabrón.*"

Ray took one step closer to the desk but stopped when Cox held up his hands like he was trying to make peace.

"Look, Ray . . . there was a slight mix-up between me and *him* . . . won't happen again. We've spoken—I took care of it. So, there's nothing to worry about for you or your lady—the blond and the boy."

Ray nodded and loosened his fists then wiped his bald head with his handkerchief and leaned on the desk and whispered. "I didn't want to bring *him* in to begin with—the cigars and all. We got a good thing going—our partnership—with this tequila business, but that's as deep as I want to go."

Cox nodded and rubbed his chin. "You're right. But now we have a bit of a situation. As I said, I talked to *him* and took care of it temporarily, but I need to know where *it* is so I can . . . you know . . . deliver it."

Ray swallowed hard as beads of sweat gathered on his forehead. "It's gone."

Cox pushed his chair back from the desk and crossed his arms. "What do you mean *gone*?"

Ray shuffled his feet. "She found it . . . I mean . . . saw *it*. *It* fell out when she was going to the bathroom and the goods broke open, and, you know, she got scared."

"Scared?"

"Yeah! She thought it was something bad—which turns out it goddamn fucking was—and she flushed it. It's in the river. Gone."

Cox stood up then slapped his hand on the desk, and a stack of papers tumbled onto the floor. "Flushed it? Why didn't she just hide it—for someone to get later? Seems reasonable don't you think?"

"Like I said, she was scared," Ray said.

Cox turned abruptly. "Let me be clear about something, Ray." He spoke in a measured tone holding back a flood of fury. "Our partnership, as you call it, has two jobs. I get the goods and you and Loretta make sure the girls know what to do and how to handle situations if things get muddy. And it appears that you and Loretta didn't do your part."

"Leave Loretta out of this," Ray said. "She knew nothing of the cigars."

Cox cleared his throat. "Well, I'm sorry, Ray, but the *gone* business creates a big problem. That'll be quite a bit of skin off our hides for what was lost. Wouldn't you say?"

Ray took a step back and looked toward the door like he wanted to make a run for it, then stammered. "Yes but, we can make it up. It'll take some time but . . ." then he stopped and continued, ". . . I mean . . . I'll make it up."

Cox's face turned stoney. "Is she still scared? Will she say something—to the police? For her and the boy's protection?"

Ray waved his hands and shook his head. "Oh, no. No, she wouldn't do that."

"Why are you so sure?"

"Well—"

Cox cut him off. "Where are they now?"

"Back at the hotel. I think. I don't know," Ray said.

Cox's eyes turned to slits as he leaned against the desk. "Here's some advice. I suggest you get your fat ass out of here, go find her, and tell her everything is okay so she won't squeal. Then buy her a train ticket to wherever the hell she wants to go! Am I making myself clear?"

Ray lowered his eyes. "Yes." He paused and whispered pleadingly, "I don't want them hurt."

Cox shook his head. "Ray, you don't get it do you? Your story about what happened—you think *Escorpión's* going to fucking believe that? He's either going to think she took it, you took it, or worse, we were in it together. So, you see, because of *your* girl, we're all fucked!"

Ray turned sheet white. "Let me talk to him, I'll tell him, I'll make it good."

A Ballad

(verse 1 & 2)

Listen and hear
what I am about to sing, these events of the boy and the great owl.
And do not say it's not true.

It happened in the desert, the home of our familia,
where our hearts are bound to the earth.
It ended with lightning, thunder, and fury.

PART II:

The Desert

CHAPTER 37

CHIHUAHUA

Where am I? Francisco thought when he awoke in the middle of the night, shivering under a wool blanket on hard ground. He stared upward through a thinly thatched roof toward a cluster of twinkling stars then rubbed his arms briskly.

Blinking to clear his mind, he remembered the images and sounds from the day before as if he were recalling scenes from a motion picture. Nothing about the day had felt like the cheerful trip to the country that his mother had described. The tension felt more like a getaway scene from a bank robbery.

There had been the taxi waiting for them outside Hotel Luna. As they crawled into the backseat, Loretta had stuck her head through the passenger-side window and spoke to Manuel in rapid-fire sentences. Her usual relaxed tone had turned wooden and heavy.

"Take the back roads. Don't stop for anything. *Nada. ¿Comprendes?*"

As Manuel drove, he gripped the wheel as though he were headed into a driving thunderstorm, and when Francisco glanced at his mother, her fingers were nervously fidgeting with her bag, and her usual full lips had inverted into a tight slit. The tension was made even worse by metal springs that poked through the ripped vinyl seats and stabbed him at every bump.

His mother wasn't wearing the light blue dress she bought in Juarez that made her look slim and beautiful, or the old grandma outfit, instead she wore a tent-like gray cotton dress and boots that were tattered and too big for her feet.

And Loretta had dyed his mother's hair black as a crow and gave her a bottle of dye for when her blond roots started showing. When Francisco saw her for the first time after her transformation, he was taken aback. Though she still had the face of his mom, she was more witch-like, but of course, he didn't say that.

Francisco wore a pair of boots as well—scuffed up looking, not new at all—and he was rid of the long braids, a change that he didn't mind since the wig had been kind of scratchy on his scalp. He was back to his usual hair along with trousers, a long-sleeved white shirt, and a wide-brimmed straw hat. He was more like his old self, which, he had to admit, felt good after being someone else for a while.

After the taxi ride, there was the train station, the bustling crowds, and the loud clock that clanged out at 5:00 p.m. with a doomsday tone—*dong, dong, dong, dong, dong*. Belching steam, a shout—*All aboard!*—then long legs, fat legs, short legs, running in a panic as if this were the last train from hell.

He remembered the dark corridor to the station's back door, a trash-filled alley, blinking headlights, his mother's voice—*this way*. Then Manuel's voice—*get in, stay down*. Then more driving—the engine revving, an abrupt turn, slamming breaks, and Manuel's voice again—"*¡idiota!*" For a moment, the car sputtered like it had run out of gas then lurched and suddenly came to a screeching stop. When Antonia reached for his hand, hers was clammy as a dead fish. His instinct was to pull away because this fish was not his mother, but a sense of desperation took over, and he gripped it tight.

By then, he knew his mother had not told him the whole story about why they were going to the country, but he was too scared to ask more.

It wasn't until he saw Javier holding the door at the church's back entrance that his nerves began to settle. But even then, Javier's smile was fleeting—on then off—like a light switch.

"*Mi amigo*," Javier had whispered hoarsely, then he held up his calloused hand. "*Señora*, follow me." He said nothing more.

Then there was the small room: shelves with neatly stacked rolls of toilet paper; mops and brooms in a corner; rags drying on hooks; a table, two stools. Then Javier's finger pointing to the stools, and a *shush* from his lips, then Javier backing out, closing the door, turning the lock—*click*—and Antonia biting her nails and bobbing her knee. Waiting, waiting—more waiting. Why were they always waiting in smelly closets?

He had looked up at his mother and whispered, "Why can't we talk?" Antonia vigorously shook her head. Then *finally*, the lock clicked again, and Antonia became rigid, and both sat still as jackrabbits in the face of danger.

"Let's go." Javier whispered.

Then there was the twilight ride: Manuel and Javier in the front seat, and he and his mother in back. Out the back window were El Paso's shadowy buildings. Ahead lay wheat fields with low slung adobes nestled within leafless clusters of cottonwoods. Then nothing but vast expanses of mesquites and desert brush dotted with bovine silhouettes. It had been a journey from light to dark, from bustle to silence, and most unsettling, from the familiar to the unknown.

He remembered being startled when smooth paving turned to gravel, and how a cloud of pink-colored dust, lit by the sunrise, billowed up behind when Manuel hit the brakes for a passing mule deer. Then the car rolled slowly, and the sound of gravel crunching under tires was all he could hear until Manuel whispered, "Is this it?"

Javier shook his head, then pointed up ahead. Soon, they turned left and came to a stop. *Click*, car lights off, engine off.

"Are we here?" Francisco had whispered. Antonia touched her finger to her lips and wore the same expression as the night they ditched Elton. He knew to remain quiet, and more worry settled in.

Javier got out of the car.

There was a cough in the distance. Then Javier whispered, "Santiago?"

A husky voice followed. "*Sí, aquí.*"

A short man with a lantern walked slowly toward them with bowlegged steps. He coursed around desert brush and cacti like he knew this path by heart.

Javier and the man embraced, and Manuel shook his hand while Francisco and Antonia stayed in the car.

"Who is that?" Francisco whispered.

"Loretta's cousin, I think," his mom answered.

The three men huddled and whispered in Spanish. Francisco remembered wondering why were they whispering. They were in the middle of nowhere—no people, no houses, no porch lights, nothing except scratchy looking vegetation and an occasional gust of wind. If anything, he thought, they should be talking louder to scare off what potentially lurked beyond the lantern light—wolves, bears, snakes—things with gnarly teeth and fangs.

When Javier waved for Antonia and Francisco to come over, the old man gave Javier the lantern then slipped back into the darkness. A few minutes later, he returned clasping a set of reins in each hand with two pale gray burros following like four-legged ghosts.

Javier pointed to the large bony-ribbed burro that stood with its neck hanging downward.

"Your ride," Javier whispered to Antonia.

There was no saddle, so Antonia gripped the burro's mane to hoist her body upward as Javier threaded his fingers together like a stirrup.

The burro shifted its weight when Manuel raised Francisco up and positioned him in front of Antonia. Antonia wrapped one arm tight around Francisco's waist then grabbed a handful of mane with the other. The burro pawed and snorted.

Instinctively, Francisco smoothed the burro's warm neck, and it let out a slow settling breath.

Javier whispered to Santiago, "*Por favor, cuídenlos.*"

"*Sí,*" the old man said softly, then he snuffed out the lantern light.

The night sky was overcast as they rode through pitch black surroundings. Only the sound of the burro's hooves on rocky ground penetrated the quiet. Sometime after, the sound turned into thuds on soft soil. It was then that Francisco's eyes grew heavy as he swayed from side to side in his mother's arms. Was he awake or dreaming when he heard trickling water, sucking sounds, then gentle splashes?

That was the last thing he remembered. Now, he was lying next to his sleeping mother in some sort of shed.

Francisco sat up and squinted. Through a wide opening at the front of the structure, he saw the moon hanging above a distant hillside. Its yellow light penetrated holes in the thatching and revealed rough stone walls and cedar posts with pitched timbers above. The air around him smelled of smoke, and he shivered and grabbed his knees to keep from shaking. Wrapping the blanket around him, he stepped outside the doorless shelter, took a deep breath, and blew out. Above, a spray of stars filled the sky and surrounding him were large boulders that looked like giant gold nuggets in the moon glow.

"Where are we?" he whispered.

"*Muchacho,*" a voice said.

Startled, Francisco turned abruptly then began stepping backwards toward the shelter.

"*Es Santiago*, come by fire."

In the moonlight, Francisco could see Santiago squatting and fueling a mound of glowing embers with twigs. When a twig flared, the light revealed a wrinkled face and eyes that drooped at the corners under heavy lids.

"I will get my mother first," Francisco said.

Santiago held up his palm. "Mama need sleep," he said. "She no sleep all night—like *chotacabras*."

Francisco shook his head. "*Chota . . . ca . . .* ?"

Santiago spread his arms and flapped. "Night . . . bird . . . *¿comprendes?*"

Francisco scratched his head. From Javier, he had learned that owl was *tecalote*, so what was *chotacabras*?

Santiago spoke louder as if the drama of his voice helped the translation. "*Night-ee-hark.*"

Francisco smiled. "Ohh, nighthawk."

Santiago clapped his hands. "*Sí, sí.*" With a satisfied nod, he sat down on a wooden stool. "Okie, you know *mi nombre*, yours?"

"Francisco."

"*Si,* Francisco, but your bigee *nombre*?"

"You mean my last name?"

"*Sí*," Santiago nodded. "*Lo siento*—my English—not like Javier's. I no talk so good."

"O'Rourke. Francisco O'Rourke."

"Ahh," Santiago said, then he squinted and gazed into Francisco's eyes as though he were looking through him. "You no look Irish."

Unnerved by the old man's stare, Francisco shuffled his feet. "No, I guess not."

"Mine bigee name *es* Santiago Bernardo Garcia." He pounded his fist against his chest. "Bernardo mean *fuerte* . . . like *oso* . . . *grrrrrrr.*"

"Strong like a bear?" Francisco said.

Santiago smiled. "*Sí, amigo!*"

There was silence for a minute, and Francisco kicked the dirt with his shoe, pulled the blanket tight over his shoulders, then looked around. There was a pale glow in the distance as the rising sun cast an array of beams behind purple-colored hills.

Santiago poked the fire with a metal rod then looked at Francisco and rubbed his stomach. "*Tiennes hambre?*"

Francisco nodded and felt his own stomach growl.

Pointing toward a pile near the shed, Santiago said, "Get *más* sticks. I get *frijoles* go hot."

At the pile, Francisco reached out to grab a handful then suddenly pulled back. "Ouuch, thorns!"

Santiago laughed. "*Lo siento*...sorry. *Aquí*..." He threw a pair of worn leather gloves Francisco's way. "I forget, your *manos* like *bebé*." He raised his hand and scratched his palm. "Mine, like leeether."

Francisco wasn't keen on the baby reference, so he skipped wearing the gloves and came back with as many sticks as he could hold.

Santiago looked impressed. "How old you? Tir-teen or *más*?

"Thirteen?" Francisco said in astonishment. No one had ever thought he was older than he was. He pushed back his shoulders with a flush of confidence. "Well, almost thirteen."

Santiago looked him up and down then turned his lips to the side. "You tir-teen—I know. Strong too. Big strong tir-teen."

Francisco's mouth curled into a smile. That was the third time he had been called strong: Gabriel, Javier, and now Santiago.

With sunrise filling the bungalow's opening with orange light, Antonia awoke, put on her boots, and stepped outside. From behind a boulder outcrop, she heard a voice. Was it singing? She crept toward the sound then peered over the top of a boulder and saw them. Francisco sat cross-legged by the fire, and Santiago lay on his back staring up at the sky.

Instead of stepping into view, Antonia hid and listened. It *was* a song, and Santiago's soft voice flowed from his lips like a soothing breeze.

¡Ah! ven querida, amable peregrina;
Mi corazón al tuyo estrecharé,
Oiré tu canto tierna golondrina,
Recordaré mi patria, y luego lloraré.

When she heard the words, her heart skipped a beat. She knew the song—"La golondrina."

She leaned heavily against the boulder in silence remembering that warm summer evening by a river, under a trestle bridge, where swallows emerged from their mud nests and swooped above the water's surface in repeating arcs of flight. As Mateo sang, she had leaned against him and rested her head on his shoulder. The song's verses poured out of him with a melodic ease as though the words were part of him. After the song was finished, they sat silently, dreamily, as if under a spell.

Breaking their silence, Antonia spoke softly. "Tell me about the song."

He lay back on the grassy embankment. "It's about a man in exile, and he's longing for his homeland. The songwriter compares his life to that of a migrating swallow."

Come then to me, sweet feathered pilgrim stranger;
Oh! let me clasp thee to my loving breast,
And list to thy warbling low, secure from danger,
Unwonted tears bringing relief and rest.

Antonia took a deep breath. "It's sad but so beautiful."

"Yes," he said, then he put his hand on her shoulder and gently lowered her to the ground. They lay together, embracing, until the chill of the night settled in. That had been the beginning of their love affair.

And now look at me, she thought. Listening to that same sad song—in hiding, exiled, a failure.

After a few moments, Antonia emerged from her hiding place and walked toward the fire. Something was steaming and bubbling in a pot over the flames, and Francisco was hungrily scooping spoonfuls directly from the kettle into his mouth.

She cleared her throat, then Francisco looked up and abruptly stopped eating. Bean juice dripped from his chin, and he looked at her sheepishly.

"Francisco . . ." she said and was about to scold him for his lack of manners until Santiago scooped up a heaping spoonful and did the same.

Santiago grunted and raised up from his stool and said, "*Señora.*" He wiped his mouth on his sleeve and positioned the stool close to the fire for Antonia to sit.

"Thank you," Antonia said.

"The beans are so good," Francisco said. "We're eating them cowboy style," trying to provide an explanation for what he knew was unacceptable behavior under most circumstances. Then he shifted his eyes from side to side and ventured one step further. "Remember, you said we'd be doing 'country stuff'?"

Antonia offered only a slight smile.

Santiago pointed at the pot. "*¿Frijoles?*"

"*Sí,*" Antonia said. The old man's soft voice was comforting, but even so, she wasn't going to let her guard down. Supposedly, this man was Loretta's family, but who knew the strength of bonds in precarious times.

As Francisco continued to scoop up mouthfuls and grin, Santiago downed whatever liquid was in his cup, wiped the rim and the inside with his shirttail, then handed it to Antonia. She restrained a pained expression. Be patient, she thought. New rules apply out here.

Santiago nodded at Francisco. "*Cuchara.*"

"Oh, *sí*," Francisco said, and then he hurriedly handed Antonia his spoon feeling a tinge of guilt in response to the old man's subtle rebuke.

While Antonia ate, Santiago disappeared into the shed and came back with a burlap sack over his shoulder. At the edge of the fire's light, he laid the sack on the ground, knelt, and slowly revealed a knife with a two-foot-long blade. He held it up to the morning light and examined the sharp edge.

Antonia swallowed hard. Was this all a trick? Were they done for? Her pistol—she needed it now! How stupid not to keep it close. She got up and moved swiftly towards the shed, searched frantically through her satchel until she found it, but where were the bullets? Dammit! No time to look. She rushed outside with the pistol tucked into her waistline.

With his back to her, Santiago stood in front of Francisco and gripped the machete in his right hand then slowly raised it.

Antonia whipped the gun out and pointed it straight at Santiago's back.

"Stop! I'll shoot!" she screamed.

Santiago turned and with a dumbfounded expression dropped the machete and raised his hands above his head.

"*Señora*, please. No shoot."

"Ma," Francisco yelled. "What are you doing? A gun?"

Antonia's hand was shaking. "Francisco, go get the burros, *now*!"

"Why?" Francisco said.

"Just do it!" she said with a panicked voice.

"But, Ma," Francisco pleaded. "He was just showing me how he harvests the candelilla. I'm going to help him with his work. You have it all wrong. Put the gun down!"

Santiago's expression turned soft, and he put his palms together. "Señora, I *amigo*. I no hurt you. I help. Please."

Antonia felt tears welling up. It was all too much—the drugs, hiding, the trip in the night, the chilling fear, the song, her memory of Mateo.

The gun fell limp in her hand then dropped to the ground. She collapsed to her knees, covered her head with her arms, and sobbed.

Francisco ran to her and knelt by her side. "Ma, it's okay. Why are you worried? Santiago is kind."

Antonia looked up and wiped her eyes. "I'm sorry, Santiago . . . I'm just . . ."

Santiago put his hand over his heart and patted his chest. "You no worry, *Señora*." He looked at Francisco and said, "Go get water for *su madre*, and let her rest more. After, you follow me."

Without saying another word, Santiago walked a few steps out into the sun-streaked desert, stopped near a ring of brush with upright stems like pencils, secured his gloves, gripped the plant by the stems, and yanked. A root still clung to the soil, so he raised the machete, *chop*, pulled the plant free, and tossed it aside.

"I can get the water myself," Antonia said. "I'm okay. You go."

Francisco ran after Santiago and watched as he uprooted more plants. After a few minutes, Santiago straightened up, rubbed his glove over the small of his back and groaned. "*¡Ay!*"

"Let me help," Francisco said. "I can do it. *Fuerte* remember?"

Santiago smiled, broke a stem off the candelilla plant, and ran his thumbnail down the stem's edge. A small waxlike curl peeled off.

"See?" he said and smiled. "Candelilla make *pesos*. Wax. *¿Comprendes?*"

Antonia watched from a distance at the gentle way Santiago treated Francisco and was relieved and touched, but she still felt fragile and wounded like a bird with a broken wing.

Was everything going to be okay like Loretta had said? They were in the middle of nowhere. How could anyone possibly find them?

CHAPTER 38

RAT'S NEST

Upstairs in her lounge, Loretta was frantically reorganizing the racks. Dresses were flung over chairs, and hangers were scattered across the floor like a rat's nest. When Ray appeared in the doorway, she threw up her hands in exasperation. "Who puts yellow dresses next to the black ones. Yellow is summer—black is winter. These girls don't give a shit." She pulled at her hair, threw herself into a chair, and covered her face with her hands.

Ray took a deep breath and whispered. "Where are they?" he said.

Loretta lowered her hands and stared at him with cold ferocity. "You will never know."

Ray took a step back. "Now, hold on, Loretta, we're on the same team."

"Team?" She let out a venomous laugh. "That's where you're wrong, Ray. Teammates don't betray each other. Family doesn't betray each other."

Ray stretched his arms out with palms up. "Loretta, come on, we need to solve this together. I need to tell Cox that things have been taken care of. I'm trying to manage this . . ." His voice trailed off.

She shook her head and pointed a bright red fingernail toward the door. "Damn you, Ray. Just go!"

His face turned angry. "I'm your brother for Christ's sake. How can you speak to me like that?"

He held his fists at his side and shouted through his teeth. "We're *all* in danger, don't you understand?"

"Crystal clear, Ray! Thanks to you."

His voice became quiet. "I'll take the money in the safe and give it to Cox. That should be a start. I'll figure out the rest later." He paused. "I'm sorry, Loretta, but please believe me, I didn't know about the drugs. I swear."

When Ray turned to go, Loretta shook her head but didn't look at him. He retreated down the hall with thundering footsteps. Then there was silence.

Loretta knew there wasn't enough money in the safe to put their problems to bed, but she didn't have time to consider other options. As far as she was concerned, her singular focus was Antonia and Francisco's safety.

Outside, an engine barreled down Luna Street like a freight train at full throttle. Another drunken fool, Loretta thought. Then there was a *thud.*

When she ran to the window and peered out, a black car swerved and screeched away with exhaust fumes pouring from its tailpipe. She looked north then south but saw nothing. The street was silent. No people, no cars, nothing.

Then a scream. "Noooooo!"

She threw open the window, stuck her head out, and looked at the sidewalk below. Angelica was on her knees, and Sam crouched by her with his hand on her shoulder. Ray's body was a mess of blood and broken limbs.

Loretta doubled over and gasped for breath. "Not my brother!"

CHAPTER 39

CANDELILLA

They had already spent three days in the desert, and Francisco was getting used to the daily rhythm. Awaking at sunrise, making the fire, Santiago heating the beans while Antonia warmed tortillas on a griddle. Next, Francisco and Santiago pulling candelilla all morning while Antonia bound candelilla bunches with rope. Then lunch: dried berries and cold beans. More harvesting, a sunset, another fire, more beans, then goodnight.

Though their meals were nothing but *beans, beans, beans*, he didn't care—they tasted good after the hard work. And the work wasn't bad either. It's not like Santiago forced him to help, he did it because he wanted to, and he could feel his arm muscles getting stronger.

As days passed, Francisco became familiar with the animals that lived near camp. Mexican prairie dogs were his regular companions. With an expression of curiosity, they popped up from their holes and glanced around like some special news had arrived from afar.

"It's just me," he would whisper as he tiptoed over their underground community.

And there was the gray fox that appeared at nightfall and sniffed around the campfire licking up any stray beans.

From Santiago, Francisco had learned the names and uses of plants. Ocotillo and its red flowers could be used to make tea, and beargrass was good for weaving baskets and lechuguilla for making rope. But steer clear of its sharp spines.

Francisco marveled at the cleverness of the cactus wrens who chose the spiny-leafed sotol for their nest. Smart, he thought, no snakes will get to your chicks.

Though Francisco had found energy and strength in the desert, his mother had become withdrawn as if someone had pulled the stuffing out of her. Her usual plucky character had withered, and she sat quietly most of the day.

But on an evening he'd never forget, her punch came back with a fury. The sun was dipping below the horizon, and they were preparing for bed. Outside the shed, Francisco was washing his chest and arms with a wet rag when he heard Antonia suddenly scream. "Bloody dammit to hell!"

Francisco ran to the shed's entrance. Antonia's face was white as a ghost, and she screamed again.

"What's going on?" he said.

Antonia stood with her mouth open. "There's a giant snake in my bed!"

"Calm down," Francisco said.

Antonia looked at him with a wild expression. "Calm down? It's a damn six-foot-long snake!"

Santiago came running with his machete, but when he spotted the snake, he held up his palms. "No poison, Missus! Snake good. Kill rats—friend of Santiago."

Antonia pulled at her hair and shrieked, "Kill it! Kill it! Kill it!" She ran to the corner of the shed, found Santiago's walking stick, and with her dark hair swishing wildly across her face, she thrashed at the snake like she was possessed by a demon.

"You bastard. You goddammed bastard—leave us alone!"

As the snake slithered around a pile of empty cans Antonia swung the stick like a bat and cans went flying.

"Stop it, Ma!" Francisco yelled. "It's not poisonous!"

She kept thrashing away. "You bastard!"

"*Stop it*! *Dammit*!" Francisco yelled again, then he used his arm to push her away.

Antonia fell backwards onto the ground and buried her head in her hands as Santiago stepped forward and grabbed the snake by the head and midsection then stepped hurriedly outside.

There was silence for a moment. At first, Francisco was frozen with shock. Regaining composure, he stepped forward and kneeled beside her.

"It's okay, Ma," he said. "Everything's okay."

She leaned her head against his chest, and he wrapped his arms around her and held her tight. "I love you, Ma."

For the first time, Francisco felt that she needed him. In the desert, he was the strong one.

The next morning when Santiago and Francisco sat by the fire alone, Santiago chuckled. "Your mama, she curse like a *loco bandido*." He playfully punched Francisco's arm. "You curse too?"

Francisco smiled. "Sometimes, not often."

Santiago smiled. "You a good *muchacho*."

Antonia's sudden craziness during the snake event had put

Francisco on edge, and he was still shocked that just days before she had pulled a gun on Santiago. She hated guns. Her lecture had always been loud and clear. "Guns are dangerous. They're trouble."

Why the change? he thought. She was definitely afraid of something, and deep down, he was too afraid to ask what it was. Was Elton back on the chase? That didn't seem possible. Elton was too lazy to come this far into the desert searching for them.

On the fourth day, Francisco had unbuttoned his shirt and was sweating from pulling the candelilla. Between them, he and Santiago had already gathered eight large piles. The sun was hanging low in the sky when Francisco saw a figure emerge from a whirl of sand like a ghost blown in on a wind witch. Whoever it was walked bent over and carried a large sack kicking up sprays of dust with every step.

He squinted then recognized the navy jacket and pants and the long black braid. Francisco shouted, "Sam?" He ran over. "What are you doing here?"

Sam rocked back on his heels then plopped the sack onto the ground. "I brought canned food, from Loretta, for you, the Missus, and Santiago."

"How'd you get here?"

"Manuel dropped me, then I walked."

"You walked all that way?"

Sam fell to his knees, "So tired. ¡*Aye caramba*!"

Francisco smiled. "You speak Spanish?"

"Little bit of Spanish, *sí*. Enough to get by."

"I'll get you some water," Francisco said. He ran to a wooden barrel, lifted the lid, and scooped out a cup of water and carried it back.

Sam gulped it down. "*Eeesh*, haven't walked so far since the war—used to walk all day. Now, I only do a few steps—laundry room to upstairs in the hotel. I'm too old for a long walk."

Francisco furrowed his brow. "Why are you by yourself?"

"Mrs. Loretta said to go alone—don't let anybody see me."

Francisco was beginning to put things together—his mother's fear, and now Sam sneaking out to find them. "Is someone looking for us?" he said.

Sam took off his hat and playfully plopped it on Francisco's head. "Don't worry." Sam shook his head. "I say stupid things sometimes. *Eeesh*. Too tired to be smart."

Sam looked around. "Where Santiago?"

Francisco pointed. "In the shade by the stone cliff. He's resting."

Sam stood. "*Eeesh*, I'll be back. Look in the bag," and he rubbed his belly. "Food for my friends," and he patted Francisco's shoulder and smiled.

Inside were boiled potatoes, shredded pork, chicken and tomato chunks, green beans, and a sack of tortillas, but Francisco didn't go through all of the contents. He wanted to hear what Sam and Santiago were talking about. He crept close and hid behind a boulder and eyeballed them through a crack.

Though he couldn't hear everything due to a gusting wind, he heard Sam's voice get shaky during a still moment, "Mr. Ray . . . bad *hombres* . . ." then his shoulders slumped. "Loretta cried. Angelica screamed like *bebé*. Javier . . . he was there . . . and Gabriel . . . they all cried. Loretta's girls said, 'don't worry, Loretta . . . things will be okay,' but now, they're gone too. *¿Comprendes?* Bye bye . . . they're scared too."

Sam paused and Santiago shook his head. "*Pobre*, Ray . . . *pobre*, Loretta."

Then Sam raised his hands in disbelief. "And now Loretta, she's gone *loco*. She spread witch stuff—*bruja* stuff—all over the hotel. Hazel—*sheeet* like that. Then she slammed—*bang*—the door and locked up and *adiós*. *¿Comprendes?*"

Santiago nodded as though he mostly understood.

Sam pointed toward the shed and pulled at his braid. "She *loco* scared for Missus and the boy!"

Francisco cupped his ear with his hand to hear why Loretta was so scared, but when Sam and Santiago began walking his way, he sprinted toward a patch of candelilla and started pulling against the strength of a long root. The machete was raised high when Santiago slapped Sam on the back and pointed. "*Muchacho* hard worker—not like Chinaman!"

Sam reared back and raised his fist like he was going to slug him, then dropped his arm, laughed, and pointed a long fingernail at Santiago. "*Eeesh*, you the lazy Mexican—you *siesta* all day and make Francisco do all the work." He pushed his thumb against his chest and straightened his shoulders. "I'm a hard worker and a good cook. Watch, I'll make food for all."

Antonia sat up when she heard the banter, then quickly ducked under the wood beam of the shed and stepped outside. She pulled at her dress wearing an alarmed expression. "I heard voices. Is someone else here?"

Francisco glanced her way and tried to sound positive in spite of his alarm. "Sam's here. He brought food from Loretta and walked all this way just for us."

Avoiding a sharp-spined barrel cactus, Antonia made her way to the fire pit where Sam was crouched. She held out her hand, and Sam quickly stood, nodded, then wiped his hand on his pants before lightly touching hers. "Missus."

"Thank you, Sam," she said.

Sam smiled and returned to his work using a pocketknife to

pry open a can of potatoes. He stared into the glowing coals as he spoke, "Hungry, Missus?"

Antonia nodded. "Yes, very. How's Loretta?"

Sam nodded cheerfully, "Good, Missus," then he closed his mouth like a snapping turtle.

That night, lying side by side and peering through the holes in the shed's roof as clouds danced with the moon, Francisco didn't tell his mother what he had heard. He didn't want to cause any more alarm. One thing was clear, something was definitely wrong. His mother was scared, Loretta was scared, and Sam and Santiago had both been upset. He now understood that his mother's story about Santiago needing help and someone to cook for him was just made-up. Santiago could cook fine. They were here in the desert for another reason. And back to the gun, why did she need it?

CHAPTER 40

BORDER AGENTS

It was late evening when one American and two Mexican border agents showed up at Loretta's house with their notepads. The El Paso police had already questioned Loretta, Sam, and Angelica at the scene of the hit-and-run incident, but Loretta knew the agents would come too. Word had it that the car that barreled over Ray had been found on the Mexican side, torched and ditched in the Rio Grande.

In preparation, she had rearranged her table full of crystals to reenergize positive forces and fumbled through her closet to find something blue to wear to ward off more bad luck—a navy sweater, a scarf with a peacock feather pattern.

The two young agents were clean-shaven and wore crisp-looking uniforms, perhaps trying to impress, but the older Mexican was the opposite. His beard was gray and stubbly down to the neckline of his open shirt, and his clothes appeared slept in. She had offered them coffee. The two young agents declined, but the older Mexican accepted. He sat down next to Loretta while the others stood.

After a big slurp of coffee, he pushed back his cap and leaned uncomfortably close to Loretta's face. He patted her hand and kept it there. "We are sorry, *Señora*, for your loss."

Loretta nodded then quickly pulled her hand away. She could smell cigars on his breath and saw one sticking out of his jacket pocket, the same brand that Ray smoked.

He faked an empathetic expression. "We have a few questions, we won't keep you long." Leaning back in his chair, he pulled the cigar from his pocket, raked it under his nose, and took a long, drawn-out sniff.

Loretta felt his eyes burning through her.

"Do you mind the cigar?" he said.

Loretta understood what he was doing. She would *not* wither in the face of his wordless insinuation that she knew about the cigars.

She stiffened. "Of course not," she said. "I'll join you with a cigarette." And when the young Mexican agent reached in his pocket for a match, she held up her palm.

"I have my own, *gracias*."

The old agent lit the cigar tip. "As you may know, *Señora*, the incident that started outside the hotel resulted in an abandoned vehicle in Mexico. So, it's a complicated matter now."

Loretta nodded.

"Do you have any reason to believe that your brother was in any trouble?"

"No, but I don't keep tabs on his every move," she said. She put her cigarette on the lip of the ashtray and her hand under the table to hide her shaking.

He squinted and inhaled. "You own a hotel together, I understand? You share a business?"

Loretta gripped the edge of the chair. "Yes, *Señor*."

One of the young Mexican agents chimed in, "But your *business*, we saw, is closed now? Why? Seems strange for a hotel."

"We had no customers, so naturally we closed it down. It's a time of mourning. Myself, and staff, we are all in shock and grief-stricken."

"Hmm," the older man said. "No customers. Odd for a hotel, don't you think?"

"Not really, our clientele mostly comes and goes with the rodeo. And when the rodeo's not in town—"

He cut her off. "Who's on your staff?"

"Angelica, my kitchen help, and Sam, our cleaner and laundry man."

"Small staff for a hotel?" The young agent chuckled, like he was onto something.

The older man glared at him, flicked the ashes of his cigar into Loretta's ashtray, then rubbed his beard between his fingers. "We are not stupid, *Señora*. We know of your *enterprise*. The women?"

Loretta stood up and stubbed out her cigarette. "You came here to ask questions about my brother's death, and if you're done, please leave."

The old man pushed his chair back and stood up slowly. "We are sorry if we are making you uncomfortable—we are only here to help." He wrapped his fingers around the handle of his pistol. "One last question. We are looking for one of your so-called customers. A woman . . ." then he stared at Loretta before continuing, ". . . and a boy, I believe? Do you know where they are?"

Loretta straightened her back. "I don't know. They checked out before the incident."

"Mexico perhaps?" he said.

"Like I said, I don't know," Loretta said.

The old agent looked at the others. "Give me a moment please, gentlemen."

After the others left, he pushed a card Loretta's way. "Well, *Señora*, if you hear of their whereabouts, I trust you will contact us. I must be frank, the more you cooperate, the better off you'll be. We will be out of your hair, and you'll be able to go on about your *business*."

He tilted his head and raised his eyebrows. "Clear?"

"I'll keep that in mind," Loretta said.

Once they had left, Loretta ran to a cabinet, pulled out a bottle of whiskey, and poured a shot glass full then slugged it back.

Gritting her teeth, she swore. "I will never tell!"

She picked up the phone and dialed. Javier answered.

"Meet me in the garden at dawn."

"*Sí*," Javier said. "*Adiós.*"

CHAPTER 41

THE GUN

Francisco couldn't get the gun off his mind. Where was it? Guns made him nervous, but with talk of bad *hombres* and of suspicious behavior, he wanted to know where it was—just in case.

He waited until his mother left to wash up and pretended to sleep, releasing a slight snore for extra persuasion. When she was out of sight, he threw off his blanket and was on his feet in an instant. It was obvious she had hidden it, but where? He had about ten minutes to search.

Maybe her satchel? Seemed too obvious, but he would check anyway and be careful to put things back the way he found them. He grabbed the bag and laid it on the blanket so that whatever he removed wouldn't get dusty. She noticed things like that—dirt that wasn't there before, something rumpled that was supposed to be folded, her money purse in the pouch with the zipper left open.

He wormed his hand around the bag but felt nothing like a gun. There was no cool steel and no hard lumps between the inner lining and outer cloth. Scanning his surroundings, he checked the cracks and crevices, and lifted a tarp that covered sacks of beans. He heard his mother's footsteps and quickly put her satchel back in its place next to her pallet and buckled the strap as it had been before.

I'll look more later, he thought. He knew a little about guns. From the magazine Loretta had given him, he had learned about gun safety.

Rules: never point a gun at anyone; *always* point the barrel at the ground whether the gun is loaded or not; *never* leave ammunition in your gun when you're not using it; *never ever* keep a loaded gun in the house.

From a bad moment with Elton, he had learned what not to do. It had happened one afternoon when Elton came home after "boozing with the boys," as he called it, and Antonia was out shopping.

Francisco was reading and drinking a glass of milk while Elton sat on the sofa wearing a bored expression.

"Come over here, Pancho," he said. "Put that stupid book down, and lemme show you some man stuff. Your ma treats you like a kitten. It's time you learned a few things." He reached behind his back and pulled a pistol from his waistband.

Francisco warily moved to the sofa, but still a few feet away.

"Here, hold it," Elton said. He held the gun out with the barrel pointing at Francisco's thigh.

When Francisco hesitated, Elton shouted, "Hold it dammit!"

Francisco grabbed the barrel.

"Not that way, dumbass," Elton said. "Turn it around and grab the handle." Elton grinned and squinted as Francisco held the gun. "Makes you feel powerful, don't it?"

Francisco nodded to prevent another "dammit" outburst, but after a few seconds handed it back.

Instead of putting it away, Elton waved it around belly laughing the whole time. He cocked his head Francisco's way. "What should we blow up? Your mama's favorite lamp? Or wait, what about that vase? It's ugly as shit. What ya think, *vaquero*?"

Francisco shook his head. Though he liked being called *vaquero* versus "dumbass" or "little bastard," he didn't want to blow anything up.

"Well, what?" Elton said. "We gotta shoot something."

When Francisco didn't answer, Elton mumbled, "You little pansy." Then he wheeled the gun around—*Pow!*—and blew a hole through Francisco's milk glass and laughed like a hyena. Milk and shards of glass splattered across the room.

Seeing the mess, Elton's expression turned sour. "Get a broom and mop and clean that shit up. And don't say a damn word to your mom about it, you hear?"

Because of the magazine, Francisco understood that guns were dangerous and safety mattered, and because of Elton, he knew people could be stupid. And he also knew he could use a pistol if he had to.

CHAPTER 42

ELF OWL

By late afternoon, Francisco and Santiago had already harvested all of the plants within fifty yards of their campsite, so Francisco ventured out further looking for the circular patches that sprung up like soda straws. He saw a large grouping between a pair of Spanish daggers that stood like centurions protecting their rough homestead. As he moved closer, he spotted something in the thick yucca stalk that looked different than the spent yucca leaves that hung down in layers like jagged tan-colored fabric. It was small, gray, and tucked into the yucca stalk, in a hole, like a wad of paper. He moved closer but couldn't tell if it was a fungus or a creature.

Slowly, he tiptoed forward along a narrow path and began to make out streaks of white and two dark slits. Suddenly, he knew exactly what it was, but he had never seen one so small. Its eyes were closed.

Santiago saw Francisco in the distance and zigzagged out along the trail to catch up. When Francisco heard him coming, he turned around and held his finger up to his lips and pointed.

Santiago smiled and nodded, and the creases around his eyes crinkled together.

"You find *mi amigo*," he whispered and smiled. "*Pequeño tecolote*," he said, then he tapped his finger on his chin. "Owl—itty bitty."

Francisco turned back to gaze at the owl. "What kind?"

Santiago let out a deep breath once again struggling to find the right words. "*¿Cómo se dice* . . . Santa and . . ." He bent his knees and shuffled on his haunches like he was a short person.

"Santa?" Francisco said, and he shook his head with confusion. "I don't think Santa is short."

Santiago rubbed his hands together and looked upward as if the clouds had answers. "No, *muchacho*, no Santa. Santa's *amigos*." Then he started pretending like he was hammering and sawing and making things and handing it to someone else.

"You mean Santa's elves?" Francisco said.

Santiago nodded vigorously, "*¡Sí!*"

"So, it's an elf owl?"

"*¡Ay, muchacho! ¡Bueno, bueno!* ¡Elf *tecolote! Sí, sí*," and he threw back his head and let out a trilling giggle enjoying his pantomiming success.

"He's so small and cute." Francisco said.

"Yes, he *dis* big," Santiago said and held his hands about four inches apart. "But he . . ." Santiago made a face, narrowing his eyes, and furrowing his brows.

"Fierce?" Francisco said.

Santiago turned his head from side to side. "No *comprendo feeerce*."

Francisco laughed. "Oh well, I know what you mean. He's little but fierce."

"Brave hunter," Santiago said. "He eat *scorpion*." He bent down, and with his fingers, clawed at the ground.

"He eats scorpions?" Francisco said. His eyes grew wide, and he winced, "Ouch."

"No ouch," said Santiago. "He no care. You, me, ouch, but not *tecolote*," and he smiled widely. "*Tecolote es mi amigo*." He put his hand just above his eyebrows and scanned the horizon then pointed to his chest.

"Your friend looks out for you?"

Santiago wore a serious expression and raised and lowered his head with long slow nods. "I think so."

"Does your *amigo* have a name?" Francisco said. "*¿Cómo se llama?*"

Santiago smiled proudly. "*Sí, se llama, Pepe*." He pointed skyward. "*Mi* boy—*Pepe Mateo—en el cielo.* Dis *tecalote es el spiritu*."

Francisco's mouth opened wide with amazement, and he patted his chest. "That's my middle name too. Mateo."

Santiago eyes grew wide—he was speechless.

"*Sí*," Francisco said. "Francisco Mateo O'Rourke."

"*Ay ya yay*," Santiago said. He covered his mouth with his hands and started turning in circles.

To the west, the sky had turned dark, and clouds advanced toward them in heavy tufts. A strong wind kicked up dust, and Francisco and Santiago turned their backs, closed their eyes, and covered their faces.

When they turned around, the owl was gone from its hole. Francisco jerked his head from side to side searching for it and ducked when he heard a flutter above his head.

Suddenly, the owl was right in front of them, perched on an ocotillo stem. Its eyes were wide, bright yellow, and just like Javier's horned owl but pea sized. Francisco stared, and the owl stared back. They held each other's gaze, then the owl blinked. Francisco blinked. The owl let out a rapid high-pitched call. Francisco cocked his ear and responded—*u ae ae ae ae ae ae.*

Santiago looked stunned. He placed his hand over his heart. "*¡Dios mio!*" He stood frozen for a moment then whirled around and started running back to the campsite with bowed legs swinging like flying wishbones. He yelled over his shoulder, "I be back."

Antonia was tying up candelilla in armful-sized bunches when Santiago came running back into camp.

Alarmed at his sudden burst of energy and what she thought were tears in his eyes, she stiffened.

"Everything okay?" she said.

"*Sí, sí*, Missus," Santiago said with a wide smile on his face, but he added nothing more. He made a beeline to where Sam was perched on a rock with his eyes closed and face tilted upwards soaking up the sun's rays.

When Santiago drew close, he began to tiptoe, then he tapped Sam on the shoulder.

Sam jerked around. "You crazy Mexican. You almost gave me a heart attack."

Santiago waved his hands. "Good news, *es* happy!" Santiago started to whisper, and Antonia could only pick up a few words.

"Tell Loretta, Javier, Gabriel—they right. *Familia*—and *mucho* more."

After Santiago's conversation with Sam, Antonia noticed that Sam was in a hurry. He quickly prepared a dinner of boiled potatoes and canned pork then ate without waiting for the rest of them.

Antonia dipped a cup in the barrel of water and took it over to him.

"You must be thirsty," she said.

"Thank you, Missus." Then he pulled out a handkerchief and dabbed at his mouth. "Sorry for bad manners," he said, "but, *eeesh*, family needs me, I must go."

"I understand," Antonia said.

"Don't worry, Missus," he said. "I'll be back. I'll bring more food. Everything will be okay."

Antonia pushed her hair behind her ears and held out her hand. When Sam gently shook hers, she smiled.

"We're grateful," she said, and when the words passed her lips, they seemed inadequate compared to the kindness that Sam had shown in bringing food and helping them.

Sam nodded.

It had never occurred to her to engage with anyone Chinese in the past. She had never spoken to the man who stacked goods at the fruit stand near their church in Tucson—a young man who was always sucking on a mint sprig. And she never said hello or left a tip for the cleaning woman at the theatre who always handed her a towel, nor did she ever buy anything from the boy who was about Francisco's age peddling trinkets and good luck charms on an upside-down box near the launderette.

But Francisco had been different. He had stopped and pointed at a trinket shaped like a butterfly and the boy let him hold it. And Francisco had noticed the banners above the launderette and knew what they meant.

"Look, Ma," he had said. "Those black squiggles on that banner mean love. See the English word below it? And that one means peace and harmony and—"

She had stopped him mid-sentence. "Come on, Francisco, we're late."

Now she was embarrassed. Sam had risked his life to walk miles through the desert and had asked for nothing in return. She wagged her head both in shame and with a sense of astonishment. This world that she and Francisco had entered had become something other than she expected. Terrifying at times, yes, but there was more. These people that she and Francisco hardly knew were caring for them.

Antonia ran her fingers through her hair as Sam filled his canteen and screwed the cap on tight, then he patted Francisco's shoulder and walked away. A few paces out, Sam turned around when Francisco shouted and waved. "Be careful . . . watch out for snakes!"

Sam smiled and waved back. "Bye bye! *Eeesh*, next time, we play checkers!"

As Sam weaved along a narrow trail, Antonia listened to his sandals flop against his heels and watched until he was just a fuzzy dot in the distance, indiscernible from the clumps of prickly pear and desert brush. And she recalled his conversation with Santiago and wondered what message he was carrying.

Earlier in the day, before Sam left, Francisco had scoured the hillside looking for something special—a gift. He found a little cactus with a ring of pink flowers, but this would be too prickly for Sam to carry. He considered plucking a green-, orange-, and yellow-striped caterpillar from an ocotillo plant and wrapping it in paper, but it would probably be dead by the time it got there, and he felt sure Loretta wouldn't like a dead bug, even if it was colorful. He remembered how scared she had been of the centipede.

Then finally he found it. A smooth, warm brown-colored stone with incised rivulets of cream-colored limestone. It looked like a piece of caramel candy with marshmallow swirls, and he instantly knew she'd love it.

He had slipped it into Sam's hand and whispered, "For Loretta," and Sam had nodded and smiled. He decided not to share his secret gift with his mother. There was something about Loretta's and his friendship that made his mother's jaw tighten—as if Loretta was, to him, the grandmother he never had. He didn't think it was jealousy, it seemed deeper, more painful. As though she were ashamed of her own family.

And he suddenly felt sorry for his mom. How could her own parents not love her?

CHAPTER 43

DAWN

In the church garden at dawn, Loretta was shaking as she told Javier about the questioning from the border agents. He reached out and clasped her hands between his.

"We can't talk on the phone anymore. Someone might be listening. They know all about the business, the girls, everything," she said. "There was even a veiled threat—cooperate or *else*. Trust me, Ray's death will be ruled an accident and finding Antonia and informing the Scorpion of their whereabouts is their main mission—the bastards."

Javier nodded. "*Sí*, it's certain."

Tears welled in her eyes as she fidgeted with the knot on her purple scarf. "Are they safe enough?"

Javier was about to speak when Sam burst through the gate then put his hands on his knees and tried to speak through a string of coughs.

"I ran . . . last four miles . . . knew Javier would be here," he said. He took a deep breath, "*Eeeesh.*"

Loretta immediately released her grip from Javier's and covered her chest. "Are they alright? Please tell me so. Please."

"Yes, Mrs. Loretta. They're fine. Good. Very good."

He reached in his pocket and pulled out the stone and handed it to Loretta. "For you, from Francisco."

Loretta held it in her hand and ran her thumb over its smooth surface and smiled. "Beautiful," she said.

Sam held up his palms. "And, there's more. I have a message from Santiago."

Loretta grew quiet with worry again and bit on a magenta fingernail.

Grinning, Sam dashed glances back and forth between Javier and Loretta, and with a playful smile said, "You ready for news?"

"Yes, please. Tell us." Loretta said. She pushed her hair back, adjusted her red- and yellow-striped skirt, and waited with wariness.

Sam couldn't stop grinning.

"You sure you're ready . . . for good news?" he said.

"Yes," Loretta said laughing. "You're about to do me in, Sam. Spit it out!"

"Francisco. He's family—your family. Santiago says he know it for sure."

"What?" Loretta said. "You mean . . . really? Really, it's so?"

Loretta threw herself at Javier, wrapped her arms around his neck, and swayed from side to side with her words, "I knew it! I knew it! I knew it!" Then suddenly she stopped and blinked. "But who is he?"

Sam beamed, "Francisco's Pepe's boy! Santiago found his grandson! His *nieto,* he say!"

Loretta fumbled her fingers nervously. "How does Santiago know?"

Sam stood on his toes like a jubilant choir boy ready to sing.

"He said the name Mateo is why. Mateo is Francisco's middle name. Mateo is his Pepe's middle name."

Loretta furrowed her brow. "How does he know for sure? There are lots of Mateos out there."

"Santiago said he knows, 'cause of Francisco's eyes, and the owl that came, and more."

"What more?" Loretta said.

"Santiago says he'll tell you himself. He wants you to come, now! He said you need to be there. He's afraid Missus Antonia won't believe him. He wants you to come—right away!"

Loretta reached out and pulled Javier and Sam in close and whispered. "But what if those men follow me and figure out where Antonia and Francisco are?"

"What men?" Sam said.

"Mexican Agents," Loretta said. "They came with questions."

Sam clasped both hands over his mouth. "*Eeeesh.*"

"*Sí,*" Javier said. "We need a plan."

"Another disguise?" Loretta said.

Javier rubbed his hands together. "Maybe, yes, maybe."

CHAPTER 44

STORM

That night after Sam's departure, Antonia awakened to the rumble of distant thunder then the sound of Santiago's voice.

"Storm coming, I sleep in here—by Francisco."

"Of course," she said.

Francisco stirred but didn't wake up. In the cool hues of lightning flashes, Antonia saw Santiago lay his bedroll next to Francisco, and then tenderly touch Francisco's cheek with his fingers.

She thought about the conversation between Sam and Santiago and wondered about the parts she couldn't hear. Why was Santiago so jubilant, and why was Sam in such a hurry? After Sam left, Santiago seemed to have a permanent smile on his face, but if she tried to speak to him about it, he'd turn to some form of work and say, "Sorry, Missus, busy for now."

She didn't want to pressure him, so she stopped trying. Maybe it was personal. A new baby in the family?

And as they ate dinner together by the fire, while Francisco jabbered on about the quail he had seen at the rock outcrop, Santiago gazed at him with a lazy, gentle expression as if he were listening to a lullaby.

"The quail had a little brown patch on their heads with a little feather toot that stuck up and made them look like they were wearing fancy caps. I tried to sneak up on them, but when one spotted me, *poof* they all were gone!" Francisco said.

And now as they lay there, the three of them side by side, it was oddly comforting to Antonia.

Within minutes, the wind picked up, and rain sprinkles blew through the opening in the shed and dampened their blankets. The shower was brief, and after it had passed, Santiago's quiet breathing turned into a gentle snore.

Antonia felt her mind drift into that place where dreams and reality mix into one. Were there voices or was it just rumbling thunder?

It was barely dawn when Antonia awoke. Francisco was still sleeping, but Santiago was gone. She got up and stepped outside to get a drink of water. The wind and blowing dust had made her throat dry, and her eyelashes were almost sealed shut with caked particles. She removed the lid from the water barrel, cupped water in her hands, and drank. Then she wet the hem of her cotton shirt and wiped her face.

She expected to see Santiago by the fire, but when he wasn't there, she searched the area behind the shed and climbed up the outcrop for a better view. About a hundred yards in the distance, Santiago was looking at the ground with his hands behind his back. He bent down, touched the dust, then rubbed it between his fingers. She was immediately alarmed.

After climbing down, Antonia approached him, and when she was within several paces, she saw them—hoof prints in damp caliche patches. The voices she had heard during the night must have been real.

She walked briskly to where Santiago paced. “What is it?” she said trying to sound calm.

Santiago rubbed his chin but said nothing.

Antonia took a step toward him. “What?”

Santiago looked down.

Her voice became firm. “Tell me, Santiago.”

Santiago rubbed his worn hands together and took a deep breath. “Border men, I think.”

“Agents?”

“*Sí*” Santiago said.

“How do you know?”

He pointed to a print with a crisp edge and then to his own shoe. “They horseshoes—our burros no wear shoes.”

Antonia’s body turned rigid. “Were they looking for us?”

Santiago didn’t say anything for a moment then spoke firmly. “We go *adiós*—leave here—go to wax camp.”

“Wax camp?”

“Where *mi familia* make wax from candelilla. More people there. More people to help.”

“Where?”

He pointed to the right of the rising sun. “*Cinco* miles—near *río*.”

Antonia turned away from him trying to compose herself. “I’ll get breakfast going, and then we’ll go?” Antonia said.

He lowered his hat trying to hide his concern. “Leave now. *Buenos frijoles y tortillas* at camp.”

They walked south in front of the burros laden with piles of candelilla for almost an hour, then along the Rio Grande for another hour, skirting the edge of the carrizo cane.

"How much further?" Francisco asked.

Santiago smiled. "*Un poquito* more."

When they reached a steep canyon and ascended a rocky trail, Francisco walked between Santiago and Antonia, and the burros trailed untethered behind. While Francisco and his mother bumbled along, slipping on loose gravel and stumbling over plant roots, Santiago moved with goatlike sure-footedness.

"How many times have you done this?" Francisco said.

Santiago laughed and waved his arm in an arc. "As many as stars in *el cielo*." Santiago's gesture and words reminded Francisco of the time he and Javier met in the bell tower that first morning of their arrival—when Javier raked his hand across the night sky, naming the mountains, the Rio Bravo, and Venus.

"You and Javier have known each other a long time?"

"*Sí*," Santiago said. "He *mi primo* and we play. Gabriel too. We do all things together—when we was bitty."

Francisco liked hearing this. His friendships were expanding in bounds. First Javier, then Gabriel, Loretta, Sam, and now Santiago. More friends than he had ever had before.

"And Loretta, did she play with you and Javier also?"

Santiago laughed and shook his head. "She hate boy stuff. She play house—dresses for dolls. Boss me, Javier, and Gabriel like she *mamasita*."

At the top of a bluff, they stood and looked outward across the expanse of the river. To the west, its brown threads snaked through eroded embankments and then disappeared into the mountains. To the east, it fanned out across a limitless desert.

Below and just around a bend, Santiago pointed to a single thread of smoke curling upwards. "*Allí, está mi familia*," he said.

Santiago looked at Francisco and smiled as if he were sharing a gift.

CHAPTER 45

WAX CAMP

Camp was a tamped-down clearing in a willow forest about fifty feet from the river, and it bustled like a beehive—men unloading their burros, boys bent over, hauling stick bundles on their backs.

At the center of the camp was a red-faced man in short sleeves and sweating despite the morning chill. He stirred a cast-iron cauldron filled with candelilla as flames flared up and licked the edges of the cauldron like devil's tongues.

"*Hola*," Santiago shouted.

Everyone raised their heads and nodded, but no one quit their work until they saw Antonia. Suddenly, everyone stopped and stared.

With a surprised expression, the man who was stirring the cauldron stood up straight, removed his hat, and lowered his head, "*Señora*."

Santiago held out his palm in the man's direction. "*Mi* brother, Dante," he said, then gently waved his palm toward Antonia.

"Dante, *está es Señora* uhhhh . . ." He hit his forehead with his palm. "O'Rourke . . ." and he pointed at Francisco, ". . . *es su hijo*, Francisco."

"A pleasure," the man said, then spoke with a half-smile to Santiago. "Why do you bring such a beautiful lady into this camp of scoundrels?"

Santiago held up his hand and shook his head, so Dante reeled off the translation in rapid-fire Spanish. Santiago grinned and shrugged.

"Come, lady," Dante said. "Sit. You've walked a long way if you come from Santiago's camp." Next, he turned his attention to Francisco. "Hungry, young man?"

Francisco nodded with bright eyes, astounded to be called a young man.

Dante pointed to a rough-hewn table under a thatched roof held up by four twisted wood posts. "Over there, fix your mother a tortilla and beans while she sits by the smaller fire. This one is too hot. Your hair will be in flames." He rubbed his head. "That's why I'm bald, you see?"

While Francisco was piling two tortillas with beans, Santiago and Dante moved back to the cauldron and turned their backs to them. Even though Francisco bent an ear, their Spanish was too rapid for him to understand, so he sat on a stool next to Antonia and watched a clump of small boys as they laughed and tried to trip each other while they carried armfuls of candelilla to the fire pit.

When one boy fell to the ground, they all cheered, including the boy on the ground, as though tripping and being tripped was nothing but fun. The downed boy hopped up then tackled the boy who tripped him, and both wrestled like puppies within a circle of high-pitched laughter. Before long, all ten were in the pile with legs and arms flying.

From the willow thicket, a taller boy appeared. "Okay, okay, enough, stop." Francisco was surprised by his English, but even more surprised when the boy stepped in to pull them apart, and his straw hat flew off and revealed a long black ponytail.

Francisco blinked and squinted. It was a girl.

When she had separated them, she gave each a soft kick in the pants, laughed, and waved her arms. "Silly boys—you want *caramelos*? Finish your work or no candy."

Suddenly, the boys jumped up, stopped their giggling, and scoured the area picking up the scattered stems in a frenzy of movement.

Francisco laughed at the way the boys scrambled like baby chicks running away from a plucky hen. The girl then turned her attention to dusting off her hat and stuffing her hair back under before heading to a shady spot where burros were grazing.

Though he wondered why a girl was out here with all these men and boys, he thought that it might make his mother feel more comfortable.

"There's a girl over there," he said.

"What?"

"Yeah, a girl. She looks a little older than me." Francisco resisted pointing and instead nodded toward the willows. "Over there. And she speaks English like Dante."

"I can't see that far. Are there more?" Antonia said.

"I don't think so," Francisco said. "Looks like just her." But he could tell that his mother was relieved to know that she wasn't alone by the way her face muscles relaxed.

Francisco wanted to go over and rub his hands on the burros' necks and talk to the girl, but an unexpected tinge of shyness set in. What if she thinks I'm as young as her herd of little ones, he thought. He decided to wait.

Back at the big fire, Dante's hands were high in the air as if in disbelief about something. His head bobbed up and down rapidly, then he gave a quick glance in their direction. Santiago started waving his arms then pointed skyward, and Dante slapped him on the back and shouted, "*¡Es un milagro*!"

They embraced then stood and stared at the rippling current in the river like they needed a moment to take something in.

Beyond Dante, movement caught Francisco's eye. There was a rustle of foliage and a dipping wispy branch as three ravens landed with beating wings in a tamarisk tree. Their heads moved rapidly from side to side, and they called out—*awwk, awwwk*—in loud shrill spurts.

"Those birds give me shivers," Antonia said. "With their shiny black feathers, beady eyes, and sharp beaks."

"Why?" Francisco said.

"Because they're all black, I guess, and evil looking."

"Evil?" Francisco interrupted as if the birds had been insulted. "They just have black feathers, the same color as our hair, and I don't think we look evil."

Antonia nodded, "You have a point, though I do look a bit witchy, wouldn't you agree, with the color Loretta gave me?" She smiled.

Francisco smiled back. Her playful side had been nowhere in sight for what seemed like weeks. "We can get you a broom," he said.

She laughed briefly.

Francisco held up a tiny piece of tortilla and one of the ravens flapped its wings, swooped over the fire, then dipped low and plucked the bit of tortilla from Francisco's fingers before returning to the tamarisk. "See?" he said. "Friendly as can be."

Antonia gazed into his eyes and appeared to remember something. "You are a gentle soul," she said. "Like your father."

They sat quietly for a while as the wind rustled in the carrizo cane, bending its stems downward then back up in a quiet dance. Except for the cheerful chatter of children and birds, it was mostly quiet. The girl by the burros was humming but stopped when Dante walked over and spoke. Immediately, she swung up on the back of one of the burros, gave it a swift kick, and headed into the carizzo cane and out of sight.

Under the thatched shade structure, Antonia sat for most of the afternoon feeling useless. Francisco had started to help the other boys move the piles of candelilla, but no one would let Antonia do anything. When she tried to get up and help, someone would smile and steer her back to her chair and with a kind voice, say, "No, no, Missus. You sit."

It was clear to Antonia that everyone, except for Francisco, knew something she didn't. Their deference, their examining eyes that diverted when she noticed, and every few minutes, a nod and broad-toothed smile in her direction like she was royalty. It made her nervous along with the unknowns. How long would they be here? Were they really safe?

Dante came over. "Are you okay, hungry again?"

"I feel like I should help," she said. "I'm capable of hard work."

"No, Missus," he said. "After dinner, Santiago will take you to your resting spot," and he pointed toward a rocky mount further away from the river. "There you will be more comfortable. You, Francisco, and Santiago will stay there during the night. You must rest, it's been a long day."

"Long, yes, but I *want* to help . . . and—"

"Absolutely not," he said, and gently held her hand and tapped it with his palm.

She finally couldn't hold it in any longer. "Tell me what's going on? I must know. I'm distressed because I have no idea what's happening or how long we'll be here."

Dante sighed. "I understand, and you deserve a straight answer. You are here with us because of the men who visited Santiago's camp in the night. We believe they were looking for you and Francisco. So, we're taking care of you, watching out for you, just like Loretta and Javier told us to do. When it is safe, we will take you elsewhere. You must be patient and trust us. It may take some time, then we will have a plan to get you to greater safety where you can live your life as you wish."

"How long?" Antonia said.

Dante shrugged. "A few weeks . . . months."

Antonia was stunned. "Months?"

"Just depends."

"Depends on what?"

"When they stop looking for you. After they've given up."

"What if I don't want to stay? What if I take Francisco and we leave now?"

He shook his head. "I understand your anxiety, Missus, but that's not advisable. Too dangerous. They will come after you and find you. You must wait with us and hide—until they don't care anymore."

Antonia wrung her hands. "Has something else bad happened?"

Dante cleared his throat and hesitated. "Yes, Missus. Mr. Ray, Loretta's brother is dead—they killed him."

Antonia covered her mouth with her hand but could not speak.

"A man we know as 'the Scorpion' blamed Ray for the lost drugs, and though we don't know for sure, they might think you took them."

"Oh my God!"

"It's best that you and Francisco stay with us. There are many of us, we are family, and we take care of each other, and we will do the same for you. Like I said, you *must* trust us. We know the people, we know the land, we know how things work."

Antonia closed her eyes and sighed, but her hands were shaking. "Alright," she said. She was exhausted and overcome with fear, and tears leaked from her eyes. Dante reached out and held her shoulders with his broad, rough hands, and when she didn't resist, he pulled her in and held her.

After a moment, she wiped her eyes and stepped back. "I'm sorry," she said.

"Don't be sorry," Dante said. "Life comes with unexpected struggles, but sometimes good things come out of it."

"What do you mean?" she said.

"You will see."

She looked into Dante's eyes. "Thank you . . ." she said, ". . . for caring, it's been a long time since I've felt that—except from Francisco."

Dante nodded and smiled.

"Your English is so good. I can talk to you. It helps," Antonia said. "I've felt so isolated, so in the dark."

"I have practiced and learned English from you Americans. I need to know your language to trade our wax. I am the voice of our family business. If I want to get a good price, English helps, so I won't get cheated. My family depends on me."

"I see," Antonia said. "Thank you for being straight."

As she sat alone, Antonia couldn't imagine what the "good things" might be.

It seemed almost impossible that something positive could come out of the disastrous decisions she had made. She blamed herself for all of it. She should never have agreed to smuggle the tequila and should have known that it would lead to trouble. And when trouble came, she panicked. She did the worst thing possible. She should have hidden the drugs and left. At least it could have been found later. And now, Ray was dead—someone Loretta loved.

And everyone in this camp was mixed up in her mess. But these kind people were still determined to care for her and Francisco. Why?

CHAPTER 46

THE LETTER

Near sunset, Francisco heard a burro snort, and when it broke through the carrizo cane, he saw that the girl was back. Behind her was another burro, with burlap bags draped on its haunches, and then another followed with a man in wide-brimmed hat and clothes that looked like Javier's and his mother's—gray pants, white shirts, canvas jacket.

The girl dismounted with a youthful ease but gave her hand to help the man off his burro. Francisco assumed he was old, perhaps a grandfather to some of the boys.

When Santiago and Dante saw the man, they briskly walked over and hugged him then stood in the shadows of the willow trees and talked for several minutes while several boys and the girl unloaded the burlap bags and hauled them to the shelter. A celebration broke out when the contents of the bags were revealed. The boys shouted, "*Papas, puerco, frijoles*," and the smallest boy raised a bag in the air and grinned. "*¡Caramelos!*" Then he ran to the girl and wrapped his arms around her waist. "*Gracias*."

Dante, Santiago, and the new man walked toward him. Suddenly, Francisco noticed several rings on the new man's fingers. Orange, purple, blue, and a green one on the pinkie. He knew who it was.

He bolted in her direction and fell into Loretta's arms. She hugged him tight then straightened her arms and gripped his shoulders and smiled with an expression of admiration.

"You look wonderful—so strong," she said.

He grinned. "I've learned everything from Santiago. How to harvest, how to make wax, and there are so many boys here my age. We have fun together. They showed me how to bait a trot line, and where to hunt for frogs, and we played chase games in the willows. And I showed them my hand signals."

Loretta laughed. "I want to hear everything, but I must talk to your mother. Help Reina rub down and water the burros—they've been on a long journey with a heavy load."

Francisco nodded. He couldn't think of a better job.

Antonia stood when she saw Francisco run and hug the old man. Who was it? Javier?

But when he took off his hat, shook out his gray hair, and revealed female features, she knew it was Loretta. She was hesitant to hear any news. Was this good or bad?

When Loretta looked her way and smiled, Antonia felt some relief but was still unsure. Why was she here? There had to be an important reason because it would be too risky for her to come otherwise. Someone might have followed.

Loretta came to where Antonia sat and pulled up a stool next to her. She reached out and held Antonia's hands. There were tears in her eyes.

Antonia looked down. "I am so sorry about Ray. I feel so guilty, so awful . . ."

Loretta put her finger to her lips and quietly whispered, "*Shhh*, Missus Antonia. It's sad—very sad. But it was not your fault. You were a pawn. You did nothing wrong."

"But maybe if I had hidden it . . ."

"There was no certain outcome. It still could have ended bad. No one blames you."

Loretta looked Antonia directly in the eyes. "I have something to tell you that may come as a shock—it's bittersweet news."

Loretta squeezed Antonia's hands. "You need to trust me. Do you?"

Antonia nodded and felt perspiration beading on her brow.

"Remember when you asked me about your friend, the one who had stayed at the hotel? I know who he is, and I'm so sorry, but he has passed."

Antonia's eyes welled with tears, then she looked to the side and bit her lip. "He wasn't a friend. He was Francisco's father."

Loretta nervously twirled the rings on her fingers. "Yes. I guessed as much."

Antonia returned her gaze to Loretta. "How do you know him?"

"Santiago figured it out. I did not recognize the name, didn't even know Pepe was named Mateo. We always called him Pepe. Down here children take two names. Father first then mother. It can be very confusing with so many family members. Your Mateo's name was Jose Mateo Rodriguez Garcia. Garcia his mother's name, Rodriguez his father's name. I knew him as Pepe Rodriguez, but when he crossed the border for work, perhaps he went by the last name Garcia—that was on his papers. Maybe it was easier to just take that name than explain to the Americans. I can only presume that is why."

Antonia blinked. "So who is he? Is there more?"

"There is," Loretta said. "I have something for you." She held out a brass oval that hung from a brass chain. "It is Santiago's."

Antonia looked at Loretta with questioning eyes.

"Open it," Loretta said.

Antonia unlatched the clasp and cupped the locket in her hands. She thought she was seeing things. It couldn't be.

Inside was a picture of Mateo. Loretta continued, "The locket was a gift to Mateo's mother during the war, but she is no longer living."

Santiago appeared at Loretta's side.

"You, Francisco, *mi familia*. Francisco my grandson, *mi hijo*. You my daughter-in-love."

Antonia's lips trembled. She stared at Santiago and repeated his words. "You are Mateo's father? Francisco's grandfather?"

Santiago smiled and nodded.

"I don't know what to say," Antonia said. "I'm so happy but also so sad—for you, for everyone in your family." She swallowed hard, "And for me—I loved him."

She paused and looked toward the river. "What happened to him? How did he die?"

"I will tell you everything now," Loretta said. "When he came home from Texas, within days, Mateo was forced to join the revolutionaries like many of the country people here in northern Mexico to fight along with Pancho Villa and his forces. He had no choice. It was death or join. A few weeks after he left, Santiago and his wife Berta received a letter from Mateo along with the locket."

Santiago handed the letter to Loretta. "I will read it to you because it's in Spanish," Loretta said. "Are you ready?"

Antonia nodded.

Beloved parents,

I thought you would be pleased to know that I have been appointed as a scout in the revolutionary army. I did not want to kill anyone, so I explained my skills to the officer—how I can see things that others can't. How I know when a storm is coming by observation—by the birds in flight. How I can read the sunlight on the mountain and understand the shadows, their depths, trails to avoid, trails to take, and to know the sources of water by following the tracks of a cougar. They agreed to the position.

And though I believe a scout's position to be less dangerous than the cavalry, there is no guarantee that I will survive. So, in case something happens to me, I need you to know something. I met a woman in Texas. We fell in love, and she became pregnant with our baby. We were going to get married, but her parents wouldn't allow it—no Mexican Papa. Three men came, there was nothing I could do. They beat me until I was almost dead. But I have sworn that if I survive this war, I will go back for her. I want to know my child.

Loretta paused to catch her breath and gazed into Antonia's eyes. "And there's more, okay?"

Antonia nodded and steeled herself, gripping her fingers together like a vice.

"There was another letter that followed two weeks later, from a young man in Mateo's regiment," Loretta said.

Santiago pulled the letter from his jacket pocket and held onto it momentarily, rubbing the paper's frayed edges with his fingers as tears pooled in his lower lids.

Loretta read.

Dear Mr. & Mrs. Rodriguez:

It is with great sadness that I share news of your son's death.

Like me, he was a scout but more brave. We were being chased by the federales from the south. Many of our regiment had been killed, and there were only a few of us left. Mateo led the way on a pitch-black night from the edges of the desert into the mountains. The federales, who had been on our heels all day, were lost in the blackness. But Mateo pushed on navigating the moonless nights by the call of a spotted owl that guided us toward the trees and hiding places in canyons.

You wouldn't believe how he did it. With calls, whistles, high-pitched barks, he communicated back and forth all night with a spotted owl. Together, they found safety for our men.

Two days later, he and I were both captured while on patrol. A hired American fighter, by the name Cook, was leading the party. They called him the Scorpion because he knew the desert and was known to be especially brutal. Following our capture, the verdict was rendered that Mateo and I were both to be hanged.

They hung Mateo from a cottonwood, and I was to be next, but a soldier recognized me as a family member, so they let me go. The guilt I feel for not having been hung beside your honorable son or not arguing to take his place will haunt me forever.

But Señor & Señora, you should know that Mateo was brave. He held his head high and spoke to God in his last words. The place where he died was beautiful. The light from the sunset was pink on the face of the cliffs, and the canyon glowed even in the shadows and water trickled from the rocks in sweet song. And I swear . . . I swear on my life . . . the owl that we had followed was there—at the top of the tree. Like a beacon to heaven.

I will deliver his body to you in two weeks. I have sent you this letter ahead of time so that you have time to prepare.

Antonia looked down and Santiago reached for her hand and smiled. "Like you, we sad—but happy too."

The three of them remained quiet for a moment, holding hands as the scent of smoke mixed with the musky smell of dried willow leaves.

"When do you want to tell Francisco?" Loretta said.

"Tonight," Antonia said. "When we go to our sleeping place

when Santiago is with us. It will be a lot to take in. He wanted to know his father so badly, but having Santiago there will help."

"Yes," Loretta said. "Through Santiago, Francisco will feel Mateo's love."

Loretta took a deep breath. "I must go back to town immediately so as not to raise suspicion by my absence. But I will stay in touch through Dante and Santiago."

"Thank you beyond words," Antonia said. "You have done so much for us." When they embraced, Antonia didn't want to let go.

Everything made sense now. It had seemed accidental in many ways, but in her heart, she knew it wasn't. Mateo had drawn her there for the truth to be revealed. And no matter what happened to her, Francisco would be happy and loved.

CHAPTER 47

THE CAVE

The cave wasn't very big but was well hidden behind a clump of alligator junipers. They had climbed about five hundred feet along the narrow trail and had to shimmy across a ledge of boulders to get to the opening. The sun was below the horizon, but a violet glow still lit the cave's entry.

Francisco could easily stand, but his mother and Santiago had to dip their heads after a few feet in.

"Where should we put our bedrolls?" Francisco asked.

Santiago pointed.

"Near the rock outcrop?" Francisco asked.

"Behind," Santiago said. "I stay here. So I see out."

Francisco started to head to the back of the cave, but Antonia touched his arm then patted the ground.

"Sit, Francisco. Santiago and I have something to tell you." She held out the locket.

Francisco glanced at both of them, then down at the locket.

"Go ahead," she said. "Open it."

Santiago lit a match for Francisco to see more clearly.

"Who is it?" he whispered.

"It's your father."

"My father? Really?"

Antonia nodded and smiled.

Francisco looked up and grinned. "He looks like me."

"Yes," Antonia said. "Very much."

"Where is he? Can I meet him?"

She touched his cheek with her palm. "This is the hard part, Francisco. He's no longer living. He died in the war."

Francisco frowned. "Oh."

Antonia waited a moment for her words to sink in. "I know this news is hard to hear, but you should be proud. Your father was very brave."

Francisco closed the locket then rubbed it with his fingers. "Can I wear it tonight?"

"Of course," she said.

Francisco gently looped the chain around his neck and placed the locket over the owl feather. He noticed that Santiago was beaming from ear to ear.

"And there's more," Antonia said and smiled. "Santiago is your grandfather. Your father is Santiago's son."

Francisco blinked. Antonia wrapped him in her arms and held him tight. "We've found home," she whispered.

Francisco threw his body into Santiago's arms feeling love—paternal love—for the first time.

Santiago held Francisco for a few minutes then brushed his rough hand through Francisco's hair. "We go sleep now," Santiago said. He put his finger to his lips. "Must be *muy* quiet."

Francisco couldn't get to sleep. He couldn't believe it. He had finally found his family. He listened to a frog trilling somewhere in the cave. Keep trilling, he thought. Maybe you'll find a companion and family too.

He also thought of what his mother had said. "Your father was brave."

Francisco wanted to be brave too.

Antonia lay next to Francisco as he rustled to get comfortable. She reached for his hand and held it tight. The news had been overwhelming, both joyous and devastating. The finality of hearing of Mateo's death jolted her to the core. Somewhere deep inside she had hoped that they might reunite, and that Francisco could know the man that he was. And she was horrified at the cruelty that he had endured at her family's hands—her father's actions, the beating, the humiliation. It made her wonder if Santiago could ever respect her.

But the letters had shown that Mateo did care, that he did love her, and that he did want to know Francisco. And now they had Santiago, and she knew they would be taken care of—somehow.

She took a deep breath, but danger still existed. The men who had been to Santiago's camp could still find them. The ground under her bedroll felt cold and damp. She shivered.

CHAPTER 48

THE SCORPION

The mounted group entered the wax camp with haste. There were four men, on restless horses, speaking loudly in Spanish as if their intent was to awaken everyone in their midst. The one in front carried a swinging lantern and yanked on his horse's reins. The horse jerked its head and reared up with a snort.

"Dante? *¿Dónde está?*" the man holding the lantern shouted.

The camp was silent for a few minutes until Dante emerged and entered the lantern's glow.

Dante spoke to the lantern holder in Spanish. "I recognize you, Josepe. Now you call me by my first name, Dante, so casually? In the past you've always showed respect calling me *Señor* Rodriguez."

Josepe said nothing.

Dante continued, "That said, what do you want? Are you interested in making wax? I thought this business was too lowly for you. Too much hard work."

The lantern flickered, and Dante squinted to see the other men. "I see you have a few boys along that look familiar—from Juarez, no?"

Josepe gave Dante a smirk. "We're not boys anymore. Now, where's Santiago? He's not at his bungalow."

"I have no idea," Dante said. A few more of the *familia* emerged from their tents along with several boys who rubbed their eyes and scratched their heads.

"You wouldn't lie to us?" Josepe said.

"Why would I lie?" Dante said. "I have nothing to hide."

"We're looking for a woman and a boy," Josepe said. "We are told they are with Santiago. Have you seen them?"

Dante shook his head. "No."

A voice in the darkness mumbled something.

Hearing the words, one of the young men behind the lantern holder swung his leg over his horse and dropped to the ground with a thud. He was skinny but muscled and younger looking than the rest. He pulled a knife from a sheath at his waistline then ran into the clump of small boys and grabbed one around the neck and dragged him toward the fire pit that was filled with glowing embers. He held the knife close to the boy's ear.

The boy squirmed and kicked and screamed, "Papa!"

"Make him stop screaming," the thin muscular man yelled, "or I'll . . ."

"*Silencio*, Pedro," said a short man who stepped forward and stood next to Dante.

Dante examined the man who clutched the boy. "I recognize you too," he said. "Didn't you dance with my daughter Elena at the Rodriguez *quinceañera*? You seemed like a nice boy then. Why are you with these bad men?"

A voice from the back growled. "He knows something good when he sees it."

Dante spoke louder so the man in the back could clearly hear. "You are a desperate man to pick on a boy. I know who you are. They call you the Scorpion?"

The man in the back grunted but didn't respond.

"Let the boy go," Dante said. "Point your guns at me if you'd like."

"Release him," the Scorpion said.

The young man with the knife released his grip, and the boy scrambled back into the arms of his father.

A fierce tension held all in silence for a moment, then there was a *click*—a trigger cocked—and the Scorpion kicked his horse forward into the light. His face was freckled, and he had a curly mop of flame red hair and blue eyes. He pointed the gun at Dante. "You peasants," he said. "You hid that bastard Villa when I was hot on his tail, and now you're hiding someone else."

The Scorpion fired the pistol at Dante's feet, and dust spirted up with a poof.

"You don't scare me," Dante said. "I'm too old to be scared. I know who you are and what you did. You think we should tremble in your presence."

The Scorpion held his finger up, twirled it, and nodded at his men. They dismounted and scurried around camp searching tents and swearing. After a few minutes, "*Nada*," one yelled.

"Check the perimeter!" the Scorpion shouted. The men dispersed in all directions, thrashing through the carizzo cane searching for footprints while the camp was dead silent except for the pop of an ember. For several minutes, the men were gone, then the last man returned and shrugged.

Scorpion kicked his horse. "*Hy*." The other men mounted and followed.

CHAPTER 49

TECALOTE

Outside the cave, the wind was restless. Extended periods of calm transformed into battering *whooshes* that filled the cave with ghostly howls. Francisco sat up and looked around the blackness. How could anyone sleep through this, he wondered, but he heard neither his mother nor Santiago rustle.

Though he could see nothing, Francisco heard a scratching noise in the hard soil just beyond the cave's entry followed by fluttering wings. The scratching continued then another flutter then more scratching.

What was it?

He got on his hands and knees and crawled toward the opening. In the dirt near Santiago's feet, he felt something graze his fingers—a box with Santiago's matches.

Maybe it was okay to light one match, just for a second, then blow it out—to see if the noise was what he thought it was.

Francisco struck it against the cave wall—*schwoot.* The match flared. Santiago rolled over, mumbled, and pulled his blanket over his head. Francisco held the match up and worked his way toward the cave's opening. He was almost there when a gust of wind snuffed the light.

Silence again. The scratching had stopped.

He crept further until he was barely outside the cave and struck another match. He held the light up. There it was—perched on a branch with wide eyes peering at him—the elf owl, Santiago's Pepe.

And inside its beak was a wriggling scorpion.

"Did you see that?" One of the Scorpion's men grabbed the arm of another. "A light, it flickered."

"Where?" a low voice growled.

"Up there," the man said.

"Lead the way," the Scorpion said.

Francisco heard a horse neighing in the distance and cocked his ear to the south. Quickly, he blew out the match, and the owl flapped its wings but remained at its perch. A few minutes later, he heard footsteps growing louder. Francisco stepped backwards, knelt down, and shook Santiago then whispered, "Someone's coming."

Antonia heard his voice and sat up. "What's going on?"

Santiago pointed towards the darkness at the back of the cave. "*Ándale*, Francisco." Then he stood with his back against the wall at the cave's entry—his machete in hand.

As Francisco crawled behind the stone outcrop and sat on his knees next to his mother, Antonia rooted through her bag. There was a *snap* and a *click* and then a shadowy outline of Antonia's outstretched arm and the dim glow of the pistol's pearl handle.

At the ledge, a lantern appeared, then a head popped up and briefly peered into the cave, then disappeared again below. Though Francisco couldn't see anyone except Santiago, the light swayed back and forth, and he heard boots slipping on rocks and hushed cursing. Another *whoosh* and howl in the cave's crevices.

"Come out!" a voice shouted.

Santiago held the machete behind his back with his right hand and stepped into the light.

"*¿Qué pasó?*" he said and rubbed his eyes with his left hand.

A man stepped forward and held the lantern up to Santiago's face. "*¿Dónde está la señora?*" a skinny, muscular young man said.

Santiago shook his head. "*No sé, Señor.* Just me."

"Bullshit!" the man said.

Behind him, the Scorpion stepped into the light. "Where's the Irish bitch?"

Everything was silent. Francisco held onto the edge of the rock wall with a talon-like grip. He knew the gun was a bad idea. He was sure all the men had pistols with plenty of bullets. One shot from his mother, and they'd face a firing squad and more than likely he, his mother, and Santiago would all be dead.

As if his mother had read his mind, she dropped the gun and whispered. "The gun's no good."

She crawled forward, and Francisco pulled on her shirt but couldn't stop her. She turned back to him and held her finger to her lips while palming the air for him to stay down.

He had expected a fearful expression, but it wasn't. Fierceness and determination filled her eyes.

Once in the light and outside the cave, she stood. "I'm here," she said. "Don't hurt Santiago. He's done nothing."

The Scorpion chuckled and shook his head and removed his hat.

Through a crack, Francisco could see his lanky figure and curly red hair. He knew exactly who it was—the man he had seen in the street in Juarez yelling angrily at the shop owner. The man who had used his fists at the *mercado* to strike someone down. The man whom everyone seemed to fear.

The Scorpion stared at Antonia. "Well, well, well. One of our own, like me, from the motherland. Who would have thought an Irish lass could be more stupid than these Mexicans?"

There was grumbling below the ledge.

Antonia said nothing but threw her shoulders back in defiance.

"Ray had you pegged to be the smart one," he snarled. "The one who could bring in the goods with no suspicion. I should have known that idiot had no idea about you. Ray probably fell in love with your Irishness." He tapped his chin in mockery. "What a sweet thought."

"Take me, I'll go with you," she said. "Leave Santiago alone."

"But we're not finished talking," the Scorpion said. "I have more to report about Ray. He was blubbering when I left him. 'Don't hurt her,' Ray begged, 'she didn't know what she was doing.'"

He shook his head. "Hundreds of dollars of *my* money flushed down the shithole. Who does he think I am? The Pope?"

"I did it," she said, "and I'm glad 'cause—"

"Shut up!" he said, then he squinted and stared more deeply into the cave. "Where's your boy?"

"Far away. Hidden."

Francisco stayed low behind the outcrop, his heart pounding in his chest as he ran his finger over the owl feather.

"I don't believe you," the Scorpion said, and he turned to the man with the lantern. "Search the cave!"

Francisco heard a distant *hoo-hoo-hoo . . . hoo . . . hoo*. Instinctively, he responded with a piercing call. *EEE, EEE! EEEEEEE!*

Santiago swung his machete, but the Scorpion grabbed him by the neck and threw him against the edge of the cave then struck him with his fist. A gush of blood poured from Santiago's nose, and he slumped.

Antonia rushed towards Santiago, but a man stepped forward, wrapped his arm around her neck, and slung her onto the ground. Francisco screeched again: *EEEEEEEEEEEEE*!

The silence was deafening—something otherworldly had spoken.

The Scorpion cocked his pistol and pointed it at Antonia.

Suddenly there was flapping! Then more flapping. Wings everywhere, small wings at the Scorpion's feet, giant wings above, beaks attacking his ankles, his knees, his thighs. Then outstretched talons scraping and clawing at the Scorpion's head and neck and against his bent-over back.

The Scorpion kicked and stomped, shrieking like a wild animal. There was a high-pitched squeak at his feet. Francisco looked down and saw an elf owl writhing under the Scorpion's boot. The Scorpion had crushed it.

Instantly, a bolt of lightning struck the desert floor. Thunder boomed.

Below the ledge, the men stared with gaping mouths, in utter terror, at the flattened owl under the Scorpion's boot.

"A *tecalote* . . ." one yelled, ". . . he killed a *tecalote!*" The frightened man crossed his heart then stood in rigid shock and screamed at the Scorpion like he was facing down the devil. "Do you know what you've done?"

Another flash of lightning and *BOOM*!

This was the moment, and Francisco knew it—his chance to be brave like his father. He touched the owl feather again and the locket around his neck for courage then ran full speed, thrust his head forward, lowered his shoulder, and threw his weight against the Scorpion's knees, pushing him backwards. The Scorpion teetered on his heels and whirled his arms trying to regain his footing.

A spotted owl flew at his face, scratching and clawing. The

Scorpion fell backwards to the ground and braced himself with his arms then found his pistol again and fired just as the owl slammed into his arm. The bullet ricocheted off a boulder, and Antonia fell back clutching her chest.

Another bolt of lightning crackled then hammered against an outcrop above. *BAM!* For a split second, all was quiet then a slow cracking sound and a rumble. Santiago ran to Antonia, threw her arm over his shoulder, and dragged her inside the cave.

Santiago looked back at Francisco and shouted, "Get inside!"

Francisco wouldn't budge. He knelt by the pile of smashed feathers then looked up into the tree when he heard a call. *Hoo, hooo, hoooo!* There it was—the great horned owl perched on the top branch—Javier's owl.

Lying on the cave floor, Antonia screamed, "Francisco, *get back*!"

The rumble turned into a roar. A giant slab of sandstone broke free and slid down the mountain.

The Scorpion looked up . . . his face white . . . his mouth open . . . eyes bulging.

A giant shard of sandstone ripped toward them like a massive knife.

Francisco locked eyes with Javier's owl.

The giant shard crashed to the ground.

The Scorpion was sliced in two.

Not even a pebble grazed Francisco.

CHAPTER 50

SIX YEARS LATER

It was a warm evening on his eighteenth birthday when Francisco went to visit his mother's and father's grave. She had died from the Scorpion's bullet, but now she rested peacefully next to his father.

Santiago had told Francisco that he had picked the spot for Mateo's grave because of its natural beauty—a place fitting for a son who felt at home in the desert mountains. It was at the base of a canyon where spring-fed pools created an oasis for the desert's creatures. And it was vibrant—visited regularly by deer, cougars, bears, and hundreds of species of birds—warblers, fly catchers, vireos. But most of all, Santiago had picked it because it was home to a spotted owl.

Francisco visited regularly, and when he came, he searched the canyon for small stones that were smooth, waterworn, and soft to the touch and placed them at the head of their graves. It was a ritual he loved, one that was quiet and purposeful.

When Francisco thought of his father, he wished he had known more of him. Loretta had read the letters that gave him a glimpse of who Mateo was, and Santiago told him stories of his father's childhood. It wasn't complete, but it was good.

But his memory of his mother was complete, whole, and enduring. As time passed, he understood her more. She had chosen to keep him as a baby because she loved him. And even though they faced trouble, caring for him had been her sole purpose. And in the end, she gave her life for him and in doing so he found family—exponential love.

Had it been luck? No.

It had been fate. Antonia had led him into the circle and the circle—his family—had found him. A few years before, he had desired to be as brave as his father. But now he realized that his mother had been the bravest of all.

Had he ever considered writing to her parents or Elton? Yes. He sat down once and scratched out a few lines but then tore up the letter. He saw no purpose in opening old wounds. He felt complete as is.

He still wore an owl feather—ones he would find in the canyon that the spotted owl had plucked and flung to the ground while pruning its breast feathers.

And often, in his dreams, he flew with the owl as he had many times before. They swooped low along the desert where tiny elf owls hopped and fluttered as if performing an ancient dance. There, Francisco raked his fingers in the soft sand leaving sprays of glittering crystals in his wake and caressing the land that was part of him. They glided upwards, circling three times around the camp and the quiet sleeping bodies that he now knew as *familia*, then soared outward West with Venus's bright light as their guide. Over the bends in the river, the owl dropped low and landed, but Francisco flew higher—home and free!

A Ballad
(verse 1, 2 & 3)

Listen and hear
what I am about to sing,
these events of the boy and the great owl.
And do not say it's not true.

It happened in the desert,
the home of our familia,
where our hearts are bound to the earth.
It ended with lightning, thunder, and fury.

The scorpion is dead.
The great owl and the boy live,
and the truth carries on.
Who will be next? Be watchful and believe.
The great horned owl will come to you in the night
with wings spread and eyes yellow as moons.
Then you will see and know.

ABOUT THE AUTHOR

Photograph by Kirk Weddle.

Catherine O'Connor is an award-winning writer and landscape architect. Her debut novel *Dust Covered Lies* received two Spur Awards from the Western Writers of America for "Best Debut Novel" and "Best Traditional Novel." She holds a Bachelor of Arts in English Literature from Duke University and a Master's in Landscape Architecture from Harvard University's Graduate School of Design. A native Texan and Austinite, she is the founding principal of Co'Design, LLC and has served as an adjunct faculty member at the University of Texas School of Architecture. Catherine lives in her hometown with her husband Jim, and they are proud parents of Claire and Patrick.

www.ingramcontent.com/pod-product-compliance
Lightning Source LLC
LaVergne TN
LVHW100405290926
849146LV00028B/336